THE WASTELAND

THEIR CHAMPION BOOK ONE

K.A. KNIGHT

COPYRIGHT

The Wasteland (Their Champion Book One)
This is a work of fiction. Any resemblance to places, events or real people are entirely coincidental.
Copyright © 2018 K.A Knight, all rights reserved.
Written by K.A Knight
Formatted by Kaila Duff

DEDICATION

To the woman who always said just one more chapter. Reading and writing became my escape, to worlds where I didn't know the pain of watching you suffer and fight. To my best friend, my cheerleader and the woman who taught me fear is OK as long as you don't let it stop you. You will never see me walk down the aisle, you will never meet my children or see me publish my first book, but this is for you. I love you and miss you every day. Thank you for believing in me.

P.S Sorry for the dirty parts, I know you would be scandalised, but would keep on secretly reading...

To my lovely beta readers who without this would not be possible, thank you.

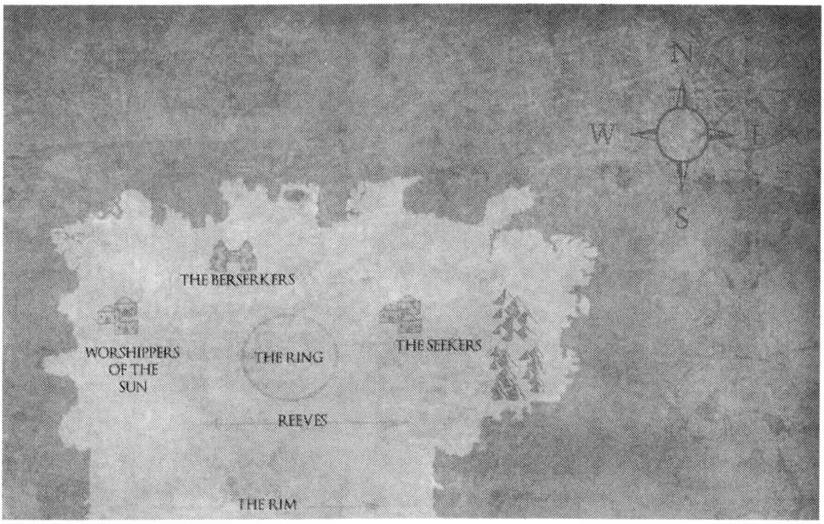
N
W
E
S
THE BERSERKERS
WORSHIPPERS
OF THE
SUN
THE RING
THE SEEKERS
REEVES
THE RIM

"I have learnt things in the dark that I could never have learned in the light, things that saved my life over and over again, so that there is really only one logical conclusion. I need darkness as much as I need light."

- Barbara Brown Taylor

Chapter One

Kill or be killed

I'M PRETTY sure he's dead, stupid fucking roadie. Kicking the body of the dust-covered man in front of me, I wait. When he doesn't move I grab his bag, spilling all the contents on the ground next to him. Pillaging through I find a bottle of whiskey, a machete and some odd bits and bobs. Popping the top of the whiskey, I down half the bottle, fully aware that it's not a good idea. Wiping my mouth on my fingerless leather gloves I glance back down at the body. He's face down in the dirt, his pants around his ankles. Classy way to die, though I know better than anyone that they don't care when they are dead.

The idiot thought I was easy prey, some meek little girl who would bend over and take it. The look of shock on his face when I stuck my knife in him was hilarious. Leaning down I wipe my knife on his pants, making sure to get rid of all the blood. When you don't have much in the way of outfits, stains are an annoyance you try to avoid, and blood is a bitch to get out. I haul my finds to my shoulder bag and hoist it back up, grunting at the weight of it. I shouldn't have pushed my scouting so long, a week in this dust-covered hellhole was a week too much.

You see, the world is dying and it's taking us with it. We weren't prepared when it happened. Back then everyone was self-entitled and had too much of everything. Over 40 percent of the population was wiped out by the floods, another 20 percent by the carnage that came after, and then came the heat. The sun scorched the earth and everything became a desert. Those who survived adapted and it's easy to understand why those who adapted *well* were the darkest of us. Those already willing to kill and steal, like my dead friend here, or me.

Shielding my eyes from the glaring sun, I know I had better get going if I want to sell this stuff in time. Gorky gets cranky if I bang on his shop when he's asleep and I like my head attached to my shoulders, thank you very much. Keeping hold of the whiskey, occasionally taking a swig, I set off to the city in the distance. The peaks of its destroyed buildings and huge gate are barely visible over the dunes. The sand kicks up as I walk making me grimace at the feel of it on my skin. Have I mentioned how much I hate sand and dust? It gets everywhere, and I mean everywhere. The last time I was out for a week scouting, I had to burn my pants when I got back, sending the tiny particles of Satan straight to a fiery death.

It doesn't take me long to reach the city limits, but long enough that I've finished the whiskey, a shame. Sighing, I chuck the bottle to the side as I saunter up to the guards stationed at the gate. The sign next to it proudly declaring 'The Rim', with 'Last Stop to Hell' spray-painted underneath. The shade provided by the huge steel gate nearly has me moaning in ecstasy, I forgot how tiring it is working in the day. Usually, I'm passed out by now, or on my way to it. The guard on the left steps towards me, he's a scrawny thing, still taller than me but skinny. I catalogue all three weapons he holds in a blink and I force myself to stand still as he licks his chapped lips while running his eyes up and down me.

He starts his pat down, leering at me the whole time. He's new, if he wasn't he wouldn't dare look at me like that, considering the last guy that did ended up pissing himself in fear at the feel of my steel blade against his manhood as I calmly told him it would make good feral bait. The newbie, or greenhorn as the roadies call them, will learn soon enough. The thought brings a smile to my lips which promptly dies when he tries to cop a feel of my breast. Before his partner can warn him, although looking in his eyes I don't think he will, I snap my head forward connecting with him before he can react. It's not the smartest move but it is effective, it's good that my head is as solid as my liver. He howls in pain holding his nose that is now gushing blood. I watch in morbid fascination as he tries to talk around his broken nose only to go back to wordlessly screaming.

When it's clear he's not going to do anything more than letting out ear piercing noises, I look to his partner. I think his name is Todd or some shit. Hell, it could be Tim for all I care. He just shakes his head and lets me pass, knowing better than to try and stop me. The greenhorn got lucky, I always have at least four knives on me and you never know when I'm going to use them. A girl has to protect herself, it doesn't help that I have serious anger issues and know how to fight dirty. I wave cheerily at the dickhead still clutching his nose while passing through the gate and then the barbed wired fence. The smells and music of the quarter hit me, immediately loosening my tired muscles and putting a genuine smile on my face.

The Rim, they call it, the haven for the lost and the damned. It's filled with whores, roadies and scavengers or scavs as I call them. It sits on the very edge of the boundary between the other cities and the waste. The last stop of civilization and humanity before you enter no man's land. There are only three reasons people come here; they have nowhere else to go, they're running from something or they're outlaws. Guess which one I am?

The streets are tiny and the city is basically a giant circle. The outer streets are houses for the people who want to stay, a mix of old broken buildings merged with shitty handmade wood and scrap metal structures. The closer you get into the circle, the more it opens up, with the very centre being the market where you trade, fuck, fight, or drink.

The wooden bridges hanging in the air from the higher areas sway in the wind above my head, the creaking familiar and reassuring. The red and white lights strung from each building only add to the atmosphere that is The Rim. The ground is a mixture of dirt, sand, and discarded debris. Men are passed out along shack walls as kids pick their pockets. Shaking my head I leave them to it, if they are stupid enough to pass out, they are stupid enough to deal with their mistakes.

I duck under a sign for the blacksmith and feel a brush against me. I grab the hand before it can pull away. My eyes following the arm to the dirty tattered kid's face who's trying to rob me.

"Too slow kid, you've got to be fast or you're going to get yourself killed." With that, I gently push him away. He runs off without a word probably looking for his next target. A drunk stumbles across my path and then passes out on the ground, without missing a beat I step over his unconscious body. Sands below, I love this place.

The music gets louder as I get closer to the bazaar, the centre of the city. Whores line the doorways shouting at the men and flashing their tits. Anything to grab attention, a lot of idiots lose their money to them. They don't rob locals or anyone they know, but greenhorns and out of towners are fair game. Once they've fucked them they don't tend to watch where their wandering hands are going. Idiots. I eye their dirty outfits. You'd think with their earnings they would buy new clothes but no, they are old and dirty, mismatched from whatever they can find. I look down at myself, noticing that I'm not much better. Dirty black ripped jeans. A top which didn't used to be cropped now torn into one, black with only a few blood stains on it. My ever present black fingerless gloves, black leather jacket and the only thing I give a fuck about keeping clean, my army boots.

"Hey Worth, I thought you'd finally decided to blow this joint." The redhead at the front of the shack laughs as I blink, coming out of my inspection, and offer her a flirty smile.

"Aww, but then I wouldn't get to see your beautiful face," I wink as I walk past earning a few chuckles from the others.

"It's free for you anytime baby!" The redhead shouts after me. I shake my head and carry on, my focus narrowed to getting a drink and into the shade.

I make my way through the crowd, the shouting of the roadies taking a break overpowering the music. I approach Gorky's shack and slam my findings down on the cracked wood counter. I don't say a word just look at the man; I struggle to hide my frown as his dirty crooked teeth play with a toothpick. His hair is slowly falling out, not that anyone will ever say anything to him. Fat covers every inch of his body, which is a feat in itself the way the world is now. His clothes are more stained than mine, put it all together and you have Gorky, the biggest and meanest trader in The Rim. Not even the gangs try to haggle or mess with him and for good reason. The last guy to short change him ended up strung outside his shack by his feet with his intestines falling out. The smell was horrible but no one dared tried telling him to take his warning down. That's what it was after all - a warning. He doesn't question me, just looks through my finds and then slides me my money. I turn back to the bazaar and make my way to a free table without bothering to say anything.

Rickety tables and mismatched chairs are scattered throughout. Material drapes across the circle from the buildings, shielding it from the burning sun. Throwing my shit down, I slump into the shaky chair and I snap my fingers at the barmaid, who is currently on a scavs' knee, as he regales his table with a story of some poor idiots he found on the road. She looks up apparently to give me a mouth full for my summons. When she realises it's me, she jumps up and grabs a bottle from her tray.

She sways her hips as she walks over to me. I manage to hide my eye roll, I really want to tell her it isn't going to happen, but I still want to be served so I watch the show she's putting on. She pops the bottle down in front of me making sure I get a clear view of her ample chest. I grab the bottle and uncork it with my teeth, spitting it into the crowd. I take a swig and look around, cataloguing who's here.

"Ain't seen you in a couple of days baby," she purrs. I don't look at her, knowing she's giving me her best flirty face. What was her name...Candy? The girls move on fast here. They come running from fuck knows what or are found on the road. They think it's a haven, sands are they wrong. Only the strong survive in this world, and this city is the motherfucking gutter. The proverbial shit on a shoe, it's not as bad as back home though. In fact, my old home makes this place look like a paradise. Her hand lands on my crotch over my pants making me glance down with my eyebrow raised. I like her boldness, but I want to be alone tonight and she is way too needy.

"I missed you. Do you want to wait for my shift to be over?" I take another drink and lean back looking at her, not bothering to move her hand as it starts to circle around.

She's good looking I guess. Her hair is dirty and tangled, what once was blonde now is brown. Her face only has a little dirt on it and her top is whole and her little shorts only have two rips. Her stupid ass heels make her teeter, which I try not to smirk at. How in the world does she run in those if she needs to? Overall, not a bad looking woman for the wastes. I don't mind whom I fuck but I don't tend to do them twice. After all, everyone's looking for someone to ride this out with, or protect them, and with my rep, they flock to me. Men wanting to prove their dick size and women wanting protection from everything. I offer them neither, I fuck them and then leave them.

"Sorry love, not tonight." She sticks her lip out, probably trying to be cute.

"Next time," she says with a pout. Some meathead shouts at her and she flounces away. She is grabbed before she gets two feet away, poor kid is going to get eaten alive. I grin as I watch her be pulled around like a prized cow. I can't remember how long ago the world went to shit. It's become our way of life now. You scavenge and fight to survive. Those who are weak are kept as entertainment or die. I was stolen from my family weeks after everything hit the fan. I was twelve at the time. The next couple of years were hell, but now they are the only reason I'm alive.

I slip my jacket off revealing my tattoos, which twist around the top half of my left arm, up my collarbone and then down my spine. Not that you can see that. They aren't tattoos in the traditional sense; each one has a meaning and a purpose and they were painstakingly carved into my skin, not all by my choice. The underside of my left arm boasts old and new scars which have lightened, so unless you look closely, they blend into my skin. Scars, white and faded from age also litter the rest of my body, all apart from my face. A hush falls over the nearby tables when they realise who I am.

Only one woman in this dead world has my warrior scars, dark long brown hair with braids running through it, a massive sword strapped to her back and a no fucks attitude. I'm Tazanna Worth or as they know me, 'The Champion' but you can call me Worth.

Chapter Two

Nan's Place

SIPPING MY BOTTLE, I wait for the inevitable and it doesn't take long. Some meathead in dirty jeans and no shirt saunters up and sits backwards on the chair opposite me. The bar through his nipple glints under the lights as does his bald head. His wide face breaks into a dirty sneer as he waggles his one dark eyebrow at me. As my dad would have said, he has a face made for radio.

"I've heard of you." His eyes drop to my chest and then flick back up to mine. I watch his movements, ready to strike if need be. When I don't speak he glances back at his friends before turning to me with renewed determination.

"You a mute? Don't worry it doesn't bother me, I can think of other things your mouth could do." Sighing, I take a drink.

"I will only give you one warning. Leave and I won't have to hurt you." My voice is as impassive as my face but it only eggs him on.

"You're not that tough, you just need a good fucking." He grabs his dick as if I could misinterpret his meaning. I flick my eyes over him, he's big—I bet one of his hands could cover my whole face. That means he's slow and by the one lonely machete strapped to him, I'm betting he relies on brute strength. This is where my speed will come in handy, you strike fast and move out of hitting range before they even realise you were there. If I wasn't so tired I might even enjoy teaching this fuck trumpet a lesson.

I down the rest of the bottle and calmly place it back down on the table. It's silent now. The vultures are waiting for a show, and any weakness means my death. The bar girls have gone to hide knowing it's going down. Everyone waits and I let them. When he leans forward his odour hits me, I have to fight the need to gag. Just because it's the end of the fucking world doesn't mean you can't wash yourself. Although looking down at myself quickly, I could probably do with one after a week out in the wastes.

"You hear me girlie?" his voice is as damaged as his teeth. Lovely. It makes me glad toothpaste is one of the things I found on my scouting. "Fuck it, I'll just bend you over like the whore you are."

Before he can move, I grab the knife hidden at my waist and lean forward. As quick as a snake bite I've grabbed his thick head and sliced. He screams as he falls back, it echoing around the now silent bazaar. Blood runs through his hands as he cups the wound. I casually fling his now missing ear on the table and put my blade away with a reminder to myself to clean it later. After all, I don't know where he's been.

"I did warn you."

His face contorts in pain as he screams raggedly. The bazaar erupts in laughter and I can't help but smirk as two large scavs scuttle forward and drag the still screaming man away without making eye contact. Signalling for another bottle, I let my eyes wander around. Everyone goes back to what they were doing before my little performance, and only four people make eye contact with me. Not locals or anyone I recognise. They sit in the far corner with their eyes locked on me, beer bottles littered in front of them yet their eyes are clear and their bodies sharp.

Their clothes are clean with no holes, so definitely out of

towners, and if I had to guess, I'd say they were from the cities. As I get a look at their weapons I re-evaluate their threat level. They are carrying at least one shooter each that I can see and so many blades that I lose count. The dark skinned one has a sword or machete poking over the collar of his shirt and one of the others has a crossbow strapped to his side. My assessment is finished in the time it takes for my eyes to flit over them. When a bottle is gently placed on my table I look away, feigning disinterest with my usual empty mask in place. I wonder what four city boys are doing at The Rim. They don't tend to survive to get this far, the stretch of roads between here and the cities is full of gangs, ferals and unforgiving terrain. Half demolished buildings block the way and finding food out there is like finding a whore without an STD. Taking a swig of the lukewarm liqueur, I decide it's not my problem.

The whores make their way into the bar seating area, looking for their next paying customer. They wind around the tables purring at men, stroking them through their dirty tattered clothes. One man grabs one of the girls and pushes her face down on the table and pulls up her skirt while throwing his money down next to her. Something moves into my line of sight and I lean back with a groan. Why the fuck can't people take a hint?

The four men from before stand around my little table, all with unreadable expressions. Either they are stupid or brave, I can't decide which yet. They glance at each other and with a nod, the middle one steps forward. He goes to open his mouth but I beat him to it.

"Fuck off," my voice is hard and cold. It makes him falter and blink in astonishment at me, obviously not expecting that.

He's really good looking for the wastes, long brown hair pulled back in a ponytail. I think it might even be combed. A neat brown beard and trimmed moustache, muscles that are obviously earned, and the best bit? I can't even smell him from here. His skin is naturally tanned, an olive colour with eyes that are darker than his hair. A wide barrel chest full of power strains against the tight shirt covering it. My eyes follow his chest and widen at the size of his arms, they must be double the size of my waist.

I let my eyes wander to his friends ignoring the questioning stare. The two to his left look nearly the same, I'd guess twins. They both have scruff instead of a beard. One has grey eyes and the other has green but they both have blonde hair-- probably lightened from the sun-- longer on the top and tight on the sides. Their skin is tanned, but not burnt and they're both tall and well built. Sleek and well-defined muscles show as they move, highlighting the swimmer's body they hide under clothing.

The one to the right-hand side of the first man is a dark-skinned man. His black hair is trimmed short almost to his scalp and barely visible. He has scruff highlighting his sharp cheekbones and a wicked looking scar running through his left eyebrow which makes him look like a fighter. Muscles contract as he moves with an almost hypnotising strain. He's taller than the others but only by half a head. I watch the way they move, fluid grace in deadly packages. They move like fighters. Great. They look like gods walking through this rough lot. Predators among their prey, their presence fills up the place. I've fought some strong men in my time, but these four? They are in a different league. They make me feel dainty and exposed. Their eyes devour me, burning away my calmness leaving only anger in its wake.

"We just want to talk." This comes from the dark-skinned man, his voice is deep, the deepest I've ever heard. It has a roughness to it like it's not used often or he spent a long time screaming-- out here either is possible. I let my eyes wander away from them and notice some of the scavs are watching us. Their expectant looks have me almost smiling. I scan the men again, I could take them or I would die trying. I know how to use their strength against them but I think I might meet some surprises. Intelligence shines in their eyes and they don't stop scanning the area as they wait.

"What part of fuck off don't you understand? Would you like me to break it down for you?" I tilt my head with narrowed eyes and then slowly enunciate every word like they are idiots. "Fuck. Off." with that I take another drink, the liquor burning a path down my throat.

The first man steps forward and takes a seat opposite me and stares. The others glance at each other again but also sit. He's got balls I'll give him that, he just saw me cut some guy's ear off, which still sits on my table like a trophy, and here he sits like we're having tea.

I stroke my blade under my arm making it obvious I'm concealing weapons. He lays his palms on the table face down -- a sign of peace. Well fuck. His knuckles are scarred like mine, showing me the amount of fights he's been in. His face is set in determination. I sigh knowing they won't leave until I hear them out. Dropping my hand from my blade, I take another drink knowing I'll need it to get through this conversation.

"You have the two minutes it takes to finish my bottle." Sitting back I take the bottle with me and cross my legs and wait.

"We need your help," I snort and he waits for me to stop before carrying on.

"We asked around, you're the one everyone told us to go to."

That's it? I must admit it piques my interest to know they asked around. I'll have to remember later to ask to see what people know about them.

"For what?"

"We want to go North. We want to go deep into The Wasteland," I raise my eyebrow not expecting that. My estimate at the size of his balls just doubled but the thought of going North again has me wanting to stab something. Memories fling themselves at the crudely built wall inside me, the one I fashioned to be able to function again, brought forward by the mention of my old home.

"Apparently that's where you're from, they say you're the only person to make it out alive. We need a guide," he glances at his friends before continuing "we need to find..." I hold my hand up and down the rest of the bottle. I watch his face as I do it and nearly sputter when it goes from annoyance to amusement. His lips quirk in a sexy as hell way and my eyes are drawn to their plumpness. I flick my eyes back to his to see they've heated with knowing, time to leave.

"Let me stop you there buttercup. I don't give a shit why you want to go into the waste," I bang the bottle down on the table and stand shrugging on my jacket as I go "and your two minutes are up." Without another word, I walk off into the maze that is this city.

My instincts are one of the only things that has kept me alive this long and right now they are screaming at me that they're bad news. Worse yet is the fact that they didn't fall for my games. One look in the eyes of the man who first approached me and I know he would fight and play as hard as I do. He's a man who knows what he wants and does whatever it takes to get it. It doesn't bode well for me.

I make my way to the edge of The Rim, people move and make a path for me as I walk, but I keep my eyes on my target. High up on the edge sits an old hotel, the shit hole I call home. Probably a posh retreat in its day, now the walls are cracked and stained and most of the floor is destroyed. The hotel itself is leaning, the outer walls scorched from the sun. The front door hangs off at an angle making me smile, it's perfect.

I make my way through the lobby and the bodies that are

sprawled everywhere. There's a guy fucking in the corner, his grunts loud in the reception. Two scavs are playing cards until one of them flips the makeshift table they sit at and flings himself at the other man. Home sweet home. Ignoring it all I make my way to the desk and ring the bell an annoying number of times.

"I'm coming, hold your tits." The old weary voice rings out spreading a genuine smile to my face. The old hunched over lady shuffles through the door and behind the desk with a fierce glare at me. No one knows how old she is, or how she came to The Rim. No one dares ask, not even me.

"Hi, Nan." She flicks her eyes up and purses her wrinkled lips.

"Whatcha want kid?" She gripes. I lean on my forearms on the dust covered desk.

"Missed you too, you old crone. I need a room." With one last glare, she turns around. She mutters as she looks for the keys. A body slams into the desk next to me and I turn slightly to keep them in my eyesight.

His eye is ballooning shut and blood runs in rivulets down his face, he slumps against the desk like he just got knocked here. Following his eye line, I see a big bastard coming for him. This should be fun, I kick my legs and lean further on the desk waiting for the show.

A shot rings out and a ceiling tile comes falling down. I turn to Nan frowning, she's holding her gun that she keeps under the desk. The old crone always spoils the fun.

"No fighting or you can get the fuck out!" She yells her voice no longer weak but full of steel, the weak old lady disappearing in an instant to reveal the true Nan. The two men nod and head back to their beds for the night.

"Aww, why you gotta ruin the fun?" I wink at her as she slides her gun away with a smooth precision born from years of using it. She ignores me and throws me a key, I catch it in mid-air.

"The usual." She shuffles off before I can reply.

"Love you too."

She flips me the bird over her shoulder and I chuckle. Grabbing my bag from the floor, I make my way down the corridor to the left.

Sauntering to my room which is the only door left at the bottom of the corridor, right next to the emergency exit. Using the old-fashioned key, I unlock the door but it bloody sticks. I barge it open and then slam it shut behind me marvelling in the peace and quiet. I throw my bag down on the dirty bed and grab the broken chair from the unused desk and jam it under the door handle. It'll give me the time to wake up and react in case anyone tries to come in. I look around and let the tension finally drain from my shoulders. All my sarcasm and bravado drops away leaving the damaged woman in their place.

Looking around at what I'm pretty sure is the best room in the whole hotel but still, the walls are peeling and a yellow colour. The carpet is dirty and covered in stains you're best not to ask about. The bed is just a metal box with a mattress on it, beats sleeping out in the open though. The four walls and roof are a godsend, protecting me from the elements and wandering hands that I would have to cut off. Plus, I can never really sleep when there isn't a locked door between me and the rest of the world. I sniff myself and instantly wrinkle my nose, trekking through the waste all day doesn't have a good effect on anyone. I eye the bed, so ready to sleep, but if I don't wash first the sand and sweat will just stick to me and be a bitch to get off. Turning to the bathroom, I start to strip my weapons as I walk.

The door to the en-suite isn't there anymore and the tiled floor is half torn up. The bath and toilet are covered in grime and the sink is partially clean, only from use. The mirror has a huge crack running down its centre from the last time I looked in it, I keep my eyes averted from it not wanting to see myself.

I flick on the light, the yellow bulb flaring to life with a buzz. I throw my jacket off and my top too, so I just stand in my bra that has seen better days. Is that a blood stain on it? With a frown, I fill the sink and plug it laying my knives down on the counter within easy reaching distance.

Cupping the water I throw it on my face and then get to work removing the grit and dirt. I wash my arms and face first before moving on to the rest of my body. I have to scrub at my breasts and flat stomach before draining the now dirty water. Looking down at my now red skin I frown, this world would be so much easier if my boobs weren't as big and obvious. It makes me stand out from the men, some slaves used to be able to bind theirs and with a haircut, it disguised them, but not me. I shake my head from my morbid thoughts and fill the sink again.

I have to shimmy out of my jeans, the sweat making them stick to me in a way that makes me cringe. I quickly wash my legs and then drain the water again. Next, I wash my jeans and then throw them over the bath to dry. Turning to leave, I accidentally catch a look at myself in the mirror. Bruises mar my tanned skin from recent trysts in the waste. My scars are easily visible with my back being the worst, it is covered in crisscrossing long ones pointing up to my slave mark, which stands out at the bottom of my neck.

A thick black circle with the Berserker symbol stamped in the middle, which looks like two diamonds connected with a sword piercing through the middle, it was the first tattoo I ever had. I know I could get it altered. Hell, if I wanted rid of it so bad, I could just burn it off, but to me, it's a reminder. Of where I came from and the struggles I've faced. My eyes fall to the lines down my spine, each one represents a person I killed. It's a tradition for a fighter to carve their kills into their skin, I struggled and begged for them not to. Why would I want a permanent mark of the blood on my hands? But I grew to see them differently and now one look reminds me that no matter how broken you are-- as long as you're still breathing you can live to fight another day.

Roses surround the harsh marks, a memoriam to the lives lost, there are so many that they run up my shoulder and down my arm bracketing my champion brand. Which stands proudly on my shoulder, a mark I happily accepted. After all, it represents my freedom, my fingers run softly over the black brand. The design is beautiful, two swords crossed in a circle of leaves with my number of fights in Roman numerals. As I pull my fingers away, my nail catches on a raised scar, I freeze and fight away the memory it triggers. Chest heaving, my eyes lock on my orbs in the mirror, their depths holding secrets that should never see the light of day. I watch the ghosts and pain reflected there, the raw emotion sucking me into my own head.

You think you can live without me? You think I will ever let you go? You're nothing, you're worse than nothing! You're a broken toy that no one will ever want and I'll make sure of it.

I push the memory away with a cry and lean my head against the cracked glass. All my hard earned walls crumble around me leaving me the broken creature he named me. No, not broken. Gritting my teeth I painstakingly rebuild them, the cracks on its decayed surface, plain as day but it holds. I shove everything behind the flimsy structure, the memories, the pain even the love. When I'm more myself, I straighten and meet my eyes once again, this time the determination and anger which keeps me going shines brightly back at me. They drop to the tattoos once again before I drag them away to drink in the sight of myself.

My long brown hair hangs in a curly mess down to my curvy hips, the ends of it lightning to almost blonde from the sun. Soon enough it will all be blonde, maybe that's a good thing. A rebirth of sorts. My eyes like the colour of the rain kissed earth from my childhood gleam with things I don't want to look at too closely. I drag them away and flick the overhead light off, vowing to myself to never look in a mirror again.

Making my way into the room in just my panties and bra, I

slump on the bed and pull a worn paperback from my bag. Opening it to where I left off, I immerse myself in the tale of pirates and a princess. The words create a world where my nightmares can't reach, my escape from reality.

Chapter Three

TOWN OF SPRING

PULLING on my still damp jeans, I almost groan at the lack of sand in them. Once I've strapped my weapons on I shrug into my jacket. Grabbing my bag from the desk, I move the chair away from the door. I check my weapons once more before I make my way down the corridor. I got about four hours sleep last night, a good amount for me. The rest was spent in a cold sweat from my memories, with faces begging for their lives and the devil himself stood in front of me with his whip. I decided after that, there was no point going back to sleep, so I got up and got ready.

It's still early which means all the roadies and scavs are still sleeping off their hangovers from last night. Striding down the corridor, my steps are muffled by the horrible green carpet. I pass an open room and glance in. A man lays in a pool of blood on the floor, a broken chair leg next to his caved in head. I don't bother stopping, but I almost laugh, Nan is going to be pissed.

The rules of her house are simple. No fighting, no killing, and no fucking staining the rooms. With a chuckle, I head to the desk. I ring the bell a couple of times which causes groans and curses from the men passed out behind me. There's a bare white ass sticking up from the pile of passed out men and the fire in the corner is just dying out enough to see they are bedded down for the day. Half of them use whatever they can find for blankets and pillows while a few actually have them. Nan charges half her normal rate for the reception compared to the rooms, which means it's always filled to the brim.

"I'm coming, I'm coming."

I turn back to the desk when I hear her tell-tale shuffle. She stops behind it, her curly grey hair perfectly held in place and I shit you not, she has on a pearl necklace and a faded red cardigan. She looks like someone's sweet little old grandmother - I asked her once why the get up and she told me people see what they want to, they never expect a little old lady with pearls to shoot them in the face. She earned my respect that day.

"The fuck do you want at this time?" I smile at her beyond happy to give her the news.

"Dead body in room three," I say cheerfully.

"Motherfuckers best not have stained my floor. Stupid ass pigs can't even take it outside. I don't need any bodies in my establishment. When I find them, I'm going to skin them alive and use their balls for earrings." She gripes.

I bite my lips to hold in my laugh as she rants. She stops and she squints as she eyes my jacket and bag and then huffs.

"Ya heading out?" Nodding, I quirk my eyebrow at her.

"Be back tomorrow, only going to the inner. Rumour has it your latest bill is there."

"Be careful will ya, heard there were some raids there yesterday. Stupid clans and their fighting," she fiddles with her pearls as she speaks and glares at the naked arse behind me, looking completely disgusted.

"Aww Nan, I knew you cared about me," I say sweetly and lean over and kiss her wrinkled cheek before she can grab her gun.

"Fuck off. You always pay your room and don't leave any bodies. That's the only reason, I tell ya."

I offer her a cheery sarcastic smile and then head out for the day. When I get outside the sun beats down on me, I can already feel the heat on my skin making me sweat. I pull my shades from my canvas bag and cover my eyes. It's going to be a long fucking day.

Making my way through the deserted streets, I wander in the silence just taking in the quiet, letting it wipe away the last of my nightmares. The city looks different in the daylight, more ruined. It reminds you of what the world is like now. No clean streets and white picket fenced homes here, no this is a halfway between hell and more hell. People don't dress in suits and talk constantly on their phones. They don't moan about delays or traffic, they're just happy to be alive.

The gate buzzer goes off when I approach it, I wait for it to swing open and then step through. It buzzes shut behind me straight away. I look out at the dead wasteland that stretches before me and with a sigh, I get to work.

THE ABANDONED HOUSE looks like it's about to fall down. The walls are covered in cracks and the windows are smashed. The wooden front door is at an angle and covered in who knows what. I look back down at the bill Nan slid under my door last night. Easy work, find the man and drag him back to The Rim. I get more if he's alive but if need be dead is fine too. Idiot must have killed someone important or pissed off the wrong man. His last known whereabouts were to the north of The Rim, somewhere in the abandoned town of Spring.

So that's where I am now, the town itself is tiny, only five buildings remaining. The others have either been demolished or burnt down. The one road in and out is filled with large potholes, big enough for a man to fall in. The road signs are covered in spray paint and bullet holes. I checked the other four buildings before finding myself outside this house. One that was once a supermarket, the aisles filled with debris and sand, the glass sliding doors missing. There was even a decomposing body down the fruit and veg aisle, I guess that counts as fresh food, right?

The others included an office building, a block of flats, and a church. I don't particularly believe in god, but seeing the bodies and ruins inside that holy building made me wince. A once beautiful stained glass window lay in shattered pieces along the pews, letting in the sand from outside. All the valuables had been looted, leaving it an empty skeleton of what it used to be. The flats made even my darkened soul cry out, the carnage inside so heinous I had to close my eyes. After I found a little girl's body, broken and mangled curled around a doll, I hightailed it out of there to check the other buildings first. I didn't bother checking all of the office building, the sand and dirt in the entrance and stairs making it clear no one had been there in a long time. It was like a vault, preserving our old lives perfectly. Mugs lay half full on desks, computers dark waiting for the staff to start their day. I wonder if I would be somewhere like that if the world hadn't gone to shit. Thinking about that sort of thing isn't good but I can't help but wonder who I would be in the old world. Would I make my dad proud? Would my family and I be the type to gather around every Sunday to catch up? Would I be married? Would I have kids? The thought sends a pang through me, I'm not the nurturing type but maybe in another life I would have been. Shaking my head and the thoughts away, I concentrate on the now.

With all the other buildings empty, that only leaves this house. I shove the bill with the guy's description back into my bag and crack my neck from side to side. Striding to the door, I bang on it three times. I hear scuffling behind it, but no one answers. Really?

"Who is it?" The scared, weasley voice rings through the closed door.

"Girl scout." Cue more shuffling.

I sigh and wind my hair around my head in a braid, just in case. I also drop my bag and pull off my jacket. They either always fight or run and I have to be ready for both. Nan gave me my first bill the day after I turned up at The Rim. She told me either I'd die or come back for more, she was right of course. The thrill of the hunt, fighting and the adrenaline is amazing. But the best bit is, for once I'm hurting people who deserve it, people like the ones who hurt me.

"Go away," the voice is higher pitched and brings me back to where I am.

Fine, let's do this the hard way. Not bothering to reply, I step back and with all my power, kick the door open. It slams inwards and I hear the man trying to run. I roll my eyes and step into the house, scanning the room taking in the cans laying everywhere and the dirty blanket on the floor. A man is frantically trying to yank open the other door, I stride towards him and grab his collar.

"C'mon, it's over." He tries to wiggle away; this guy does not know when to give up. He jumps forward and I let him go, he turns towards me and holds out a tiny knife. I'm pretty sure it's a kitchen knife, his arm is shaking so bad it wobbles. I'm betting he's never even used it, how the hell he made it out here this long, I'll never know. By the smell in the room, I'm guessing he ran and holed himself in this house and hasn't left since.

"Just leave," he pleads, his eyes wide showing the white. They dart around searching for an escape.

"Can't do that Jim, you've been bad, so they sent the devil," I say, stepping to the left, sometimes my words and acting hard are enough for them to give up but not this guy. He follows me with the knife.

"Do it or I'll cut you," his voice gets higher and his head swings as he searches for a way out of this mess.

"No thanks, I've got enough scars," I say conversationally. I step back and his arm lowers slightly thinking his threat has worked. Honestly, it's a little insulting.

Before he can lift his arm again, I snap mine back and punch him straight in the face. He goes down hard with a bang, like a bag of rocks. Kicking the knife away from his hand I crouch down in front of him.

"Couldn't just do it the easy way could you?" with a disgusted noise, I stand up and shake my hand out. I turn to the room and spot a dirty looking rucksack in the corner. I make my way to it as I ignore his crying.

"Don't move Jimmy boy," I point to him and then crouch down to the bag. I'm searching through it when I hear him trying to push himself up.

"You crazy bitch," his voice is nasally, huh, guess I hurt his nose. Why am I always a bitch or a whore? Can't they get creative with their insults? I stand back up after seeing he has nothing of value. He's laid half propped on the floor, blood dripping slowly from his nose. Damn, I didn't break it. I must be losing my touch.

"C'mon dude, time to go back to The Rim," I march over to him, bracing myself as I haul him up, my muscles straining in the process. I take one last look around for anything of use and when nothing stands out I march him out before me. On the way out, I kick the door shut behind us.

I push him down the road, the once white lines that used to indicate the middle worn away. We walk around the holes on the way out of town. The sun is high in the sky beating down on us making me overheat, so I take my jacket off and shove it in my bag. I leave my hair on top of my head to get some air on my neck. I eye Jim wearily; he's sweating like a pig and crying to himself. Convinced he's not going to try anything, I search through my bag looking for the tin I shoved in earlier. Aha, I yank it out and unsheathe my knife and stab it into the lid, lifting it easily. When it's off, I put my knife away and using my fingers eat the canned peaches as I walk. He stops and stares at me, the hunger evident on his gaunt face.

"You going to share?" he whines. I roll my eyes but don't answer. I was right, it's going to be a long day.

Chapter Four

No Means No

HE'S MOANING like one of the whores from The Rim, I'm really debating cutting his tongue out, but I don't want his blood on me. Plus, he'd probably still find a way to annoy me. I made him walk in front of me so I can keep an eye on him and halfway back to The Rim, he tried to run. I threw my knife. It missed my target by inches, but it embedded in his leg. I blame the sun getting in my eyes, so now he's limping and crying. At least he won't try to run again, sands below, it's too hot for that shit. You ever tried running in scorching sun? Not fun, let me tell you.

"They'll kill me!" he screams his dramatic ass off. I ignore him and keep walking, counting backwards from thirty to stop me from killing him here and now.

"You're condemning me to death." He turns to look at me, tears leaking out of his eyes, he's pathetic. Why do they always cry, do they think I'll feel sorry for them? They did the crime, now they have to face it.

"I don't know what you did and I don't care. I get paid to bring your sorry ass back, so that's what I'm doing." He stops, so do I. We face each other, the wind blowing dust at us from the side and the sun burning down on our heads. A howl echoes off in the distance and he flinches.

"I could pay you," he says quickly, the desperation clear in his voice.

"With what? You have nothing." I walk towards him, he starts walking backwards to avoid me with his arms tied behind his back.

"I have money, it's just hidden."

"Sure thing, let's get right on finding that then," I shove his shoulder and he turns back around with a stumble and a cry.

I spend the rest of the two-hour walk back to The Rim debating all of the ways I could shut this guy up, seriously. One of my most creative ones involves a toe and some stitches. The sun continues to beat down on me and I look at it shading my eyes and sigh carrying on walking to my new soundtrack, Jim's wailing. I block him out as much as I can and think about before.

We were lucky we were in the North of the UK when it all happened. Before all communication cut off, I saw the devastation left by the polar ice caps melting. Extreme weather hit the world, tsunamis, flooding, hurricanes, all leaving devastation behind. Then the ice caps were gone, just gone and raised the sea level by over 216 feet, submerging entire countries and continents. Buenos Aires, Uruguay, London, Denmark, and Netherlands were all gone. Venice was reclaimed by the sea while the water left mostly mountains in other countries, leaving most of Africa completely uninhabitable. The world as we knew it, wiped away by the encroaching water, the world we knew no longer existed. Like Mother Nature reclaiming her land.

No one knows what happened when all of the communications cut off. No phone, no TV, not even any radio. The world became silent with only the cries of the dying to be heard. People started fighting each other for scraps of food and slavery and death became the norm. People only started migrating back to the cities ten years ago when a new government was 'established'. They flocked to them, thinking they were saved. It was more like they took power and no one dared to stop them. Rumours reach even

The Rim of the dictatorship within their walls. They tried to bring back a civilised society, but so many people are used to this way of life, it was a hard battle. Which only a few managed to escape from and flee north. They even tried to make The Rim bow to their command, when their diplomatic party was sent back to them in pieces, they gave up.

The burning in my face brings me back to Jim's cries. Wasters tend to avoid midday travel, but if I want to be back before all the roadies and scavs I knew, I had to set off. Plus, if there have been raids out here I'm more likely to avoid them while they bed down for the day. I could have ridden my bike but then Jim would have to sit with his arms around me, not my idea of a good time. Eventually, I see the spikes of the shacks and houses peeking over the horizon. I quicken my pace, pulling him along with me. We reach the back of The Rim and head around to the gate.

When I see the two guards at the front gate, I pick up the pace and count down the steps to them, wanting to be away from this guy.

"Here," I shove Jim at one of the guards and he grabs his arm automatically. He looks at the guy in disgust and then nods to me. The other guard steps forward and starts counting out my money. He's a regular and is usually the one I give the men too. I kick back against the wall and let the shade cool me.

"He give you any trouble?" he asks, not looking at me. I snort and don't reply. His lips twitch. Done counting, he passes me my reward, I double check it to be sure. At least Nan sent the money to the gate before I got back, it's annoying having to drag their asses back to the hotel to hand them in.

"So, what did he do?" I ask curiously, still counting. The guard looks back at where Jim is being escorted through the gate. He's now pleading with the guard and pointing at his swollen nose.

"Raped some young clan girl, got a big bounty on him." The disgust is plain to see on his face and when his words click my face contorts to a snarl, I should have punched him harder. Maybe even cut his cock off. The guard steps back and eyes me warily, touching his side where his weapon hides. My lips twitch and I straighten up, he steps further back and spreads his legs in a ready stance.

"Don't worry cupcake, I'm not going to cause you any trouble. They'd have to replace your pretty face and we can't have that, can we?" He takes a deep breath and drops his arm a relieved smile twisting his lips. I pat his shoulder on the way past and he shakes his head at me. I wonder if it's too early to start drinking.

I'M LOOKING for a new top, the one I'm wearing is on its last life. I do have one in my bag, but it's my emergency top. You never know when someone is going to rip yours in a fight and honestly, fighting with your tits hanging out isn't fun. It wouldn't do to just walk around in just my bra. They might get the wrong idea, and then I would have to play smack a bitch. So a new top it is.

I pick up the black ribbed tank top. I always tend to go for black, hides the blood stains easier. It's a bit shorter than I usually wear, hanging just above my belly button, but it will do. I'm digging through my bag for my money when a hand reaches past me and pays the bored shop merchant. I glance up and then snarl when I realise it's the dickheads from last night. If they are stupid enough to buy me a shirt, who am I to refuse? I nod at the owner and move around them.

"You're welcome," the olive-skinned man says. I turn and walk backwards.

"I didn't ask you to," I turn back around and make my way to the next shack needing a new blade for my boot. I'm just admiring a small throwing knife when I feel them behind me again. Do these guys not get the picture?

"You're not a talker are you?" The voice is different, darker and less growly so I look up. It's the dark-skinned guy. He flashes pearly whites at me. Well hello, if he had been just passing through, I would have climbed him like a tree. He sure is pretty, in a scary sort of way.

"No."

"It's refreshing." The voice is different again, smoother. It's one of the twins though I wouldn't have a clue which. Turning back to pay for the knife, I bend to slip it into my left boot. Then I strip off my chest harness, which is handmade with two holes. One for a back weapon-- I put my sword in there-- and one on the left side, my second largest blade rests in that one. Placing it gently down on the table with my bag and yanking my ruined t-shirt up to throw it aside, I grab the new one and pull it down noticing it fits well. I put my harness back on and look up. The guys are just standing there looking shocked. Really, where are they from? Surely they've seen a naked woman before.

"What do you want?" I ask gruffly.

"Did you think about what we said last night?" This time it's the leader talking again.

"No," I say honestly. I push through the middle of them and make my way to Nan's. They fall into line with me, the leader walking next to me the others behind. I just ignore them and keep walking. One of the whores steps out and pushes against him and he tries to sidestep her. I watch in amusement and carry on walking, leaving him behind. I'll have to thank her later.

I step through the front door of Nan's and with chagrin realise they followed. Can't a girl catch a break? One of the twins steps in front of me blocking my way.

"Just hear us out," his voice is the smooth one from earlier. I hear a whistle and with a sigh yank him out of the way of the flying blade. He turns and looks shocked at where the knife is now sticking out of the wall where he was standing.

"Look greenhorns. I don't know where you're from, but here in The Rim no means no," I walk around them grabbing the knife as I go.

I test the weight in my hand and look up at the person who threw it. Two big men in leather stand there looking like it's the funniest thing in the world. I smile my shit eating grin at them and then throw it with deadly accuracy. It embeds in the wall in the tiny gap between both of their heads. Their expressions make me laugh as I make my way to the desk. I ring the bell and wait.

"Yeah, yeah." Nan shuffles around the corner and glances at me.

"You get that raper?" I nod and lean on the desk, sliding the bill across to her. She nods and throws it on the pile on the desk.

"You got any more?" I grab my knife and clean my nails as she looks behind me. I wonder if I knocked myself out on the desk, would they leave me alone? Nah, probably would sit around staring at me creepily until I woke up, persistent hot bastards.

"Ya brought company girl?" She asks, no doubt stroking her gun under the desk. They don't exactly fit in and Nan knows I don't take anyone back to my room. There's something about having a sanctuary that no one else can go in, plus it means I know there's nothing hidden in there.

"Not with me," I say and turn to watch this go down.

"What ya motherfuckers want?" she snarls at them. It's safe to say they look shocked at her language, I laugh before I can stop myself.

"They are just passing through Nan, ain't that right boys?" I arch my eyebrow at them, the leader steps forward.

"We are her new job," he says nodding at me. Motherfuckers, Nan was right.

"That right girly?" I narrow my eyes at her in warning.

"No." She ignores me, smiling she stops stroking her gun.

"Sure, sure. Ya boys need a room, ya pay." The dark-skinned one leans forward and offers her some money.

"The one next to hers." He jerks his head at me, asshole. I put my knife away and push off the desk, done with this whole conversation. I stomp off towards my room, ignoring everyone.

"I'll slip that job under ya door girly," Nan shouts after me. I flip her off over my shoulder. I can hear them murmuring something to her, but I pointedly keep walking.

Chapter Five

RUSSIAN ROULETTE

THERE'S a knock at my door. I ignore it, knowing the only people in this joint stupid enough to do that are the four guys from before. They carry on knocking and I heave myself up pissed; slamming open the door with a snarl. Before I can talk, they barge past me and into my room. The silent twin offers me the job slip from Nan. Snatching it, I quickly glance through it. It's easy enough: last seen whereabouts in the Wastes, travelling to The Ring. That's usually where the jobs start, a clan puts in a bill or a job there and then they slowly work their way around to The Rim.

"So you're going that way anyway." The leader says. I stay near the open door with my back to the wall and let the bill loosen in my hand.

"So?" I cross my arms over my chest, which puts my hands closer to my blades.

"So you can take us," He says. The twins sit on my bed and I nearly fling a knife at them. Pushy bastards don't seem to know what personal space means.

"No," I say instantly.

"Why?" The twin with the green eyes asks with his head cocked.

"You guys stick out like a sore thumb. That's a sure way to get killed. It's easy for me to get in and out. But you?" I scoff.

"That's why we have you. Also, we can fight." Green eyes proudly shows off his arm muscles as he speaks. I eye their muscles and weapons and don't doubt it, but even the best fighters can be outnumbered out here.

"I don't tangle in Wasteland business. You got an issue with any clans up there-"

"We don't." The dark-skinned man interrupts. I grind my teeth and debate my options. I know they won't leave me alone until I say yes. That much is evident. Maybe if I charge enough they'll fuck off.

"My pay is one hundred for each day."

The leader nods. Sands below, I should have asked for more.

"Done." He looks smug. I'm so fucked. This is such a bad idea. I let my hands drop from near my blades. What the hell am I going to do? Eying them again, I decide what the hell. The likelihood of them wanting to carry on when we get out there is slim; I'll probably be bringing them back in a couple of days. At least I will have some good money to show for it. Calmer now that I have a plan, I nod my head in agreement.

"You get injured, do anything stupid, or lag behind and I leave you. Understood?" I say sternly, fighting the urge to punch something. It would probably be his smug pretty boy face.

"Sure thing, Cap." The talkative twin says with a smile, his green eyes alight with amusement. Why is he so happy all the time? Just another thing about them that pisses me off.

"Ok. We leave at six a.m., now get out," I point at the door just to make sure they get the point. The twins stand and both stop before me, making my room feel claustrophobic with their tall frames blocking everything.

"I'm Drax," green eyes points to his own chest, "this is Jax." He gestures at the silent grey-eyed twin who just watches me. I nod and Drax smiles as he struts out the door, his twin silently following. The dark-skinned man stops by me and offers me a small smile.

"I'm Thorn, darling." He walks through the door without saying anything else. The leader steps up and offers me his hand. I hesitantly shake it.

"I'm Maxen, you are?" I look into his eyes which blaze with determination, a look I used to see in my eyes before I came to The Rim.

"Worth." That's all I offer him. His lips twitch and he nods.

"See you in the morning, Worth." He closes the door after him. They're going to get me into trouble, I can just tell.

AFTER THEY LEAVE, I start to clean my weapons, preparing for the journey ahead. I even bathe knowing I'm going to be stuck in the waste for at least a week. When I'm as clean as I'm ever going to get, I pull out my map and plan my journey, avoiding the major clan areas.

The job from Nan is in The Ring, which is a couple hundred miles into the Wastes, a straight up journey. But to get there you have to pass through clan territory. Maxen never mentioned where they were going. I'm hoping they'll get to The Ring with me and decide they want to turn back and return to wherever they came from. Reading through the reason for the bill makes me feel sick. The son of a bitch killed a whole family. Not just killed, but tortured as well. I shove it in my bag, done with the in-depth description of his crime.

Stripping down, I lay on the bed letting my thoughts turn to where they always do when I'm alone and sober... the past. Closing my eyes, I try to remember my family. My dad and brother's faces come clear to me, but I can hardly remember my mum's now. I focus on my dad as he smiles at me as we sit around a fire in the back garden of some empty house. It was just after we decided to head North and avoid the chaos in the cities. My brother throws a twig at me as our dad smiles and watches us bicker. The memories change and I see him shouting for me to run as four black bikes charge towards me. Men are jeering as I cry. I turn back to see my dad and his face changes so I'm looking at the smirking face of the man who haunts my every moment. Those deep black eyes locked on mine, his long black hair pulled back in his 'warrior braids', some coloured with blood until they shine red in the light. His crown made of skulls moving as he leans towards me.

"*Miss me pet?*"

I can almost smell the blood on his breath and feel his slimy hands as he cups my face lovingly from where I sit shackled to his chair like a dog. He leans forward, his whip coiling next to him like a snake. My eyes snap open as I swallow the bile in my throat, breathing through it and counting back from thirty.

I'm free, he can't hurt me anymore. I'm free, he can't hurt me anymore.

I repeat my mantra until the need to be sick disappears and then I jump up and grab my pack from the floor next to me. I might as well do something useful if I can't sleep tonight, so I go through it and note what I will need to take with me. It pays to be prepared. And I would do anything to keep my mind firmly in the now and away from the pain of my memories. Looks like I've got everything I will need, I just need to fuel up my bike and-

Bike, shit. I need a new bike. Mine's rusted and probably would make it but it's not fast and if there're more than me travelling, I need to be the fastest, just in case. The slowest will be the one who dies and I don't plan on dying. I debate my options and with a snarl at what I will have to do, I get dressed while making sure to strap on my weapons. I lock the door and head out to the buzzing city. The scavs and roadies are out in full swing now that the sun has set.

Heading to the other bar in town, I slip through the crowd like a ghost. The sign above the bar proudly declares it The Hole-- I know, us roadies aren't very original. Making my way through the quieter area of the bazaar, I descend the steps to the lower bar. It's different than the one up top. People come here for reasons other than drinking. The Hole is what it says on the tin, a hole in the ground where you come to prove yourself and if you're good, you win. You lose? You guessed it, you tend to die. Either that or they make you their bitch as they take your belongings. Games range from Russian Roulette to a ring. It's a way to let out the aggression without bringing the city to its knees. Most fighting between scavs and roadies is settled down here.

It's busy tonight, there must be a gang passing through. I circle the crowd trying to decide what game I want to play. I need a new bike which means that I need a roadie, scavs sometimes have bikes but not always. I don't want to risk it. The music is muted down here so that you can hear the winners and the crowd, the cheering almost sending me spiralling back to my past.

The Hole is one large square underground room which runs below the bazaar. A bar is placed at one end of the room to the right of me with a skinny man working behind it. No serving girls work down here. This place is strictly for the games. You don't want to accidentally kill a woman, after all. The floor is a combination of stone and packed dirt and is covered in dried blood from the fights over years. The only tables are the five which feature the games. They are placed in a diamond shape with the main one in the middle. Along the back wall directly opposite me is the raised staging area for the fighting. A crowd is gathered around as they watch two men beat the shit out of each other. It's a poor imitation of the fights at The Ring. I steer clear of it unwilling to go down that rabbit hole again. Bright flood lighting hangs from the rafters, making it easy to see and I have to crinkle my nose at the smell of dirty unwashed bodies and blood.

One of the assholes who threw the knife earlier is at the table in the middle. I can tell he's a roadie from the others gathered behind him. I heard him boasting earlier about heading out tomorrow, which means he has a bike. With a smirk, I head his way. The crowd parts for me and I stand behind the empty chair, which his unconscious opponent just got kicked out of.

"Who's next?" he shouts triumphantly. I don't say anything, just pull out the chair and sit down. He glances at me and swallows, his smile slipping for a second. He regains it well and sits down with his grin fixed in place.

"You want to play?" I nod and lean back. The ref steps forward from the waiting crowd, I nod at him out of respect; he used to call the fights I was in and he's always been fair. At least there's something going right today.

"Winnings?" he asks in a bored voice.

"My bike," I declare loudly to be heard over the crowd.

"My bike too," the roadie boasts. He's confident and I can't wait to wipe that away. The others are shifting in the crowd either knowing why I'm unfazed or hearing it. I nod my agreement to the ref. The mummers increase, but I tune them out. The ref nods and steps back after placing the knife on the table. About the size of my forearm, it's a mean looking bastard. I should know, it's mine after all. The ref tosses a coin and my opponent calls it before I can, just like I knew he would.

"Heads," he shouts looking mighty pleased with himself. Some people cheer, the group of morons. I watch the ref, his lips twitch as he puts the coin down to reveal tails.

"Worth first," he calls over the crowd. My opponents face darkens and he finally loses his grin.

The rules of the game are easy. It's all about ways to intimidate and show how tough you are without fighting your opponent. It's a fucked-up version of Russian Roulette. You get to slash your opponent's arms until they either faint, die, or withdraw. You can go deep, but you can't hit arteries, that is it. I take my jacket off, gently putting it on the chair. His shirt is already thrown off from his previous match. I look at his arm. His last challenger only got two cuts on him, what a pussy.

He lays his forearm down, palm facing up, and smiles at me.

"Give it your best shot," he leans his body back leaving his arm outstretched, trying to act casual. I can see the tightening around his eyes and mouth, though and it's obvious he doesn't understand why most of the crowd isn't cheering for him. I grab the knife, flick it in the air, and catch it. He gulps, I hide my smile and lean towards him. Without touching his arm, I use the knife and run it lightly across one of the cuts already made, deepening it and reopening the wound. He doesn't make a sound, but he makes a fist as more blood wells, leaving tracks down his arm as he clenches.

"My turn," he grits out, pulling his arm back and grabbing the knife from me with sweaty hands. I reveal my left arm, placing it palm up and let him see the scars. He pales before he looks back up at me, finally realising who I am.

"Your go," I'm openly laughing now and the crowd laughs with me. He hesitates before leaning over me. He makes a big cut; not deep, just long. I don't look, knowing that would make me seem weak. I don't even move as the blade parts through my skin like butter. He watches my face for a reaction and pales further when he doesn't get one. I grab the knife and wait for him to lay his arm out. He does it slowly, almost reluctantly. I smile at him sweetly as I widen the cut from earlier. I wiggle it around, cutting deeper as the skin parts. This time he grunts in pain. From my years of experience, I know cutting over the same spot hurts more than a new one, and this big bastard of a cut has got to hurt like hell. The blood runs faster down his arm and onto the already stained table. The red harsh against his skin.

He grabs the knife and yanks my arm out. I don't make a noise, just let him do it. He doesn't give me any time before slashing down vertically. I grab his arm and yank it out like he did to me. Done with playing, I slowly drag the blade from elbow to wrist, making the pain wretch higher as it crosses over where I cut before. He howls and yanks his arm back, making the knife drag in deeper. He looks at his arm and goes deathly pale.

I lean back and count to myself.

Three, he watches the blood, not even bothering to try and stop the bleeding.

Two, he swallows rapidly as his skin tints.

One, his head hits the table.

I grab the drink from his side and down it, watching his unconscious body. The ref offers me something to bind my wounds and I nod my thanks while turning to his friends.

"Tell him to bring his bike to the gate. Six a.m. sharp or I'll finish the job." They mutter a reply, looking uneasy.

"Thanks, boys," I wink and turn to leave. There, watching at the edge of the crowd, is my new annoying tagalongs. Rolling my eyes, I go to walk past them.

The silent twin steps in my path, I think his name was Jax.

"Why did you do that?" His voice is rough, probably from disuse. It so different from his twin that I hesitate.

"I needed a new bike if we are going to get anywhere. I knew he would lose," I say confidently. Drax steps up next to him. "They always lose," I add when they don't say anything. With both of their stares locked on me and their bodies hovering over me, I have to fight not to step back.

"You can't know that," Jax frowns at me.

"I created the game, one that doesn't focus on physical strength but inner. I have never lost, so it was a fair bet I wouldn't tonight. If I did, all he would get is a rusted piece of shit bike anyway."

Jax's intense stare flares with amusement but none shows on

his face. Drax laughs throwing his arm around his twin. Unnerved by their reactions, I squeeze through them and head back to Nan's to get some rest. Most people run far away when they realise how brutal I am, so why did they look interested instead?

"See you tomorrow, boys," I holler over my shoulder.

Chapter Six

Mad Max Love Child

THE GATE OPENS with its usual buzz, and the sound reverberates around my tired mind. I spot the guys standing a little further out, in front of a line of four bikes which they are leaning on. In the front of them and closer to the gate is a black bike, I have no idea what kind. Most bikes in the Wastes are rebuilt with what we have and no longer look like the sleek kind you used to see in the pre-scorch magazines. They look more like something out of Mad Max. The roadie from last night is leaning against it, the fury clear on his face. Ah, so I'm guessing it's my new ride, I eye it with new appreciation. It looks fast, a sleek black and grey body with places to hide weapons built in.

Heading his way, I nod to the guards as I do. Stopping a couple of steps away from the roadie, I put my hand near my knife which is tied to the waistband of my pants, just in case. He straightens up and slowly makes his way to me. Really? He's wearing leather pants and no top. The leather pants are ridiculous in this heat. Tops are okay. Vests better but the pants just make you sweat and then they are impossible to get off. Just because it's the apocalypse doesn't mean we need to dress like some fucked up love child of Mad Max and Sal from Doomsday. Which is a great film by the way, me and my brother snuck in to watch it as kids. Of course, I never expected to be living it or I might have paid more attention.

He steps to my side and without saying anything, tosses me the keys. I catch them and offer him a nod, he snarls at me and spits at my feet as he stomps past. What a sore loser. I shake away the dust in my head, and saunter over to where the guys are waiting. Nodding at them, I turn to look out at the land in front of us stretching as far as the eye can see. The heat is bouncing off the earth creating a weird mist over the ground, the blackened remains of dead trees swaying in the slight breeze.

It's strange, roadies and scavs are okay in the Wastes, but happier in The Rim. Me? I love it out here. I might moan and gripe, but it feels like home. The unforgiving terrain, the brutality of it all - after all the land doesn't care. I face the never-ending scorched earth, a real smile graces my lips. There's something about this lawless land that draws the wildness in me; I could easily live out here if I wanted. I would miss human interaction though, as much as I might seem to hate it. Plus, it would make it easier for certain people to find me, which is why I put the miles and miles of land between me and him. I'm surprised it has stopped him, but I know it will only work for so long. Turning, I put my back to the blazing heat and face the guys.

"Okay, so what do you know about the Wastes?" I talk as I walk back to my new bike and drop my bag to the ground beside it.

I copy their stance and lean back against the bike. My sunglasses are in place and my hair is braided behind me, putting my weapons on clear display. I feel badass I admit, it was how I dressed when I was a fighter. Just with more weapons and no face paint. I also didn't miss the way Drax and Jax's eyes tracked me as I walked out, nor did I miss their slight inhale and pupil dilation; it made me feel good. Thorn looks me up and down and flashes me a quick smile. Maxen just continues leaning back against his bike. I can't help but stare at him. He's wearing white high waisted pants which are tight around the waist and then flare out, which weirdly worked for him. He's shirtless, showing off some impressive ink and shoulder holsters. I have the urge to step closer and see what the tattoos are, but I hold my position, instead satisfying myself by looking him over again. I can see the bulge in his pants where he has more weapons stored. Tied to his bike is a leather jacket. All in all, he looks badass.

Both twins are in matching white vest tops and black jeans. I don't see a weapon, but I know they must have some; they would be stupid not to. Thorn has a black leather vest on which only highlights his skin. He's wearing black jeans and when he moves, I see the blades peeking out of the vest and the hilt of his sword is visible over his shoulder.

"Other than the obvious?" Drax asks, I'm guessing it's Drax as Jax doesn't seem to talk much and it's too far to check their eyes. I really need to find a way to tell them apart without getting close enough to see their eyes. I raise my eyebrow and wait.

"We call it No Man's Land. Because no man comes back," Jax's deep rough voice rumbles. So I was right - yay me. When I remember his words, I nod.

"The territory is divided up," Thorn states, flashing me his signature smile.

Shit, they really don't seem to know much about it out there. That doesn't bode well, there are too many unwritten rules and social expectations within the clans to cover right now.

"Okay, quick Wastes 101. There are four clans past this border. Reeves, The Seekers, The Worshippers, and The Berserkers. You were right the Wastes are divided up and they protect their territory fiercely. We are heading straight into Reeves land to get to The Ring. You will do what I say and not speak. Understood?" I wait for them to nod.

"Should we worry about them?" Thorn asks.

"They are okay, the territory is made up of mostly scavs and roadies and they tend to be the ones here at The Rim. Their leader is an older man, scary as hell, but you can bargain with him.

They're the most social of the clans, but don't mistake that for weakness," I don't have enough time to cover the others with them, so I hope we don't run into them. All it would take would be one mistake and the other clans will be circling them like vultures.

"Oh, and don't wander off," I added. Turning back to my new bike, I swing my leg over it, knocking the kickstand off.

"Why?" I hear Maxen's rumble over the engine of my new ride.

"There are all sorts out there, just waiting to eat you. Literally. The cannibals, they love to snatch people when they are alone. Stray packs of dogs. Worse," I say with a look back and see they are all perched on their bikes, waiting.

"Dogs?" Drax laughs. I frown at him.

"Stray ferals. They work in packs and I've seen them tear men bigger than you to shreds in seconds. They aren't the pets you remember, they are complete beasts now and they will use your hesitation to kill them against you," I turn back around but not before seeing his raised eyebrows. I pull my bandana up from around my neck and cover my nose and mouth. It's not a necessity but the bike will kick up a lot of dirt and I don't want my mouth to taste like grit.

"Let's go!" I start off and I hear the rumble of their bikes as they follow.

This should be fun, I think with a humourless laugh.

WE ARE STOPPED behind the ruins of an old building. I'm laying on my jacket, staring at the sky with my arms crossed under my head. The drive to The Ring should take just over a day from here, which means we need to camp somewhere tonight and most of tomorrow. There's no point heading into The Ring during the day, it will be empty, and we are more likely to hit the patrols from the clans' territory we are in.

The Waste is basically one big rough-edged square, the border to the south is where The Rim sits. The rest is divided up between the four clans like I told the guys, with the exception of the middle which boasts The Ring, and the mountains to the east. It's not easy to survive there and that tends to be where the cannibals are.

To the left of The Ring is the cult clan, The Worshippers. They really call themselves Worshippers of The Sun. Catchy right? They love this new world and believe the sun bestows power or some shit. They steal women for their leader's little wife selection. The men are rough and some of the best fighters you will see. The only upside is they tend to keep to themselves.

To the right of The Ring, and with plenty of room from the mountains is The Seekers. They are mostly hunters and assassins. You pay them the right price and they will do just about anything. Their clan is run by a man not much older than me, a scary bastard called Dray. Rumour is, he killed his father and brother who ran the clan. I met him a couple of times and it was enough to earn my respect. For some reason, he always seemed to be at my fights. I only noticed because he's a hard person to miss. Eyes as cold as the sea, I remember when I was younger, a wicked looking scar running from temple to mouth where someone tried to cut him in two making him look like a Viking warrior. Oh, and he's a complete psychopath. I saw someone stab him and he laughed, like a full belly laugh. I learned never to mess with him.

The North is what you should worry about though. Home to the meanest and toughest bastards you will ever meet. They don't show mercy or leniency, they are true warriors. They master weapons and fighting as kids and only grow to hit harder and faster than any other fighters. It's made up of all men, women are only permitted as the help, or should I say, slaves? They pounce on any weakness. I've seen their men kill for a drink, so yeah... not people to mess with. Their leader rules his clan with an iron fist and they are completely loyal to him. Their territory is the largest, and although the other clans won't admit it, they have a grudging respect for them and an unspoken policy not to fuck with them.

Their border from The Ring is set miles back and there is only one road into the main area. It's lined with bones of their enemies, like some sort of macabre welcoming committee. The land surrounding the road is booby-trapped, and let's just say being blown up is a horrible way to die.

They call themselves The Berserkers. Their leader is the coldest, most evil man you will ever meet in the Wastes. Oh, and did I mention it's my old clan? You can see why I'm such a ray of fucking sunshine.

The Ring, or purgatory to the fighters, is a peace zone. You don't start fights there unless it's in the pit and you sure as shit don't piss off the other clans. The only place death is allowed is in the pit, and most fights are to the death. Leaving an opponent alive means you're weak, and sometimes it's a mercy killing them there and then. The peace there is hard-won and the only reason it works is that they're so focused on the people beating the shit out of each other in the pit, that they don't care what the other clans are doing.

There are two different types of fighters: the slaves and the freemen. The freemen do it for respect or to prove to their clan the size of their dicks. Slaves are different, they have no choice. Most masters throw in men that are useless to them, or women who piss them off. Any slave can win their freedom from their masters after thirty fights, but many don't make it past the first. If you make it over ten, you earn a following, twenty and you're famous. To win all thirty? You become a champion. It's how I won my freedom, but the decisions I made in the ring left me scarred. You don't come out of something like that the same.

I shake myself out of my morbid thoughts and concentrate on

planning our next steps. I'm deep in thought, when I feel the air change above me. Instantly, I roll to a crouching position a couple of feet away from where I had been laying. Crouching near where I had been laying is Thorn looking confused. I tilt my head, more animalistic than human. He stands and holds out a canteen for me. I stand, and only then do I realise I have a knife palmed in each hand out of habit. I slide them away and walk the few steps to him. I grab the canteen, my fingers sliding against his in thanks. His skin is coarse and filled with callouses.

I take a few sips, never taking my eyes of his. He stands there with a relaxed smile in place. I lower the canteen and wipe the back of my hand across my mouth.

"You shouldn't try and sneak up on me. It could have ended differently," I say in a low voice.

"Noted. There's only one reason people have reflexes like that, and who move that fast from being half asleep. What happened to you?" His face is serious as I hand the canteen back to him. Pushy bastard, who just asks about someone's past like that? I look up, calculating the time and then look over at the others where they are sitting a couple of feet away, watching our exchange.

"You don't want to know, now let's go," I wait for them to nod, but Thorn offers me a searching look. Ignoring him, I head over to my bike picking up my jacket and shaking it as I go. I can still feel his eyes burning a hole in me. I start to get annoyed. Gritting my teeth, I set off without them. Let them play catch up if this is how it's going to be.

Chapter Seven

HIS PROTECTOR

CROUCHING ON THE HILL, I watch the house in the valley down below. Usually I would just camp outside, but with this many of us it will attract too many eyes. It doesn't help that there have been more and more rumours of raids and the only clan brave enough to do that are The Berserkers. So, the house it is.

Tilting my head, I consider our options. I know the layout of the house below from passing through before and I don't see any bikes outside. That doesn't mean there is no one there, it just means they are either smart enough to hide their bikes or they are on foot. I eye the house again still hesitating, it's an old run-down shack. Only enough to keep the elements out, but scavs and roadies tend to use it on the way to The Ring or when heading back to The Rim.

I hear a howl in the distance and wait to see if more follows. If they do, we are out of here. One feral I can handle, but a pack? Not even I like those odds. I watch for another ten minutes, not seeing any movement inside. Maybe we got lucky. I snort and stand. The men are sitting on their bikes behind me. Thorn looks confused, the twins look bored and Maxen looks blank. I glance at the sky one last time; the night is close and we need to get to shelter before then.

"Looks empty, but that doesn't mean it is. Someone needs to

stay up here with the bikes while the rest come with me. Draw your weapons, make sure you stay behind me, and only attack if I say so," I turn away, drawing my sword as I go. "Don't need to start a war." I mutter. I don't look back to see if they follow me, either they do or they don't. Sliding down the hill on my side, I crouch at the bottom, the sound of the men following me making me smile. With a quick look, I see both twins and Maxen. Guess Thorn gets bike duty.

I know there's no back door to this place, it was sealed shut long ago, so front door it is. I crouch walk over the remaining distance and perch under the window next to the door. The two windows on either side are opaque with dirt, so no help there. I crouch walk to the other side of the door and hold my hand up for them to stop on that side. They watch me, waiting for whatever I decide. Tilting my head listening, I frown when I hear nothing. Maybe it is empty. I hold my hand up, all four fingers pointed up. I drop down to three and they nod in understanding. I'm just dropping another finger down when the front door creaks open.

Springing up, and before whoever it is can decide if they are going to attack or not, I use the hilt of my sword to smash it into the guy's startled face. He howls and falls back into the house, me following him in. Fuck, there are four of them. I have to trust the guys to handle the other three for now. The man I attacked is holding his nose where it burst like a ripe grape.

"You bitch!"

I zone out the sounds of fighting behind me and concentrate on this man. He comes running at me, no thought or planning in his attack. He's relying on brute strength. I keep on the balls of my feet, knowing my speed is the reason I'm alive. Men tend to swing first and ask questions later, no finesse and planning to their moves. I move like silk, easily sidestepping his attack. He swivels, and with a roar, comes at me again. I slide past him, this time cutting his side as I go. The blood starts to soak through his shirt and it only enrages him and makes him sloppy. He rushes me again. I feint left and then spin right, cutting him again as I go.

A noise draws my attention to the other fight and that split second is enough. The punch snaps my head to the side, and I spit out blood. He doesn't hesitate and punches my stomach, knocking the wind out of me. He yanks his arm back for another punch. It leaves his midriff open, and from my bent over position where I'm shielding my sore stomach, it's the perfect angle. I push forward and bury my knife, to the hilt, into his stomach. He makes a high pitched keening noise and I skip back. He's still standing. He's tough I'll give him that. Maxen ghosts up behind him, looking like some avenging angel. Yanking the man's head back, he cuts his throat, eyes locked on me.

Quickly, I retrieve my knife before he falls. I turn to the other fight while Maxen is still behind me with the dead scav. One of the twins is fighting hand to hand with two scavs. With a frown, I glance near the door.

Gripping my sword, the blood dripping to the floor, I notice the other twin is pinned beneath a scav. The scav is perched on his knees and has a two-handed grip on a knife, which is slowly descending towards who I now realise is Jax's throat. Sweat coats his forehead from the effort in his arms as he desperately grabs onto the knife trying to stop the killing blow. I blow out my cheeks and palm a knife from my side. Tossing it up and down a view times in my palm, I swing my arm back and let it lose. The thud and squelch let me know it hit its intended target. The body of the scav slumps, his hands loosening on the blade. Jax quickly pushes him off to the side, where he flops down; dead. Jax snaps his gaze to me while still laying on the floor, chest heaving. I look around in time to see the two remaining scavs sprint out the front door. I don't go after them, there's no point. Instead, I look back to Jax.

Not bothering to speak, I simply walk towards him, offering him my hand. He stares at me for a second, obviously realising now there is a reason I'm comfortable out here. For a moment, I think he will bat my hand away; I see the inner battle in his eyes. Blood slowly makes its way down his head and there's a small cut at his throat where the blade had obviously gotten close. He gently puts his hand in mine, his decision to trust me clear in his stormy eyes. I brace and pull him up; he uses his other arm to help. Still not saying anything, I walk around him to the body. I kick it to be sure and when it doesn't move or make a noise, I use the toe of my boot to kick him so he rolls over face up. I ignore the emptiness in his eyes and the blood pooling around his head. Crouching down, I grab the handle of my knife where it's embedded in the side of his neck. With a tug, I manage to slide it free. It does get caught on the way out, but the blood allows it to slide easily enough. I wipe the blood coated blade on the dead scavs' shirt. It's not like he will care. Standing back up, I face the guys. I don't bother trying to read their expressions.

"We need to move the bodies, or it will start to smell. Then, we bed down for the night. Someone signal Thorn." With that, I turn and grab the feet of the dead man closest to me. I start to tug, grunting at the effort; the man is big, so he's hardly budging. I look up in time to see Jax grab his head; he nods at me, and together, we lift him. We toss the two bodies out back. I don't care about them out here. If the ferals don't eat them, they will start to smell and rot but we will be long gone by then. I use the canteen I brought out to wash the blood and smell of death from my hands. I silently hand it over to Jax, who doesn't bother to speak. Fine by me. I like quiet. He grabs it and copies my movements before passing it back. I spin, and head back inside to where Maxen and Drax are setting up our stuff in the opposite corner of the room from the blood. I hear the rumble of Thorn's bike and turn as he swings his leg off. He whistles at the sight of the bodies.

"Trouble?" He asks us.

"Not anymore," I make my way up the hill, letting the adrenaline still drive my body, and mount my bike. Riding it down to the house, I park it around the side. The others watch me, and then go to do the same. Smiling slightly, I head inside to get some rest. At least I don't have to worry about the other two scavs heading back. They know they are outnumbered, and by the time they reach anyone for backup, we will be long gone.

"IS this some sort of bandit safe house?" Thorn asks around a mouth full of canned beans. The laughter makes its way up my chest and bursts out of me into the quiet room. They all stop what they are doing and stare. I slowly let my chuckles die off, embarrassed by their shocked expressions.

"Bandits?" I can hear the smile in my voice. Thorn looks at me in confusion.

"Yes?" He draws the word out, obviously confused as to why I'm laughing.

Leaning back on my arms, done with eating, I stare at him. We are sitting on our makeshift beds for the night. Mine in between of Thorn and Maxen's; the twins make up the rest of the semi-circle we are sitting in.

"What do you call them?" Drax asks with a smile on his face.

"Roadies and Scavs," I say conversationally. The food and good fight have put me in a better mood. What can I say, I'm a little crazy.

"Why two names?" Jax has been throwing me looks ever since I helped him, so I don't bother looking at him now.

"They are different types," I shrug. It's easy to forget they aren't from around here until they start asking questions.

"What's the difference?" Maxen's voice is his usual grumble as he cleans his knife on a spare bit of cloth. My eyes keep drifting back to watch, it's hypnotising. The moving of his muscles as he works on the blade, the concentration on his face. I blink, and drag my eyes away again.

"Scavs are scavengers. They don't tend to roam in more than packs of five. They aren't the best fighters. They tend to be dumb and big; plus, they have no leadership. It's not uncommon to find scavs killing each other. They don't always have rides either. They are the lowest on the totem pole with the exception of slaves."

Maxen nods at my explanation and flicks his eyes up at me, before carrying on with cleaning his blades. Lust sparks through me as I watch him. Why is the sight turning me on?

"Roadies?" Thorn asks, the word sounding foreign on his tongue. It brings me out of my haze, and I keep my eyes averted from Maxen, just in case.

"They roam in bigger groups, usually ten or more. They are a little smarter but not by much. They always have a leader, and are usually the fighters or the bounty hunters," I reply, hoping my confusion and desire doesn't show on my face.

"So, which are you?" Jax asks. I finally glance over at him and hold his gaze. I try to decipher the look in his eyes, but something in me tells me I don't want to.

"Neither." My voice is emotionless, the thought of talking about me making me defensive "Anyway, how did you four meet?" They glance between each other.

"Well, obviously Jax and I are brothers. We were raised in a shitty area in the cities. We met Maxen when we were about ten, after he tried to beat me up, and then Thorn a year later. We didn't really have anyone else, so we became each other's family and have been together ever since." Drax's voice is overly cheery, but I can see the pain in his eyes. What sort of upbringing forces four kids to band together for safety? For the first time, I realise we might not be as different as I thought. With that unsettling thought, I decide to end this little party.

"I'll take first watch, then we swap every three." Not waiting for a reply, I stand and make my way to the door. We left it open to let the smell out and it makes it easier to see. With the light now out in the house, it means I can see anyone approaching, but they can't see me until they're too close.

I hear them all bed down for the night, and soon their snores fill the house. It's good that they can sleep, some people struggle. They will need to rest, tomorrow will be another long day.

I'm staring at the moon, when I hear rustling behind me. Knowing it's one of the guys, I don't say anything. I'm sitting sideways in the doorway, and he sits down next to me, squishing against me in the narrow space. I look out of the corner of my eye and see it's one of the twins. He doesn't say anything, and I know it's not the time for his watch, so I just carry on looking, the silence comfortable. His eyes catch the moonlight and the silence makes me guess Jax. Drax feels like the sort of person who needs to fill the room with jokes or small talk. His personality is huge. Jax is the polar opposite, his eyes are always watching, calculating, and learning. He rarely speaks, and when he does, it's for something important. He has a seriousness about him that his brother does not. I like both, it's like the day and the night.

"You should laugh more, I like the sound of it." His whisper doesn't wake those behind us, so I turn to him a little bit. I ignore the warmth his words cause, it wouldn't do to fall into that trap again.

"You should talk more, I like it," I say honestly. He looks at me, the intelligence in his eyes astounding.

"I don't have a lot to say, so I leave it to my brother." Our whispers create a bubble around us. I nod and look back outside, the silence and darkness making me brave.

"I can be that way sometimes," I reply honestly.

"I know."

I sigh, knowing he sees too much; he's too smart. They all are.

It's silent again for a while, just our breathing letting each other know we are still there.

"Couldn't sleep?" I ask, honestly happy for the company; watch can get boring. Back when I was a Berserker, I was always on watch alone. Only because being a slave turned slave fighter made me an outcast. Half the men feared me, and the other half hated me right up until I won my freedom. Loneliness is my ever-present friend, but at this moment, I don't feel it. That scares me, but I'm not about to run away. I'll get my fill and then when I go back to my solitude, I will use this to help. I eye him again, wondering why he's awake. I'm used to running on empty with sleep often evading me, too many bad dreams. It doesn't help when every little noise wakes me, fearing an attack.

"No." When he doesn't say anything more, I let the silence stretch. I see him look at his brother, his face filling with tenderness. "We always had this rule; one awake, one asleep. It's how we survived, I guess I'm just used to it."

I nod in understanding, but my curiosity is piqued. I don't bother asking any questions; if he wanted to share, he would. I know better than anyone that pushing won't help.

"Why do you live out here?"

I can see him looking at me out of the corner of my eye. Genuine curiosity laces his words, not the scorn I was expecting. I think about my answer before replying.

"It's easy to lose yourself out here. No one cares, I can just be me. Plus, I'm too rough to live anywhere else, too much darkness. Out here, I can use that to help people." I don't elaborate, and he doesn't ask, but I see the small smile on his face.

"I can understand that. Drax fit right in the cities, but me? I had too many demons, ones I tried to protect him from." He says softly. He goes to say something else but we both freeze at the sound of a whimper. I turn into the house to see Drax tossing and turning, crying out in his sleep. Looking to Jax, I see the pain and guilt on his face. When he sees me looking, he doesn't bother locking it down like I thought he would.

"I couldn't save him. I couldn't protect him from everything." The pain etched on his face has me reaching out to him before I notice. I cup his cheek and turn his face to mine. Watching his brother's struggle with nightmares has stripped him bare. I see the damaged man in front of me and my heart softens, making me bold; making me forget my rules to keep my distance.

"You can't protect him from everything, Jax. I'm betting he doesn't blame you and the fact that you still sit here, protecting him, says a lot more about you." Cursing my need to wipe that look of his face, I lean forward and put my forehead to his. He watches me like you would a lion, the vulnerability and fear clear to see. When you are so used to people fucking you over and hurting you, showing any weakness is hard. For him to let me see that? I swallow hard.

"I'm betting we all have nightmares. The question is: do you let them control you, to own you? Or do you let them build you up, stronger than before? Drax lets it build him, he might struggle, and yes, I've seen the flashes in his eyes, but he's okay. You need to let this guilt go before it eats you up. Trust me, I know." He closes his eyes as a tear escapes.

"How-" he croaks. "How do you forgive yourself for not protecting someone you love?"

I laugh bitterly. "When you know, you tell me. For now, all I can offer you is your safety. Tonight, here in this house, I'm not the monster everyone knows me as, and you're not Jax the protector. We are just a man and a woman." His eyes open slowly. I inhale and move away, trying to bring my aloofness back and create some distance. Drax whimpers again and my head and heart start to pull me in two directions. My head is telling me all the reasons why I shouldn't let them in, to get too familiar, but my heart doesn't care. That last soft part of me aches at the pain in that sound and begs me to help. I stand up before I can question my actions. As I am moving over to his brother, Jax grabs my hand. I look down at him as a smile so brilliant it changes his whole face appears.

"Thank you."

I nod and shuffle away in embarrassment. When I reach Drax's side, I crouch and move the hair out of his face. He looks so young in his sleep, his ever-present smirk and attitude absent, to reveal the man trying to outrun his nightmares. I can feel Jax watching, but Drax and all the others being asleep helps, and when he whimpers again, I tell myself he will never know that I helped. I gently kiss his forehead and murmur to him, stroking his cheek. My words don't make much sense, just reassurances and funny stories. Eventually, his eyes lose their tightness and his face slackens. When I drop my hand from his face and go to stand, he reaches out in his sleep with a cry. I swallow hard and look at his brother. He watches us with a gentleness to his face I've never seen.

"I'll keep watch if you protect him from his dreams." He turns and looks out the door. The trust knocks me sideways, to leave me with his unprotected brother? I watch his back as I move over Drax. Hesitating, I look down at the sleeping man. Why do I care if he's upset? What makes them so different? My internal war carries on as I lay behind him and wrap my arm around his waist, so I can still see his brother and the doorway. He murmurs and shifts onto his back before smiling and falling into a deep sleep. My neck starts to ache, and I find myself laying my head on his chest. His arms wrap around me, cocooning me in their warmth. My chest loosens at the feeling of safety; a feeling so foreign to me it takes me a while to realise what it is. I close my eyes and breathe through the feeling, wanting to remember it. When I open them again, Jax is watching us, a look of longing on his face. When I blink, it disappears and he nods before turning back to the door again. Convincing myself I will move before anyone else knows, and I will put my shields back up again, I get comfy.

We spend the rest of my watch like that. Me wrapped around his brother and him watching the outside, defending his friends from the wasteland. It's one of the best nights I've had in a while, and in Drax's arms, my heart races as feelings I thought had been tortured out of me long ago emerge.

Chapter Eight

My Weakness

I WAKE up before anyone else to see Jax still on watch, and the sun starting to rise. The rays hit his face, making him look like a fallen angel. My heart clenches and I quickly look away. Scolding myself for falling asleep, I lift my head. I frown when I notice my leg is thrown over Drax, and even in his sleep, he's a cocky bastard with his hand cupping my arse. I shake my head with a small smile and shuffle away slowly so as not to wake him. He curls into the spot where I just was as I step over him and make my way to his brother.

"Why didn't you wake anyone to trade watch?" My voice is just above a whisper. He shrugs not looking at me.

"I wasn't tired. If you're awake though, I'm going to hit the head."

I nod as he stands and stretches, his top lifting to show me his lean muscle. I drink in his clean lines and the V that points downwards. His finger tilts my chin up and he winks at me. Well, looks like Jax has learnt something from his brother. It's like someone else is in my body; all those hard-earned walls seem to have disappeared, leaving me frantically trying to deal with all these emotions bombarding me.

"Sitting watch all night was worth it to see you look at me like that." He wanders outside before I can reply. Cheeky bastard. I find myself smiling though, liking this playful side of him. Arms wrap around me from behind and a head lands in my hair. I jump but manage to hold in my shout. Motherfucker, I'm going to kick his ass for that. Why are they so touchy-feely? Part of me likes it, I mean somewhere deep down. My head starts to ache at trying to sort through all the emotions and questions.

"I don't know what you did, baby, but I've not heard my brother talk so much in years."

Baby? Fucking hell, I'm going to stab him. I try to convince my traitorous heart that it's not a good thing. I watch the sun rise as I debate his words, steering clear of the warmth in his arms around me are creating. I'm frozen, and ramrod straight. It must be like hugging a brick wall.

"I know he doesn't talk much, but I figured that was because of me." Drax's arms tighten and he kisses the top of my head. My heart races and I tell myself I'll kick his ass later.

"Nope. We had a shitty childhood. When you are punished enough for talking, you soon stop. I went the other way, but he retreated into himself. He barely even talks to us and we are his brothers." I feel him take a deep breath, his chest moving against my back. "I saw the way he watched you, I was worried that you would think he's stupid." I turn in shock and his arms loosen enough to let me. He tilts his head down and watches me with a seriousness more like his brother.

"Jax isn't stupid. Hell, he's probably smarter than me and you put together."

He smiles at me, one not full of mocking or teasing. Just a happy smile. The twins are doing some serious damage to my breathing this morning. I don't remember a time I was ever affected like this by someone. My body is so highly-strung right now, unsure how to cope with everything that's going on. Especially being touched, being held. It's been so long. I feel like that scared little girl again, everything raw and stripped bare.

"I know that, the others know that. But outside of our group people tend to think he's an idiot because he doesn't speak. I was worried you would be the same. That would hurt him more than you realise. I don't know how you've done it, baby, but you've gotten under his armour."

"Wha- I didn't, I mean-"

Drax laughs quietly at my blathering. Seriously, what has happened to me? Has a heart to heart and a night in a man's arms really turned me into this wreck? I fucking hate it.

"You have. I've never seen him smile so much or open up to someone. He even hides from me. He thinks he's protecting me. He always did, you see; protect me. He tried to take every beating, every punishment, even when it was my fault. He blames himself for any that I had to suffer like it was his duty to take all the pain. So, for him to show any type of happiness?" He shakes his head. "It's a fucking miracle. I don't know your past, I don't know if you will turn around and leave us, but somehow you've managed to wrap us around your little finger without even meaning to." He takes a deep breath, his confidence retracting a bit as he looks shy. "Thank you for not leaving me last night." Stepping back, he throws me a look filled with need and tenderness before turning around and moving over to his bag.

A noise behind me has me spinning, my blade flashing in the sunlight. Jax stands close to my back, his eyebrow raised at my knife. Fuck, I didn't even hear him come back. What are these guys doing to me? I honestly don't know, but I feel like I have whiplash. Grumbling, I retreat to the corner of the room. Packing my bag, I keep my eyes downcast as I try to rebuild the wall between me and them. I can feel them throwing me looks, but I don't know what will happen if I look up with all these emotions coursing through me. So, instead, I keep to myself, and for once, they let me.

MY BIKE RUMBLES beneath me as we ride through the empty Wastes. We spent the morning looking through the scavs' belongings and packing up. I managed to regain some of my composure and push my emotions back a bit. Unlike normal, they rest just below the surface as if now that they have been called forward, they refuse to go back to hiding this time. Just after mid-day, we set out for The Ring. Maxen rides next to me, the others spread out behind us. We pass the ruins of buildings, some destroyed by the floods, some in the scorch, and some in the fires after. The scenery shoots by, but I stay on alert, letting the concentration of watching for other clans wash away the need to dissect everything that has happened since last night.

A shout has me snapping my head to the broken earth to the left. Squinting, I try to make out the blobs in the distance, blurring together. When a scream comes, I swear and slow down, pulling over to the side of the road. Parking under a dead tree, I sit and watch, telling myself to keep going. I know better than to interrupt. I know better than to stop. But I can't keep driving. Leaving someone when they clearly need help, leaving them to a fate worse than death would break that last part of me that clings to the light. The part that uses the darkness to fight for people who can't. Swearing, I hop off and grab my swords off my bike. Putting on the sheathe, I turn to the guys, who are already off their bikes watching me.

"Stay behind me," I warn. Turning before I can change my mind, I jog towards the silhouettes. The screams get louder the closer we get, as do the sobs and grunts. Shit. Speeding up, the people finally come into view. A woman is on the ground, a man holding down her arms as one tries to pry her legs open. Another stands over them laughing, with a fourth man on the ground, not moving. Anger burns through me. Fucking pigs. Pulling out a sword, I sprint towards them. Maxen sprints past me, Thorn right after him, both with swords in their hands and fury on their faces. An arrow whizzes past my face, nearly touching me before it hits the man at the woman's feet. He cries out as he falls away from her, batting the arrow out of his shoulder. Using his distraction, I leap towards him. My sword cleaves into his unprotected neck. He freezes and gurgles as I pull it back out and chop again. Blood squirts out and pumps steadily as I hack at his neck. Panting, I pull the sword back. He falls to the floor, his face frozen in a look of shock as his blood drains from him.

My blood lust chases everything else back, leaving nothing but anger and the need to hurt someone. I can imagine that my eyes are wild as my hair streams behind me in the wind, my sword raised to hurt someone. Anyone. Maxen is pulling his sword from the man at the woman's head as Thorn swings at the other man. He dodges him and dances away. The woman is still screaming, the sound echoing around and raising horrors from my past. Breathing heavy, I let my sword drop towards the floor slightly, loose in my hand. I watch Thorn dance with the man, playing with him before finally sneaking forward and burying his sword in his chest. When he turns, he's not even out of breath. He grins at me, his mouth opening as a scream comes from the woman again. Swallowing, I turn to her. Crouching at her feet, I try to push back my blood lust. Her eyes flicker between us all, obviously wondering what we are going to do to her. Taking a breath, I blow it out before trying to make myself as unassuming as possible.

I hear footsteps behind me and watch as her face turns white before she lets out a moan and tries to scramble backwards on all fours.

"Please, please stop!" She cries, her nose red with her sobbing as it shakes her whole body. Maxen steps as far away as he can, and I hear the rest doing the same behind me.

"Please, leave me alone." She wails. My breathing picks up as I try to fight off the memories, her words echoing the ones I used before I learned that it didn't matter. My eyes stay locked on hers, her panic feeding mine. My grip turns brutal on my sword as I try to stay in the here and now.

"It's okay. we won't hurt you," but my voice is soft and unsure, all my concentration on my inner battle.

A hand lands on my shoulder and something in me snaps. I can feel myself moving, but it's like I'm watching a movie, my body lost to instincts and memories as my mind screams at me. Spinning, my sword raises before I've even turned.

"Maxen, watch out!" Comes a shout, but my whole world narrows to the hand on my shoulder. My mind is tricking me, thinking it's Ivar's, even as my body rebels. A snarl twists my lips as I leap to my feet, swinging my sword at him. Maxen blurs until all I see is Ivar, that cruel mocking smile twisting his lips. I barely remember the next couple of minutes, until a voice calls me back.

"Worth, you're safe. Feel the ground, smell the air. Remember our names, you're safe. Where are you? What's your name?" The questions don't stop, even as my mind tries to slip away, back into the horrors of my past.

"Where are we going? Who are we? What's your name?" Blinking, the face above me comes into focus and I look into Maxen's worried eyes.

"Worth, my name's Worth," my voice cracks, quiet and painful, but it's there.

"What's my name?" He demands, pushing the memories back even further, the awareness slowly returning to my body.

"Maxen," I whisper.

"Where are we?" He asks, his voice less panicked now.

"Wastes, going to The Ring." My voice gets stronger until it's near my usual one. Blinking, I look down. I'm laying on the sandy earth, his legs trapping mine as his hands pin mine above my head. I look back at his face as I realise what happened.

"Sorry, shit, I'm so fucking sorry," I whisper, banging my head back down. Why did I think I could do this, be around people? I'm too fucked up for that. Even my mind is broken. Shit, I attacked him! What will they think of me now...

"Hey, Worth, look at me," he demands. My eyes raise to his out of habit. I'm too raw to try and hide anything at the moment and I know he must see the war in my eyes. He lets go of my hands and cups my face.

"You're okay, you didn't hurt anyone. I know that wasn't you. I'm sorry I didn't think before I-" He takes a deep breath, "I'm sorry."

"You're sorry? Why?"

"I know what it's like to be triggered by something. I didn't know, but I should have noticed the warning signs."

"I'm fine," I growl.

"It's okay not to be. Look, I can see you trying to turn away now, trying to lock back down. Just know that none of us blame you. Take what time you need, but we understand. We all have our demons, yours won't scare us away." He offers me a grim smile before climbing off me and standing. He offers me his hand, and I watch it warily, his words running through my head. I don't see any revulsion or pity in his face. Like he said, all that I can see in his eyes is understanding and... hope? My hand lands in his before I can change my mind, trusting my poor damaged heart as it cries out not to shut them out. He's trying to help. He hauls me to my feet and squeezes before turning to the others.

I steel myself for their looks, but Drax offers me his usual smile and Jax winks before turning away. Thorn grins even as he helps the man on the floor sit up. Maxen looks down at me with a soft smile.

"Seems you're one of us now." He offers, before letting go and starting to walk away.

"One of you?" I ask. He turns as he walks backwards, his ponytail flipping over his shoulder.

"One of the lost boys."

We stay while the man regains consciousness, me hovering at the edges, allowing myself the time I need to put myself back together again. As soon as the man fully woke, he leapt at Thorn, who battered him away softly like you would a fly. Once he calmed down, he realised we didn't want to hurt him, but he obviously wasn't taking any chances. He grabbed the woman's hand and ran away before we could offer them a lift.

"You're welcome!" Drax yells cheerfully after them. Turning, he smiles at me. "Come on then, back on the road we go!" He claps his hands as Maxen rolls his eyes. Nodding, I turn with them following.

"Back to the five of us, the five amigos," he carries on as I roll my eyes and tune him out. I turn when I hear a smack to see Drax rubbing his head and shooting Thorn a glare as he smiles innocently at me. Drax sticks his tongue out before skipping up next to me. He doesn't even hesitate to throw his arm over my shoulder and steer me back to the bikes. I hear Maxen start to warn him, but when I don't react, he shuts up.

"You're like a ninja. You guys see the way she leapt through the air with that sword of hers? Marry me?" He asks, offering me puppy dog eyes, wringing a small smile out of me. He clutches his chest and staggers backwards before turning to the guys.

"She smiled at me! I got her to smile!" He brags. Groaning, I speed up, the bikes parked where we left them.

He jokes around with the others as we mount up and only shuts up when the roar of the bikes overpower him. Turning back to the road, we carry on with our journey but there's something different, some shared understanding pulling us together. They throw me smiles as we ride, and I find myself returning them. My attack only seems to have brought us closer, like seeing my demons has broken down a barrier between us. I just wish I knew what.

Focusing back on the road, I try to pinpoint our location. The mountains can be seen in the very distance on our right, letting me know we are on the right track. They always give me the creeps, purely because I know what hides in their depths. We're about halfway through the Reeves territory by now and I'm hoping we don't run into a patrol. It's not a life or death situation, I just can't be bothered with the gaining passage talk. They would demand a payment which would piss me off. Luckily, me and the South patrol have an understanding. They let me pass and I don't kill them. It will be the North patrol on the way out that's the problem. It's an ever-changing position. Lots of scavs die on that patrol due to the proximity to The Ring.

Debating my options the whole ride, I stop just south of the normal North patrol route. The others stop next to me, but I don't say a word. I bite my lip and look all around us. I can't see or hear anything, but they could be on us faster than we can get away. So, I start my bike back up and the guys follow suit. I drive along the border, searching for the path I know is there. It's technically some old rail tracks. It's on the edge of their border and for some reason is never really patrolled. I think it's because it's feral hunting grounds. Lucky us, it gives us the break we need to slip past.

We drive for another couple of hours before I see The Ring. I stop in the middle of the no-man's land between Reeves territory and The Ring's neutrality. I slip off the bike and stretch my legs. Turning to the others, I watch as they do the same. I almost drool at the muscles being flexed before I mentally slap myself; this is not the place to have daydreams.

"Okay, we are almost there." They nod, "Rules. Don't talk to anyone, and I mean it. You don't know who is who and I really don't want to have to deal with a pissed off worshipper or berserker." They look confused, but I wave it away. "Don't go anywhere alone. Don't kill anyone," I nod to myself, thinking through anything else that could go wrong. Which is everything.

"Okay," Thorn says smiling at me. What's he so happy about? Ugh, men.

"Sure thing, Captain," Drax chimes in. Jax and Maxen just nod. This should be fun. I groan, but swing back on my bike and start it up; heading towards The Ring's entrance.

The tops of the buildings appear on the horizon, and within a few minutes, the fence slowly appears. When we get closer, I slow down and roll up to the side. Bikes and vehicles are parked to the left like an impromptu car park. I park away from everyone else and the guys follow suit. Glancing at the sky, I notice the sun is starting to go down. Hopefully, that means my target will be nearly here. I grab my jacket and pull it on as I wait for them to get their stuff together and then we silently head off towards the gate.

"It's a zoo?" I don't know who says it but the disbelief in their voice is cute.

"Yep. Most of the animals either died or fled. Couple years ago, it got turned into The Ring." Not saying anything else, I head over to the guards. They look bored, there's one on each side of the gate and at least four on the gate post above. One holds his hand up and I stop obediently, so do the guys behind me. They spread out, protecting my back. The guard hikes his dirty pants up and then spits on the floor. His torso is naked, apart from the two nipple piercings which are tied together with a chain hanging down his stomach. His Mohawk is edged in blue, but he still looks young. Or maybe I'm getting old.

"Clan?" His voice is full of attitude. I arch my eyebrow, but step forward, my hands out to the side.

"None."

He hesitates as he runs his eyes over me, a little too intently too be anything but checking me out.

"No clan, no entry," he snarls. I drop my hands closer to my legs and the weapons that rest there.

"Ask your boss, boy, before you make a fool of yourself," I say politely. He snorts and steps closer, showing me the knife strapped to his stomach.

"No clan, no entry." He licks his lips "You thick? Maybe you're just desperate for a master, ey," he cackles. I just stare at him and wait for him to finish.

"Ask him," I say again, my voice strong and sure, not showing the annoyance building in me. His smile disappears, and he walks straight up to me, towering over me.

"Boss doesn't give a shit about a twat," his voice is lower. He probably thinks it makes him sound deadly. I slowly shrug out of my jacket. He grabs his knife and my lips twitch. I make sure he gets a good look at all my weapons before I turn slightly and lift my hair, showing my tattoo. The other guard steps forward at this, before grunting when he sees it. He quickly turns away and shouts something to the others on the gate post above. The kid in front of me still isn't getting it.

"Get your boss, kid, before you get hurt," I warn, the purr of violence clear in my voice. I don't have time for this shit. He leans forward and spits on my boots. Did he just...? Everything in me goes still; the quiet that engulfs me when I kill. I manage to push it down and fake a sigh, looking at the other guard with a bored expression. Fake it till you make it. I learnt that early on and it's worked well for me, with the exception of the guys spread out behind me. I could be terrified, and you wouldn't know. Instead, I'm hiding much worse. My reputation won't allow me to accept such an insult, if I let this one slide and it will soon spread from the guards to the fighters, like wildfire, until they see it as weakness.

"He has exactly thirty seconds to get away from me," I make sure my voice is loud enough to carry to the other guards. I hear running feet, but I don't look away from the kid. He snarls at me and goes to grab me, but I'm no longer in that spot. Instead, I'm behind him. I tap his shoulder and he spins. I step back. He steps closer to me, his face growing red as his chest heaves.

"What the fuck is going on?" The shout stops everyone and brings memories I would rather forget rushing to the surface. Sands below, it's like a trip down memory lane today. I turn, giving the guard my back, showing him how unafraid of him I am. I walk slowly up to Major, eyeing the man who was there through all my days here. Once, we were close, I even used to trust him. I thought he would save me, the childish hope in me clinging to him. Now, doubts and logic that comes with age clouds our strained relationship. It saddens me, but also sets my anger alight. There is so much left unsaid between us. As soon as I won my freedom, I turned my back and slipped away in the night. I didn't even say goodbye.

His usual suit is in place, making him look like a gangster from one of those old movies, the shirt and pants only showing a few wrinkles; evidence of his rush here. His hair is greying at the temples and his face has more wrinkles than before. He must be about forty now. Regret and sadness chase each other in his brown eyes until he drags his gaze from me, flicking over everyone else as if it pains him to watch me. He waits until I'm in front of him before talking.

"You causing trouble?" He asks, but smiles to show he's joking.

"Always," I sigh and decide to at least be polite. After all, he never let anyone hurt me outside the pit when I was here. What happened outside his territory he couldn't control, but in here, he stopped it - to an extent. He carries on smiling at me, the one he shows the world, reminding me of a shark, then snaps his finger at the other guard and points at the kid. The guard runs over to him and grabs him, yanking, so he stands next to me.

"You blocking our champ?" He asks. His voice has lost his teasing edge and the kid must be stupid not to hear his death in it. I look at the kid, as his eyes widen. He swivels them from me to Major, his mouth flapping open.

"She's the champ?" He squeals. I roll my eyes and grab one of my knives. Major watches me as I start to clean my nails with it, beyond bored. I flash my teeth at the kid and wait.

"This is your third infringement," Major's voice is casual, as if discussing what to eat. With a sigh, probably because he hates getting blood on his suit, he pulls his gun. He and Nan are the only ones I know with them. Realistically, I know there are more, but you don't see them around. Before the kid can say anything, he shoots him point blank in the face. I get blood splatter on my right arm and face but don't flinch. He holsters his gun and looks back at me, ignoring the body. Guilt flashes in his eyes before he straightens again.

"Sorry 'bout that, kid. You here for work or pleasure?" He tugs on his sleeves, making them straight as he asks. The nickname has me gritting my teeth against the old familiarity. It has my hackles rising and the facade I put on in front of everyone else returns full force. I push the pain at seeing him deep.

"Why can't it be both?" I wink. He laughs, but it's strained and he almost flinched at the mask I slid into place. He wipes his face clean, and then turns to the other guard exasperated.

"Get rid of the body. Inform the others the champ is here." He smiles back at me. "I'll see you inside, kid." He stops, and with the soft smile he saves for me, he lets me see past his facade to the tenderness below. "I missed you." He spins on his heel, which is good because I don't know what I would have said. Our relationship is so complicated, I don't even know where to start.

He walks slowly back into his kingdom. Ignoring the body, I step towards the gates of purgatory, my old home of sorts. I guess I should feel something about the kid's death, but it's just the way the world works. For three infringements with Major, he has to have raped, killed or started a clan war. Poor kid was destined to die.

"C'mon." I shout, not bothering to wait for the guys.

YOU CAN HEAR the crowd from here, their drunken blood lust coating every shout. The path to the pit, which is what the fighting ring is called, is short. I reach the edge of the crowd and look around for potential problems. The pit used to be an enclosure of some kind. Major built a rickety circle to contain the fight and the general spectators are pushing against each other to the get to the front. Tables are dotted here, there and everywhere, with three in the back on a hill, offering the best view. The higher ups of clans stand or sit where the visitors to the zoo used to watch the animals; I guess we are the animals now. The steel barrier separates them from us, the way I like it. I could go and sit up there, Major would love it, but he knows better. I always sit with the "common folk", as he says. I can blend in, and at least I know what to expect from them. Plus, it's less likely that I'll run into anyone from my past.

Satisfied with my surveying, I turn and walk through the crowd with the men hot on my heels and head over to the tables on the hill. The noise from the fight and cheers from the crowd permeate the air along with the smell of blood, death, and unwashed bodies. I push my way through to a table high up, and with a snarl and a flashed knife, kick out its inhabitants. I sniff the jug on the table, and with a shrug, pour myself a glass. Looking over the crowd again, I notice some usuals.

Some woman is bent over on the next table, her fake moans spurring on the fat bastard fucking her. He ruts on her and with a groan, comes. She rolls her eyes and stands up when he moves away. He slaps her ass and goes back to watching the fight as she prowls for her next prey.

"What the hell is this place?" Drax asks. They have finally sat down. Drax, Jax and Thorn opposite me with Maxen sitting next to me. Smart man sits to my right, not blocking the view. My smile is genuine, but more a baring of teeth. This place was my home for years. I thought more than once that I would die within these walls. Yet, I'm comfortable. Call me crazy, most people do.

"Welcome to purgatory, boys. Drink up." I demonstrate by downing my cup and pouring another. Thorn pours one hesitantly. I watch as he takes a sip then spits it back out in disgust.

"That's horrible," he groans. I just laugh, home-brewed spirits aren't for everyone. They do the job though.

"What, not hell?" Jax asks, looking disgusted at the men near us. My smile disappears, and my face closes down.

"Hell is to the north, and you wouldn't make it out alive." With that, I turn back to the poor bastard getting the shit beat out of him in the pit. The sand in the pit absorbs his blood as he's dragged away, and another is thrown in. The cheers increase, and people start screaming out bets and encouragement. A man wanders up, a bottle clutched in his hands.

"On the house, not that piss excuse for a spirit for the champion."

I nod at the man as he puts the full bottle down in front of me. He wanders off through the crowd.

"They call you the champion, why?" Maxen asks.

I laugh bitterly as I answer him. "Because I'm the only one to ever make it out of the pit alive." They all look from the pit to me and back again. I carry on before they can ask, it's not like it's not common knowledge.

"You can win your freedom when you're a slave, like I was. The man who owned me threw me in the first time as punishment. He found it amusing when I won my first fight, and I made him some good money, so he did it again, and again. He never expected me to live, but I did. I kept on living, fight after fight. Not even he could argue against my freedom then. It's the rules," I down some of the bottle and refuse to make eye contact with them. I don't need to see their pity.

"How many did you have to win?" Jax asks, his voice normal and steady. I look into his eyes and he lets me see his emotions. I see no pity, but there is plenty of respect.

"Thirty," I say solemnly. I hear someone inhale and someone else curses, but I don't look away from Jax.

"You're a survivor." His respect is evident, and it smooths some of my jagged soul.

I nod. "I do what I have to, I always have," my voice is quiet.

"Not many people could," Jax takes a drink and I look back to the fight as the screaming gets louder. I hear them whispering between themselves, but I tune them out, lost to the rhythmic sound of flesh hitting flesh. It reminds me of my life here. The constant pain, the fear, the determination to never lose. The man I lost along the way.

"Who's that?" I follow Maxen's eyes to see he is looking at the balcony. I drag my eyes across until I stop dead in my tracks at the ghost there. Dray, the man I thought I would never see again-and he's looking straight at me.

"Fuck."

Chapter Nine

Pain or Pleasure

I QUICKLY LOOK AWAY, letting my eyes run over the people on the top layer. Luckily, I recognise no one else. Looking back to where he was standing, I notice he has disappeared. A tension I didn't realise I was carrying disappears with him, but something in me was happy to see him again. I never knew why he came to all my fights, I was always too afraid to ask him. His stare felt like he could see into my soul, when everyone else flinched and whispered words like 'monster' when meeting my eyes, he looked proud. It was the time in the changing room that confused me more than anything. I had just finished a fight. It had been easy, two low-level scavs trying to prove themselves. I only got a couple of wounds, one being a split lip. I was in the middle of changing when the door opened.

I turned to give whoever it was a bollocking when Dray walked in like he owned the joint, his cold eyes already on me. He drank me in like he was a starving man as he prowled straight up to me. He asked if I wanted my freedom, I said yes. He told me to agree to his contract and he would free me. I was confused as hell, but nodded anyway. I would do anything to be free from Ivar and this place. I heard the sound of the gate to the pit opening again, and he must have too. He put his finger to my cut lip and rubbed it, brushing my blood across my lips like lipstick. My lips automatically parted, and he smiled, full of promise. He told me he would be back, and then I never saw him again. I won my freedom the next month.

Most people would be terrified to have his attention. After all, his reputation alone is enough to make a grown man piss himself. He is wild like the world we live in, and something in me loved that. Maybe my own wildness. He didn't apologise for his brutality and it called to the darkness in me. The way he watched me, his eyes never leaving me while burning a path across my skin, drew me to him. I wasn't stupid enough to try and get involved, knowing it would result in my death, but it would have been a hell of a ride.

"No one you need to worry about," I pass the bottle to them and gesture for them to drink.

"So, who are you here for?" Drax asks. I go to answer when a hand lands on my shoulder, the heat and rough skin burning into mine like a brand. It echoes Maxen's move from earlier that triggered me, but I'm able to control myself to a certain extent this time. I instantly unsheathe my knife and spin, putting it to the person's dick. I look up into those cold eyes that I had just been thinking about. Dray, The Seekers' leader. My heartbeat speeds up, I can never tell whether he wants to fuck me or fight me. I don't think he even knows. He rubs his dick against my blade and I lick my lips without thinking.

"Haven't seen you in a while?" His voice is deep, deeper than even Thorn's. It's smooth like honey and there's a lilt to it that I could never work out. Like the remnant of an old accent. I focus on his words. He's right, I haven't been back to The Ring since I won my last fight.

"Why are you here?" I tilt my head to him, keeping the knife on his balls. Not that he cares. In fact, he seems to like it.

"Got a fighter."

I feel a little silly with my knife to his balls, but I've heard the stories of him ripping people to shreds; so yeah, the knife is staying. He leans down and whispers against my cheek.

"Your knife is turning me on."

Again, not lying, the evidence is pressed against the sharp tip of my blade. I thought I was crazy, I don't have a patch on this guy. He stands back up.

"You going to chop my balls off?" he seems more curious than anything.

"I'm thinking about it." With a sigh, I drop the blade and lean back into the table, keeping my eyes on him. He's like a wild animal, and you don't ever turn your back to a wild animal. He licks his finger and leans towards me. What the hell?

He swipes my cheek and it comes away red. Ah, the blood from the guard.

"This yours?" He doesn't seem overly bothered. I shake my head mutely. He pouts. This grown ass mass who has two swords strapped across his chest actually pouts at me. Sands below, I'm terrified and turned on all at the same time.

"Shame."

"Who is this?" Maxen asks from next to me. I manage to hold the narrowing of my eyes in slightly. What the hell did I say to him about not talking? Dray's eyes flick to him, a different kind of predatory gleam in them. He's looking for a fight tonight, the menace rolling off him in waves. His muscles are tight and strained. Did I mention he's shirtless? Why does he have to be so hot? He has those delicious V lines that make me want to drool - or stab him - I haven't decided. He strokes the blades strapped across his chest like you would stroke a cock. Okay, why am I turned on by this? I wasn't always this fucked up, I promise. Or was I? Either way, my panties are toast. They don't notice my internal debate, but carry on.

"Who are you, high school musical?"

My mouth drops open. Did he just call Maxen high school

musical? I don't even know how to respond. Clearly, Maxen has the same issue.

"Who's your fighter?" Safe conversation changer. He sighs, and stops stroking his blades.

"Some lowey. I need him to die." He leans over me, grabs the bottle from the table, and takes a swig. I watch as he swallows. Jesus, even that is making me all hot and bothered. It has definitely been too long.

"You look like you're ready for a fight," my voice is low, the one I use when threatening someone. Or fucking. He looks me up and down and licks his plump lips.

"You offering?" The lust in his voice not covered at all. I'll admit I'm curious about who would win, but not that damn curious, and I'm not even going to think about the fucking part. I feel like that would be a fight all in itself, but my nipples have other ideas and pebble beneath my shirt.

"I'm retired," I keep eye contact, not showing any weakness. It's a game I learned early on. One of his lackeys comes up to him. I know it's one of his because of the similar cut down his face. It's said it's a ritual for when you pass into the higher ranking of his clan.

"Two fighters up for you," his voice is even and he flicks his eyes at me before flicking them down. A submissive move. My lips twitch. Dray unstraps his blades and hands them over to me. His lackey looks shocked. I bet he's not the only one. To offer someone your weapons is the highest honour. Only lovers or clan brothers do it.

"Hold these." Not waiting for a reply, the bastard struts to the pit edge and expertly jumps over the short wall. My eyes are locked on him, unwilling to look away. I've only ever seen him fight once; it was magnificent. He was sleek, fast, and brutal. I'll admit to watching some of his moves and trying to replicate them for myself.

He doesn't bother with any show boasting or playing the crowd. He stands there on the balls of his feet, hands loose at his sides, with a crazy smile twisting his lips. If I had walked into the ring to that, I would run the other way.

Two big men step through the gate, less gracefully than Dray did, and stand next to each other. One has his hands balled into fists at his side, the other has a knife in his hand. The bell rings and I find myself unable to look away from the brutality that is Dray.

He plays with them, circling, and sneaking in for the odd punch. Dray darts out of reach every time and laughs as they try and corner him. The one with a knife manages to get a cut on Dray's arm and it's like something breaks free in him. His smile is more a flashing of teeth and I can barely breathe as he sprints at the two men. Grabbing the knife from one man, Dray stabs him in the eye. He falls to the floor, covering it, and screaming. Dray turns to the other, who is standing there, looking horrified. The man tries to run, but Dray isn't far behind. He grabs the back of his shirt and flings him like a rag doll across the arena. He's on him in a second, pummelling him with both fists. Even from here, I can hear the bones crack. Blood splatters everywhere and coats him like some kind of demon. Finally, he stands, his chest heaving and his fists clenched at his side. He rocks his head back and howls. It's returned by his brethren in the crowd, who start stomping. The man on the floor lays dead at his feet. Dray turns back to the other man and glides towards him. The guy tries to scramble backwards, but it's too late. He has his prey in sight.

He yanks the knife out of the other man's eye, taking it with him, hanging onto it like a trophy.

"Stand," he says loud enough for everyone to hear. The crowd stops stomping and silence reigns. No cheers or claps for this fight. The man somehow obeys, but I can see his body shaking like a leaf from here. I also see it when he pisses himself. Dray stabs the blade into the man's stomach. Disembowelling him, he lets him feel the pain for a while as he plays with him. Stepping back, he eyes his handiwork before sliding forward and slitting the man's throat. Dray turns his back on the man and drops the knife on the ground.

Dray looks directly at a man on the balcony. I have never seen him before. I file that away for later. Then he looks to me. He doesn't break eye contact as he hops the wall and walks towards me. His chest and arms are covered in blood, his eyes alight with his kills. He likes it, that much is clear to see and a dark part of me whispers that I do as well. This wasn't just about pleasure though, he might be a bastard, but he doesn't usually play with them. This killing was for a reason, I just don't know what the reason is. He holds his hand out and then frowns at the blood coating his hands, obviously not wanting it on his precious blades. Before I can hesitate, I stand and step up to him. This close, I can smell the copper tang of blood on him and see his chest heave as he catches his breath. His skin shimmers in the light with his sweat, and I have the strangest urge to lick it. I quickly strap on the holster, not caring about the blood on my hands. It's not the first time, nor will it be the last. I can feel his eyes boring into me, so I watch him as I fasten the buckle. His eyes heat, the lust and longing evident as he watches me. I can't seem to look away and neither can he, the monster in me wants to rise. To fuck and fight and show these bastards how it's done. It's like he can see the internal fight and takes pity on me.

"I have a job for you," his voice is a growl. It breaks whatever spell I'm under and I stagger back to the table and sit down heavily.

"I'm on a job," my voice is steady which I'm proud of. He nods.

"When you are done, come to my clan. You are guaranteed safe passage." Then he turns and walks away, taking his crazy with him. It's like the world rushes back. If he had stayed, I think I might have jumped his sexy ass. I turn back to the table and grab the bottle, leaving a bloody handprint on it. Dray has a job for me? That is not good. I down as much as I can. I can feel the looks been thrown at me. I have no time to worry though as I see my current target walking through the crowd. Just the distraction I need.

"There he is," I say to the others with a nod at the lowlife we are hunting. He's wearing an eye patch and all leather. Seriously, what's with the leather?

"So, are you going to take the job?" Drax asks. I sip the bottle and watch him.

"Maybe," I mutter. Honestly, I'm curious, but not curious enough to venture into Dray's territory, even with his blessing.

"You saw what he did in the ring, right?" he asks. I nod.

"It was a warning, a message," I drop the bottle back to the table and scan the crowd for my mark.

"To whom?" Jax asks. I tilt my head to make sure I was right. Yep, it was definitely Jax.

"I don't know, Dray doesn't usually go in the ring. It's beneath him. That brutal way of killing the men was a warning to whichever clan they were part of," I mutter distractedly as I watch the man with the patch.

"That doesn't bother you?" Thorn asks I turn back to him in confusion.

"Why would it? There are always fights between the clans. It has nothing to do with me," Thorn looks at Maxen for a minute.

"Are you taking the job?" Maxen asks, making me lean back with a sigh.

"Honestly, I don't know. I'm not stupid enough to walk into his territory, but if I don't, he will just hunt me down. That would be worse," I think about it, then wave my hand. "It doesn't matter at the moment, he doesn't know how long my current job will take, so I have some leeway." I run my eyes over the crowd again, easily spotting the eye patch man.

He's drinking alone at a table in the far corner. I turn back to our table to see the guys leaning over, muttering between themselves. I don't bother listening. Instead, I watch the guy out of the corner of my eye. I read the bill on him, it even mentioned what he did to get it, which is unusual. Apparently, our one-eyed friend over there walked into a house in one of the outposts. He tied the family up. He made the kids watch as he tortured and killed their mom and dad. The son took his eye and so he took the son's life. When he walked out, none of the family had survived. I might kill for survival like the others in the Waste, but purposely killing and torturing for pleasure? It's a problem for us all. I don't bother telling the guys, I caught them reading the bill from my bag earlier, so they know what he did. I'm going to use that to my advantage.

I watch him for a while, thinking of a plan. A whore approaches him and he doesn't even look at her. I tilt my head when his eye sharpens. He's watching a scav that is beating the shit out of another. A tremor runs through his body and he licks his lips. Violence, that's the way to get him to drop his guard enough to knock him down. This isn't a return mission after all - this a kill order. Usually, I wouldn't take a hit, but Nan knows my feelings about kids. Didn't help that it described what he did to the little girl in detail. Even I have a heart. No, he's got to die before he does it again, and he will, as I watch him now, I know he will. The need for bloodshed and violence is in his blood. He's had a taste and now he wants more.

I have to knock him out. I can't kill him on The Ring land. That means somehow transporting him out into the neutral zone. Luckily, I have four big men with me. Rumour has it the mark has a car as well. A rough plan forms in my head as I turn back to the guys.

"Do not move from this table, when I knock him out I need you to carry him out of here while I watch our back."

Jax raises his eyebrow at me. "How do you plan on knocking him out?"

I wink at him. "Leave that to me." They are all staring at me again.

"Then what?" Maxen asks. I turn to him, my face hardening, and my mask slipping into place. The one that makes nearly every man scared, they all know what it means. Death. I know my eyes have gone cold, but he doesn't react.

"Then I kill him." With that, I stand from the table and make my way through the crowd slowly, my eyes on the target. I snag a bottle off a nearby table. The scav it belonged to stands, infuriated, but takes one look at me and sits back down. Smart.

I add a sway to my steps as I get closer to his table to make it look like I'm drunk. Flopping down on his table, I grab on to the edge for stability. I smile a glazed smile at the man and take a swig of my bottle, leaning forward.

"You alone?" I slur. He leans back, disgust clear on his face.

"Fuck off. I'm not interested whore," he says looking around, clearly dismissing me.

"Hey, I'm not a whore," I slur at him indignantly. I lean forward again, admiring the blades strapped to his chest.

"Nice knife." I lean farther forward, balancing precariously on the edge of the table.

"Can I-" I cut my hand on purpose on his blade. I hiss and lean back, holding my hand up to the light where he can clearly see. The blood is slowly making its way down my hand, to my arm. His pupils dilate and blow, locked on the blood. He licks his lips. I smirk and grab my hand pretending to try and stop the blood. Instead, I squeeze more and let him see. His eye follows it down my arm, to my bandage.

"You're clumsy; what's under there?" His voice is low and thick with lust. I look down like I just remembered it was there.

"Accident," I say slowly. He grabs his blade and leans towards me. I hold my position, but drop my other hand to my blade at my side. He cuts the bandage away, cutting my skin as he does. My cuts are exposed, dry blood crusted around them. His breathing picks up.

"Give me your hand," he demands as I protest half-heartedly. He snatches it and pulls it towards him, twisting my arm to a painful angle. Usually, I wouldn't make a sound, but a pained noise escapes. Like I expected, he moans. He squeezes the cut on my hand and I let the little scream escape when pain shoots through me. He looks like he's about to cum in his pants. Lovely. I let him distract himself with my hand. He touches the edges of the cut, prying it further open. I slowly inch my hand across the table. He doesn't notice, too engrossed in playing with my wound. I grab the bottle I brought with me and lean forward with it clutched in my free hand.

"Hey, asshole," I say, my words no longer slurred. He looks up and I smash it over his head. His eye widens in shock and then blanks as he slumps forward, unconscious.

"Sick bastard," I mutter. I bind my new cut with my bandage. Great, another scar. I hear shuffling behind me and spin, my blade already out. I let my breath out when I see it's just the guys. I jerk my head at the guy.

"Grab him and follow me," they don't move until Maxen nods. Drax and Jax go around the table and grab him under each arm. Maxen and Thorn just stand and stare at me. I don't break eye contact. Maxen slowly blinks and then rips a bandage out of his bag. Still staring at me, he kneels before me and binds my hand and arm. I don't speak, I barely move or breathe at the intensity in his eyes. It's different than with Dray. This feels less sexual, more emotional. Like he's seeing all my wounds, all my insecurities.

"Ready?" Drax mutters, the strain from holding the man clear in his voice. I blink and look around, realising I had just been staring at Maxen. I stand.

"Let's go."

I slowly make my way through the edge of the crowd and then down the path to the entrance. Once there, the guards take one look at me and open the gate. I stand at their back as the men make their way through.

"Not on our land!" One of the guards shouts. I turn back to him; he flinches at whatever he sees in my expression.

"I know the rules," I turn back to the others.

"What shall we do with him?" One of the twins grunts. I step up to them and search the man's pockets. Finding what I was looking for, I click the key and then follow the beeping noise. His vehicle is at the end of the lot. The black frame is twisted and new metal is melted onto it in places. Spikes line the roof and also stick out of the tires. Spray paint swirls over the black, making it look like blood.

"I'll drive, put him in the passenger side." Drax and Jax nod and drag him. I turn back to Maxen.

"You can either stay here or follow me. Either way doesn't matter," I say casually. He steps up to me.

"We stick together, Mi Alma." He heads over to his bike, Thorn following him. Drax and Jax look grim as they head over to me after putting the man in the car. Drax eventually smiles at me and heads over to his bike. Jax stops at my side and stares at the retreating back of his brother.

"You really going to kill him?" I don't bother looking at him.

"I have to. What's one more mark on my soul?" With that, I head to the man's car and start it up with a rev. I wait for the others to pull up beside me and then slowly make my way out of The Ring. I head down the road, leading them to the other end of the territory. The side of The Worshippers. After all, they have fewer patrols. I use the time to harden myself, blocking out all emotions. I can't kill someone otherwise, and in this, I can't afford to hesitate. The journey doesn't take long. The man is starting to rouse when I pull the car over to the side of the path we are on. I get out slowly and make my way around to his side of the car. Opening the door, I watch as he falls out onto the ground, swearing.

"What do you want?" he slurs. He leans back against the car, ignoring the blood running down his head. His eye sharpens as he comes around; the monster in him awake. I shiver from that look, there's nothing human in him.

"My job," he smiles at me. "On your knees or stand?" I ask. He slowly pushes up from the ground. He laughs when he stands.

"You should join me, you obviously have a love for blood and death too." I ignore his words, and the men I can feel at my back.

"We are very different," I mutter, pulling my knife from my side. It's times like this when I wish I had a gun.

"How so?" He asks casually.

"I kill only when I have to, you do it for the pleasure." Not wanting to talk to him anymore, I step forward and jam the knife towards him. He moves at the last minute and while it was supposed to pierce his chest, it now sticks from his stomach. He stands there, clutching the blade moaning like it's the best sex he ever had. Lust is in his eyes again. I grab the knife and twist, trying to free it. He grunts and then moans again. Bile rises in me and I have to swallow hard; he's enjoying this. I yank the blade out and he screams, but not from pain. Sands below.

Not waiting another minute, I jam the blade in his good eye and through to his brain. I step back as his body falls. I stand there, my breathing even as the blood leaves his body. The horror and guilt don't surface, my soul so used to death that not even a little part of me is bothered. I thought something in me would cry out, but there's only silence. I don't know whether that's a good thing or not. When I remember who is behind me, my shoulders tighten. I know it had to be done, but the blackness in my soul will just keep growing at this rate. Something makes me hesitate to turn around. I don't want to see the expression on the men's faces. I hesitate for another minute, no one saying a word. I brace myself for their horror and turn to see them. Their faces are blank. I run my eyes over everyone, searching for their disgust for me now. When I don't see any, my shoulders slump, the tension leaving my body. I don't want to examine why their opinions mean so much to me. Maxen steps forward and my eyes are drawn to him like a moth to a flame, my light in the darkness guiding me home.

"What are we doing with the body?" His voice is even. They want to help me? Even after what I just did?

"I need proof of his death." My voice sounds odd to me, like it's muffled.

Jax tilts his head at me in question. "How?" I consider it, but hell, they just saw me kill someone in cold blood so…

"I would usually take their head, but I don't want that sick bastard near me."

"You kill people a lot?" Thorn asks. I look at him, knowing this is an important question. They might be okay with me killing this bag of dicks, but I need them to know I'm not just a monster.

"Only if I have to. I don't enjoy it like the sick bastard at my feet, but I will do it if it means someone else doesn't have to." He nods like that makes sense, and I turn back to the body.

"I'll take his eye patch and that will have to be enough. The car, I'll drive back to The Ring and give to Major." I nod as I list off what needs to be done.

"The body?" Maxen asks. I consider it, I would usually bury the rest of him. This bastard doesn't deserve that. Who knows how many people he has tortured and killed? I'm not wasting my time on sending him to the sands below.

"Toss it over the border, let the ferals get him."

Chapter Ten

THE NEW ME

DRIVING the dead man's car back to The Ring with the guy's bikes rumbling behind me, I let the time and silence soothe my thoughts. The evil from the man feels like it is staining me, coating my skin, making me ache to scrub at it. I pull up right to the gate of The Ring and slip out of the car. The guards watch me as I approach.

"Get Major."

One of them nods, I lean back against the hood of the car and wait. Jax joins me to my left and Drax to my right; Maxen and Thorn stand next to the car. We only have to wait five minutes before I see him. He strolls down the path with his guards flanking him, his suit still impeccable. It pisses me off that he still looks so put together when I feel like I have blood and death all over me. When he stops before me, I chuck the keys at him. He manages to snatch them before they hit his chest.

"It's yours, but I want a room for the next month held under my name and someone to send word to Nan that the job is complete."

He nods at me with a small smile. At least this way I don't have to ride back to The Rim. I was planning on it but it would be pointless now. I figured the guys would have seen the Wastes and demanded to be taken back, but it looks like they are stronger than

I gave them credit for. The fact that it will piss Nan off to see some courier rather than me is just an added bonus.

"Anything else?" He flicks some dust off his shoulder as he asks, before delicately passing the keys to the nearest guard. As I step closer to him and I can sense all the men tensing behind me.

"Yeah, a bottle of your best. Oh, and food sent up." With that I walk around him, my men following. I only stop because Major calls my name. I don't bother to turn around. At this point, I am almost counting down the steps between here and my room, needing to be alone to try and push the feeling of the man away. The way his eyes lit up, the noise, all of it feels like a violation in my mind.

"I'm glad you killed that bastard, he was bad for business." His voice rings out loud and clear.

I swallow down my protest, I know he doesn't care what the man did. It took me a long time to realise everything he does is for the good of his business, so the times he stopped the abuse of me inside The Ring? It was because his customers couldn't see it happening, after all, they are paying to see people hurt - what good would it do if we came into the pit already broken? I know this deep down but I still like to think a small part of him wanted to help. Breathing in deep, I force myself to start walking again, heading towards the back of the zoo, bypassing the pit.

Hidden behind the empty enclosures is a building. I don't know what it was before, but now its room and lodging for the fighters and the clan leaders when needed. A three-story white building covered in peeling paint. With large rounded windows, stone steps leading up to the building. Two guards with massive swords stand at either side of the wooden door to keep the slaves in and the rabble out. I don't bother waiting for them to tell me which room is mine, I head to the one I always use. It's at the back of the property, with only one way in or out. The best bit? It has an old balcony off the back window that overlooks the Waste. It always allowed me to lose myself in the view and made my problems seem small in comparison.

The men are silent as they follow behind me. I leave them to their thoughts. The bright green door of my once upon a time refuge has me taking in a deep breath. Using my spare key I let myself in.

The stale air hits me first, making me wrinkle my nose. At least I know that no one else has been in here. The grey carpet is still soft and I kick my boots off by the door so I don't trek mud and dust through it. The room is large and runs all along the back wall of the building. There is an open-plan living room with a table and chairs and even a sofa. An old TV hangs on the wall, useless as it is now. There's a mini fridge hidden in the corner as well. Two doors face each other at opposite sides of the expansive room, one to the bathroom and one to the bedroom.

"Make yourself at home. There's a shower through there. It's cold, but it works," I say over my shoulder.

I head straight for the back of the room where two double doors sit propped open, leading onto the balcony. Stepping through them, the stone cool on my bare feet, I let my head fall back and breathe in the crisp air. The others talking breaks me out of my bubble, so I wander to the edge of the balcony and lean over the wall looking at the world spread below me. The stone wall is the only thing stopping me from falling to my death. When I stayed here as a slave, I used to debate just stepping over the edge. It would be so easy, but every time I went to do it something held me back. I used to claim the excuse of revenge and the thought of one day being free but the truth? I was terrified. It made me realise I didn't want to die. No matter how shitty my life was, I wanted to live.

Someone's boots stomp onto the stone behind me but I stay facing the land. I was always alone here and that was fine by me, but now that I know what it feels like to have someone have your back, an intense wave of loneliness hits me. I was the one who ran away. Away from here, into my own little world, so used to it being alone. To bottling everything up and only relying on me. So now I don't know how to let them in, to lean on them when I need them. When I feel him step behind me, my heart slows from its galloping pace and it's easier to breathe, I almost gasp as the air hits my lungs. I used to be so good at hiding my emotions, the hard-won mask I wore only to be taken down when I was alone. Now, the familiar comfort of nothingness is gone, wiped away by a few comments and smiles from them. That place I escaped to during the hardest days of my life is cold and empty and no longer appealing. What have they done to me?

"You want to shower first?" I turn in shock. No one turns down a shower, but I figured I would go last. Jax stands waiting for my answer, somehow I knew it would be him. He gets me. The silent warrior understands me better than I seem to understand myself.

"Why?" There's nothing I can do to hide my suspicion and desperation in my voice. I have an almost clawing need for him to tell me why he cares.

"You need to wash away the feel of him." His voice holds no pity or judgement, just truth.

That's all he says before he turns and leaves me to my thoughts. He's right of course, my skin is almost crawling with the memory of him. I watch Jax's retreating back, how did he know what I needed before I even did? Most of all, why does he care? Questions swirl in my head as I hesitantly step into the room. Even though they didn't seem to care what I did, I feel like at any minute they will turn on me, calling me a monster like so many do. To see disgust and hatred in their eyes would break me. Sometime along the roads in this godforsaken place, I've come to care and rely on these men, they've stripped me bare before them. My horrors, guilt, and loneliness clear to see. That scares me more than any Berserker ever could.

They're spread around the room, busy unpacking. I don't make eye contact with them, I keep my head down and my focus on the bathroom. My world narrows down to me and the steps leading to that door. If I don't look, I'll never know the feel of them rejecting me. Rushing through the door, I shut it behind me. Leaning my head against the cracked wood, I close my eyes and take a deep breath.

One breath at a time Tazzy, you can do this. In and out, in and out. Good girl, you can do this, baby. You can do whatever you set your mind to.

I let my dad's words soothe me as I follow his instructions, letting the words that he used to say to me when I was scared wash through me. Once I feel more whole, I strip off my clothes, leaving them in a pile on the floor. I don't want to look in the mirror but my eyes rise anyway. I look different, there's no denying it.

The last time I looked in this mirror, my hair was shorn short from where I hacked at it with a knife so that no one could ever use it against me again. Now it hangs in waves to my hips, the top a dark brown and then lightening to blonde. The hopeless defeated look has left my eyes, now they sparkle with hope and determination. No bruises, whip marks or wounds litter my body like Ivar's favourite painting. Instead, my skin is tanned and glows with health. My face has filled out, no longer starved. So have my hips, I now have curves, no bones peeking out for all to see. My boobs have grown too. My muscles are still there, but bigger. All together I look healthy, something I never thought I would be. I don't cringe or feel sick, not even the slave brand makes me turn away. My body feels like mine once again, not his. When I do turn away, it is out of choice, not repulsion.

I hop in the shower and when I'm under the cold spray, my body starts shaking. I let myself think it's because of the temperature of the water, not that too many emotions race through me at once leaving me weak. I forgot what it was like to feel anything and now it nearly overwhelms me. When I manage to get some semblance of control, I scrub my skin, washing away the feel of that man. My skin turns red from my ministrations, but the look in his eye is forever burnt into my mind. Just another horror to add to my memories. I quickly wash my hair, and get out, not wanting to leave them waiting for long. Using one of the two towels in the room I quickly dry off. I look at the clothes on the floor in disgust, I really don't want to wear them again. With a sigh, I steel my spine and stick my head out the door.

"Could one of you bring me my bag please?" I ask. They all stop what they were doing and look around for it where I dumped it at the door. They all dive for it at once and I have to bite my lip to hold in my laugh. Drax makes it first and struts up to me, the bag outstretched.

"You want some help getting dressed?" He winks. I laugh this time and shut the door in his face. I dress in my back up clothes, forgoing a bra. After quickly washing my dirty clothes in the sink, I hang the towel over it to dry. Before I leave I look at myself once more, a small smile on my lips. Grabbing my wet clothes, I slip out. Heading outside I hang them on the balcony to dry.

This time I don't stay outside. I wander in and sit with the guys, letting their banter and camaraderie wash through me. Thorn throws me his smile and Drax winks at me as he makes fun of Jax, who sits through it all with an unreadable expression, but I see his eyes twinkle with amusement. Maxen just shakes his head at us all, but when I catch his eye, he offers me the softest smile I've ever seen. One full of something I don't want to think about, but I find myself returning it. Is this what it feels like to be happy?

LATER ON, when everyone has showered, we sit around an actual table eating the food the guards brought up. The men talk quietly, including me in the conversation. They keep it light and for that I'm glad. We laugh and joke until the sun starts to set, throwing its last rays through the balcony doors.

The guys spread out on the floor in the bedroom. There is a bed, but the mattress only sleeps two. I protested when they said I could have it, but they didn't listen. Maxen eventually told me to shut up and take the bed, so I did. Now I'm laying there, staring at the ceiling when Thorn's voice breaks the silence.

"Where are you from?"

I know he's talking to me, but I don't respond. I really don't want to open that door. Something in me whispers that I fear once they know everything they will look at me differently. It's starting to get really annoying.

"Is Worth your real name?" Drax asks.

"No," I take a deep breath "I chose it to remind me to always be worth the blood and death spilt for my freedom." My voice is soft but it echoes around the room.

It's quiet as they take that in and I wonder how they will react when Drax's cheerful voice sounds from somewhere at the end of the bed "What is?" I snort, beyond grateful for his ever-present amusement. But I remember what Jax said about his brother and his nightmares. The thought is sobering.

Sometimes some of the happiest people hide the most pain, their joking attitude a way of covering so that no one will ever know the truth. It physically hurts me to think he feels the need to do that with me, I need to remember to ask him, to dig deep and find the real man behind the laugh.

"Seriously, I don't think I can keep calling you Worth," Drax laughs. I smile in the dark, he never gives up.

"Tazanna, my name is Tazanna. My dad named me. It means princess, he said it was because when I was born, I became his princess." The words tumble out of me and I want to snatch them back immediately.

"That's a beautiful name," Maxen rumbles. I'm quiet for a bit, but in the end, I decide to take a leap of faith. Jax shared his pain with me and they had my back today, sharing something about me is the least I can do.

"My mum named my brother, I guess it was a fair trade...you tell anyone my real name and I'll kill you," I mutter. They laugh and I even smile again, what are these guys doing to me?

"What's your brother's name?" Jax's quite voice rumbles.

"It was Von. It means hope."

My voice cracks over his name, it felt foreign on my tongue after so long. Like saying it out loud gives it power, it conjures his smile and soulful brown eyes. I quickly push them away, the pain and loss so great that my heart clenches painfully and my breath catches. The air hard to suck in, I hear the men inhale and then the sound of flesh meeting flesh. It brings me out of my misery, bloody men can't even let me suffer for one minute. The air tumbles back into my tight lungs and my heart releases its painful grip.

"So Taz, where are you from?" Drax asks again, his voice purposely cheerful. I ignore the nickname and groan at the question. I hear a smack again and snigger to myself.

"She doesn't have to answer if she doesn't want to." Maxen's voice is strong and leaves no room for argument. He's offering me a way out, but the dark makes me brave and I find myself spilling my secrets to these men who are worming their way into my cold broken heart.

"You know how I told you the divisions of the clans up here?" I ask, my voice taking on a faraway quality as I try and push the past back. There's a reason I don't talk about it.

"Yes," Thorn sounds hesitant.

"I'm from The Berserker clan," I hear them inhale and the air practically trembles with their unasked questions.

"How?" Maxen sounds shocked. I roll over and face where I know his body is. It's easier to talk when I can imagine it is just one person.

"I was stolen from my family when I was thirteen. My mother died in the scorch. My brother, father and I headed North to avoid the chaos in the cities. We survived for a while, but the further North we got, the worse the chaos. We were running every day, hardly stopping to eat and sleep. I could see it taking its toll on us. One day, I begged them to stop, to let me rest, and eventually my dad caved. He always did when it came to me. That's when Ivar found us. Him and his men surrounded us before we could even run. He beat my father, as my dad screamed at me to run. My brother ran at them, trying to stop them and buy me some time. I'll always remember the look he gave me as he did, he knew what would happen but he was hoping he could save me. My stupid, protective big brother." Silence reigns as my story takes on a life of its own, I couldn't stop now even if I tried.

"I did, sands help me, I ran. As fast as my legs would carry me, but I was already exhausted and running on empty. They laughed as they chased me. When they caught me, they dragged me back by my hair and made me watch as they killed my brother. I had to watch the life leave his eyes as he realised he couldn't save me." I take a deep hiccupping breath, tears slowly making their way down my cheeks, and carry on, "I was thrown over the back of a bike. I never knew what happened to my father, but I can guess. Ivar kept me as his pet, chained to his chair and forced to lay at his feet as he sat in his throne. Days passed into months which passed into years of just trying to survive the hell that is that clan." I feel better after getting it out in the open, like I needed someone to hear my sob story. That I needed to remember my family's sacrifice, despite the pain. Even at night when I laid in the dark on the floor in Ivar's bedroom, I didn't, in case he saw my tears. It soon became easier to just push all the memories away; to forget. But I want to remember, I want to see the good as well as the bad. My dad's cheeky grin, my brother's ever constant eye roll. Memory after memory bombards me like I threw open the doors and they are eagerly rushing out.

"How did you get from there to here?" I appreciate Maxen's steady strength, it allows me to shove the memories back. But I don't lock them away again, just enough to give me room to think.

"I was his slave at first. When I grew up, I went through the same pain and training his men did. He thought it was amusing that his pet could fight. I soaked in their knowledge and brutal nature like a sponge, hoping I would be able to use it on them one day. When I became a fighter, he taught me more, only so I could win him more money. He reluctantly allowed me to join his warriors. My days were filled with just getting through the next moment. Killing and fighting to survive. I don't think he ever knew I planned to win all my fights and my freedom, but I'd spent enough time under his hand, experiencing the pain he gained pleasure from. It gave me all the determination I needed to get away." I snap my mouth shut to stop the word vomit from coming out. They don't need to know just how broken I was or what he did to me. What I let him do to me. Deep down, I know I couldn't stop him and it wasn't like I sat there and asked for more, but it's hard to explain that logic to the primal side of me. The guilt, hate and self-loathing whirling, crying out for vengeance.

"You said you were thrown in the pit as punishment?" Jax asks, his quiet timber reminding me that I might be alone in this bed, but they are still here. And of course he would remember that. That question locks me down faster than anything. I don't want to see his face again. To remember the pain of losing the only man I ever trusted, my light in the darkness.

"Yes," my voice is clearly saying drop it, but he doesn't.

"What for?"

I turn over again, facing the ceiling. Bright blue eyes flash in my memory along with a soft smile, the one only I saw. I remember his tears of hopelessness as he patched my broken body, crying all the tears that I never could. I close my eyes in pain, I can't see it again. It was bad enough living it the first time.

"I fell in love," I ignore them after that, burying my head in the pillow beneath me. Eventually, I hear their breathing even out, and lulled by it, I soon follow.

I WAKE UP SLOWLY, my head cushioned by something soft and my legs and arms wrapped around something hard. I crack my eyes open and then slam them shut in panic. Shit. The body I'm wrapped around like a koala moves beneath me.

"You were screaming and moaning in your sleep. You stopped when I touched you, so I stayed up here." Maxen's voice is soft and his calm even breathing helps stop my panic. This is no big deal right?

"Sure," I fake my calm and his chest moves as he laughs.

"Calm down Mi Alma, it's only a bit of cuddling."

Calm down? I'm going to stab him and then see how calm he is.

"Yes, well, some of us don't cuddle with a lot of people," I gripe before trying to move out of the circle of his arms. He tightens them, caging me in.

"You've never cuddled before?" His surprise only pisses me off. I wiggle trying to get free. He moves one of his hands and swats my ass.

"Stop moving and answer my question."

I huff in annoyance and look at his face. It's open and there's a tenderness in his eyes.

"No. Okay? No. I either couldn't or didn't want to," I stay rigid in his arms. He peers at me, his eyes at half-mast. His hand strokes down my back softly. I grind my jaw against the purr that wants to come out.

"Couldn't?" His voice is soft, creating a bubble around us.

I nod and he just waits. Ugh. "You don't exactly get to have what you want when you're a slave." My voice is hard and I know my eyes must be flashing with barely controlled violence right now. His lips quirk despite that.

"Fair point. Now go back to sleep, will you? I'm comfy."

My mouth flops open when he closes his eyes, his long black lashes causing shadows on his cheeks. Stupid pretty bastard.

"Let. Me. Go." He tightens his arms again but doesn't open his eyes. Motherfucking cocksucker. I eye him, wondering how I can get out of this without killing him with the knife hidden under my pillow. He smacks my ass again and I yelp. Narrowing my eyes on him, I lean forward and do the only thing I can think of. I bite his neck. I don't press hard enough to hurt, but hard enough for him to feel it. He shivers under me and his arms tighten again.

"Mi Alma," he groans. I let go and smile wickedly. Ah, so Maxen likes teeth.

"Let me go or I'll do it again," I warn. He slowly smiles, the effect devastating on my traitorous body that is enjoying this way too much.

"You can bite me all you want." He licks his lips as his eyes heat. Fine, he wants to play this game? I dart forward and bite his shoulder, harder this time. He groans and buries his head in my hair.

"Fuck, Taz." His voice is rough. I press harder, and his hips jerk as he thrusts beneath me, sending a spike of pleasure through me. I let go and pause, licking my suddenly dry lips, wishing he would do that again. Shit, I wanted to wind him up, not me. Knowing that he's turned on only makes me hotter. My clit throbs as he rubs his dick against me and his hands slip down. Before I can run away, my head spins and I find myself blinking up at him in shock.

He grins down at me and settles between my parted thighs.

"If you want to play dirty Mi Alma, you should have said." His head lowers and I turn mine just in time for his lips to hit my cheek. He smiles against me and kisses my skin softly. I don't know why I'm fighting him, but it's turning me on like nothing else has before. He kisses down my cheek to my neck, his teeth gently scraping, making me moan. He smiles against my skin. Cocky bastard.

"Are you going to play nice?" His voice is smoky and sinfully sexy. The fact it's whispered against my skin sends an onslaught of sparks through me.

I shake my head, but my legs wind around his waist keeping him pressed against me. Traitors. It's my turn to rub against him like a cat in heat when he bites my neck. He let's go and softly kisses where he just bit. Then he does it again, lower, each time leaving a gentle kiss to wash the sting away. I'm panting by the time he lifts his head, my breath shuddering out of me with need.

"What about now?"

I bite my lip to stop from demanding he carry on, and he grins again. Those lush lips parting in a grin.

"Keep fighting babe, it only makes me harder." His head lowers to the other side of my neck this time. As he kisses and nips down it. The feel of his erection rubbing over my clothed crotch sends sparks shooting down my spine, my nerves alight. I lift my hands and try to push him away, but without looking, he grabs them and yanks until they are above my head. He holds them in one of his large hands while the other strokes my side, getting closer and closer to my pebbled nipples. Goosebumps break out on my skin in their wake.

Trying to twist away from him, I move from side to side. His free hand digs hard into my hip, stilling my movement. I know it will leave bruises, but fuck it's hot that he doesn't treat me like I'm glass. At the same time, he bites down hard, and I arch beneath him as I let out a cry of pleasure. He lifts his head again as my lips part. His face is inches away from mine and he stares at me like a starving man.

He lowers his head slowly this time, giving me every chance to turn away. When his lips ghost over mine, I'm lost. I raise my head and chase his lips. The kiss turns hard and brutal, all clashing teeth and lust. I open, and he plunges his tongue in, battling with mine. I bite his bottom lip hard, which has him thrusting against me again.

I break away and turn my head to the side, gulping in air. I moan again when he nips my ear, his breath hitting my sensitive lobe.

"I want you so fucking much. It's crazy how hard you get me. I knew I was fucked when I saw you cut that guy's ear off." He lifts his head, the sight of his swollen lips making me momentarily forget what we were talking about. A clear imprint of my teeth on his neck has me grinning like a fool before his words register. I face him in shock, he must see the question on my face.

"Oh yes, Mi Alma, that turned me on like nothing else. Watching you fight? Fuck, it's like porn." His lips smash into mine again and I'm lost in the taste of him, like sex and booze all wrapped in one unbelievable package.

I hear the door to the main room open, but he keeps kissing me until he has to break away to breathe. Leaning his forehead against mine, we breathe each other in, our eyes locked in intimacy. I can still feel him hard and hot between my thighs and it keeps my body wet and wanting.

"You can fight this all you want, I will just keep coming. I knew when you told me to fuck off, I would make you mine."

I snarl at the thought of being a possession again. He pinches my nipple with his free hand hard through my shirt, leaving me writhing with need. He waits until my eyes focus on him again.

"I am not him, Mi Alma. I am yours as much as you are mine. You just don't know it yet."

"That's crazy, you don't even know me!" I protest. He kisses my forehead gently.

"This world is crazy. I know what I need to."

He kisses my face with each compliment. "You're a fighter." Kiss. "A survivor." Kiss. "Strong." Kiss. "Loyal." He pauses above my lips, "and just as batshit crazy as us. Taz you are ours whether you like it or not, so you might as well get used to it." He gently caresses my lips.

"Guys, are you still asleep -" Drax's teasing cuts off and Maxen grins down at me before turning his head to Drax. I peer over Maxen's shoulder to see him leaning against the door frame, looking smug.

"Well, well, well. If I knew it was that sort of party I would have been back sooner. Care if I join?" My pussy throbs at the thought of having both of them. I'm pretty sure my panties are toast at this point. Maxen distracts me by turning and offering me a quick kiss before jumping up. He stands there in his boxers, impressively tented at the front, completely unashamed. I lick my lips as I take him in, all muscle and glowing skin. He stretches his arms above his head, making his erection bob with him. I swallow hard and watch all his muscles move with sinewy grace. Fuck, he's so fine. He turns and winks at me and I know the bastard did it on purpose. I yank my blade from under my pillow and throw it. It grazes his cheek and sticks in the wall behind him. He bends over laughing so hard I see tears run down his cheeks. He straightens with a chuckle as I fume on the bed. Sauntering to my knife, he gives me a good look at his firm, peachy ass.

I blink as he walks towards me. I should be scared of all that power heading my way and the knowing smile on his lips. Instead,

I lean back on my arms, thrusting my breasts out and letting my legs spread a little. After all, two can play this game. He stumbles and almost falls as his attention drops to my chest and then my legs. He swallows hard, his Adam's apple bobbing, before stopping in front of me. He leans over me, his head next to my ear as he slides the blade back under the pillow.

"You're playing a dangerous game here, Mi Alma. I'm tempted to throw you up against the wall and fuck you until you forget why you're fighting in the first place." His voice whispering naughty things in my ear as my eyes lock on Drax's makes me shiver with need. Drax watches me, not hiding the lust in his gaze as it drops to my body and slowly slides down to my parted thighs. Maxen pulls away, dropping a kiss on my lips as he goes.

"Fuck," Drax moans, rubbing his face as if trying to get rid of the image of me.

"You're just jealous," Maxen teases as he saunters past Drax, leaving me spread out on the bed looking bewildered. What the hell just happened?

Drax pouts at me.

"He's right, you know. I've been wanting to kiss you since that shit hole of a town, and seeing you like this? I'm going to be imagining you riding me while Maxen whispers dirty things in your ear all day."

I rub my thighs together, trying to relieve some pressure. He watches and then points at me as his name is called in the other room. "I'm next."

Then he follows Maxen out.

When he's gone, I blink, bringing myself back into the real world. I bang my head back against the pillow in frustration. Why is the thought of Drax joining Maxen in playing with me so hot? The bigger question is am I going to let them? I bang my head again, don't I have enough problems without wanting to start some sort of harem?

Chapter Eleven

Play Time

FINISHED FEELING SORRY FOR MYSELF, I drag my horny ass to the bathroom, grabbing my clothes that are folded on the sofa on the way. I slam the bathroom door behind me. I have a quick cool shower. It's not cooling my lust in any way.

When I come out dressed and washed, the others are sitting around the table with food spread out between them. I slump into my seat next to Thorn and grab a plate. He leans over and quickly kisses my cheek before going back to eating. I look around and the others don't even blink at it. Jesus, did Maxen mean all of them? I shake my head and start eating.

Jax slides a piece of paper towards me as he munches on some fruit. When I quirk my eyebrow at him, his lips split into a small smile before going back to eating. I put down my food and pick it up.

I know your job is finished, meet me at the training grounds tomorrow – D

Well fucking shit balls, that's my plan of avoiding him out of the window. I stare at it long enough that Thorn ducks his head and catches my eyes.

"What's the plan?"

Nibbling on my lip, I debate our options. Turning down his invitation wouldn't be smart. So, it looks like we are waiting unless they want to go without me. The guys must notice my mood because they stay quiet and watch me with wary eyes. Feeling the need to do something, I stand up and move over to my things.

"I have to wait. I'll find out what Dray wants and then get you wherever you need to go. Either that, or you go on without me. Your choice," I strap my weapons on as I speak, unwilling to admit I want them to stay with me.

"We stick together," Thorn declares. Jax nods and Drax throws me a wink. I look to Maxen.

"What he said." He smiles at me and I find myself smiling back.

"Looks like we have nothing to do today, apart from Taz," Drax smirks, clearly eyeing me up. Finished with strapping on my weapons, I saunter to him, making sure to meet his eyes while I lick my lips.

His nostrils flare and he quickly stands and steps forward. I stop in front of him and lean up on my toes, using his chest for support. I breathe on his neck and he shivers. Leaning forward, I put my mouth to his ear so with every word he feels my breath hit his sensitive flesh.

"You couldn't handle me. I like it rough and hard," I step back and throw him a smirk as I turn away and head for the door.

"Holy shit, I think she just might kill me." His voice is strained and the others laugh. I hear them scramble to follow after me.

"So, where are we going?" Drax asks, obviously recovered.

"I'm going to see Major. Something is obviously going on and I need to know what. Why don't you go check the bikes?" I stop and turn to them when I hear grumbling.

"I'm with Taz!" Drax shouts and darts to stand at my back. Maxen grins at me and I almost smack him.

"Me and Jax will check the bikes. You can have Drax and Thorn." I cross my arms and glare at him.

"I don't need babysitters." The snark is obvious. Maxen steps up to me and I concentrate on his bare chest, grinding my jaw to stop myself from snapping. He tilts my chin up until my eyes meet his.

"You don't have to fight us, Mi Alma. No, you don't need babysitters, but I want Thorn with you in case anything happens. You just said yourself something is wrong. Trust us Taz, please?" I swallow my anger and look into his open expression. So full of hope and tenderness and I just can't turn him down.

"Fine," I grumble, uncrossing my arms. Arms wind around my stomach from behind as a body meets my back.

"What about me?" Drax whines.

"If anything, she's looking after you." Maxen throws Drax a smile before leaning down and kissing my forehead.

"Be good Mi Alma, let us know what you find out." Jax steps to his side and offers me a meaningful look before following Maxen's retreating back.

"Now we can play," Drax whispers while nuzzling my hair. Thorn watches from where he is standing leaned against the wall with his arms crossed. My eyes run along him, lost in all that bare muscle. When I flick my eyes back up, he's watching me, the hunger clear. He drops his arms and pushes off the wall. Stalking towards me, moving like a predator, his strength is clear to see. He stops when our feet touch and I have to lean my head back against Drax's chest to see him.

"Why?" I clear my throat, then try again "Why all of a sudden are you all coming after me?" He stares at me, obviously assessing the question.

"Maxen."

I blink, er okay? Drax's chest rumbles as he lets out a bark of laughter.

"What he means is Maxen made his move. Plus, I told them all how much you liked the idea of us sharing you, so now you're free game."

My eyes narrow with anger and I'm pretty sure they are spitting fire.

"Get used to the idea, baby. We all want you and now we aren't hiding it anymore. Now let's go get your information shall we?" Thorn throws me a sweet smile which pops my anger like a balloon.

"Fine." I wiggle out of Drax's arms and stomp down the corridor. A thought pops into my head like a light bulb and I spin to see them stumble back at my quick movements.

"You know that means you are all free game too. I can play with all of you." Thorns smile is slow and sexy this time but Drax looks shocked at my forwardness. I throw him a wink and strut off in search of Major.

AFTER SEARCHING for over an hour and asking at least four guards, I give up my hunt for Major. With a grumble, I turn to the training grounds as the midday sun beats down on us. With an annoyed huff, I walk towards the wooden fence. Leaning against it, I look down into the sand-covered enclosure.

Easily the size of a football pitch, the enclosure is where fighters - mainly slaves - train for the fights. Weapons are laid out on a table just below us, from swords to a mace. There are a few fighters dotted around here and there, watching intently as they spar with each other. It brings back memories, but I push them away and focus on a woman down below us.

Sweat drips down her body as she ducks swing after swing from the skinny kid in front of her. She's tall, probably a bit taller than me, with short spiky black hair. Her green eyes flash in fear as the kid's fist heads towards her unprotected stomach.

Something touches my hand and I glance down in surprise. I'm gripping the fence so tight my knuckles have turned white. I look to Thorn who doesn't even bother glancing at me as he uncurls my fist and twines his fingers with mine.

A scream has me spinning back to the fight to see the kid is on the ground holding his bleeding leg. Well, shit. The woman is bent over, her breath sawing in and out as she sucks in air. A knife clatters to the floor. Ah, so that's how. My heart stutters when I realise what she just did. Before I can shout a warning, a big guy marches out of the shade and towards her with deadly intent. When he reaches her, he backhands her and she falls to the ground, cupping her now red cheek.

"Why did he do that?" Drax sounds angry, but I don't look away from the woman.

"She's a slave. Weapons in the training grounds are only for chosen fighters, which are hardly ever slaves." The big guy stands over her shouting, so hard spittle flies from his mouth. He spits on her and then kicks her stomach. She curls around herself, crying openly.

Shit, don't interfere Taz.

I try to count backwards in my head but as insult after insult is thrown her way, punctuated by kicks, my anger rises. Memories of me being punished flash through my head and I know I can't let this happen. I might be able to kill without blinking, but I can't sit by as someone suffers. Maybe I'm not a monster after all.

Steeling myself, I hop over the fence and land softly on the balls of my feet. All the other fighters stop and watch as I strut confidently to the big man. He doesn't even notice me, too engrossed in his slave. My fury ratchets up a notch when he unthreads his belt and palms it. He lifts it in the air. Rushing forward, I catch the lash mid-swing, the leather slapping against my palm with a resounding smack. I don't let the pain show, instead, I use his surprise to yank on the belt. He stumbles forward as it drops to the floor.

"You stupid bitch. Do you know who you are messing with?"

His face darkens to a deep red as his eyes bulge. I turn sideways so I can see the girl but keep the master in my eye line.

"You okay?" I try to make my voice as soft as possible.

She nods, still cupping her cheek. She eyes me cautiously as she pushes to her feet. The guy moves as if to push her back down and I waggle my finger at him.

"Nope, you stay right there."

He turns his fury on me, forgetting about the slave. This time, I keep my eyes trained on him, the bunching in his muscles letting me know he doesn't plan on letting this challenge lie.

"Go." The girl looks at me as if I am part of this and tricking her only to drag her back and beat her. Sighing, I offer her a small smile. I know that distrust and that look. I nod and she hesitantly takes a step backwards. When I don't move, she turns and spins. She sprints to the edge of the arena where Drax and Thorn wait. Drax catches her arm and keeps her between them.

I crack my neck from side to side as the man advances on me.

"You're going to pay for that, cunt."

Bouncing on the balls of my feet, I grin at him.

"Can't wait," I taunt.

He falters for only a moment before running at me with a roar. I sidestep his charge and he spins wildly, his nostrils flaring. I feign disinterest and eye my nails. He steps forward, more reserved this time, and when I don't move, he launches himself at me with surprising speed for a big bastard. I manage to twist out of the way and grab the belt from the floor in one move. I run it through my hands as I watch him, he's getting even angrier now. Good, it will make him stupid. The first rule in the fights was to let your rage be present but not rule you.

He starts to circle me, obviously looking for a weakness. This time when he rushes me, I don't move. I block the punch aimed at my head with the belt, wrap it around his arm and twist it behind his back. Using it as leverage, I kick off, pushing him away from me.

I want him to suffer, to be humiliated. I can hear the crowd from here as more fighters and trainers stumble over to watch. Keeping light on my feet, I stay out of his reaching distance. He starts to get frustrated and overreaches himself trying to hit me. He puts more power in his wide swings, overexerting himself until he starts to slow. I let him closer and he grins obviously thinking I've made a mistake. I duck under a punch and instantly straighten, throwing a powerful punch at his unprotected head. He stumbles back, the shock evident. I don't give him time to recover, I whip my leg up, kicking with all my strength. He falls back further, bending over, clutching his wounded ribs. Rushing forward, I bring up my knee and hear a crunch when it connects with his unprotected face. He howls and falls to his side. I step back and watch in grim amusement.

"Get up." I jump up and down on the spot as I snarl at him.

He groans, but manages to glare at me.

"Get up, pussy," I shout. The crowd laughs and chants at him. Snarling, he pushes to his feet but staggers. I wait until he's standing to end this. With the belt wrapped around my arm, I run and twist around him, leaping on his back like a monkey. I lock my legs around his waist and wrap the belt around his wide neck.

He jerks and twists, trying to throw me off. I hold on, keeping the pressure around his neck. He staggers over the ground heading to the wall. Ah fuck, this going to hurt. Turning as he gasps for breath, he throws himself backwards, my back smashing against the dirt wall. The breath is knocked out of me, but I manage to hang on. He starts to get desperate as he claws at my hands until he falls to his knees, his breathing harsh and wheezing.

"Do you give up?" I shout to be heard over the crowd. When he continues to claw, I increase the pressure on the belt until he falls face first into the dirt. I ride him down to the floor, planting my feet on either side of his body. When I'm sure he's unconscious. I let go of the pressure and hop off.

Strolling away, I hum to myself. The crowd goes silent as I reach the girl.

"Thanks for letting me take that, I haven't had that much fun in a while." Drax is bent over laughing so hard, I see tears.

"Oh god, I think I'm in love," Drax says between chuckles. He wipes his eyes but I can still see the laughter in them. Thorn smiles at me as he eyes me, the desire clear. The girl blinks at me incredulously so I throw her a wink and turn and run and jump at the wall. I catch the bottom of the fence and pull myself over. The spectators part as I stroll through their midst. Knowing that Thorn and Drax were watching and found it hot has me turned on as all hell, the adrenaline still coursing through my body, wiring me up, the lust from this morning rushing back with a vengeance.

I need to let out some of this excess frustration and pent-up desire and I know just the people. I'm really hoping they follow me. When I hear running feet behind me, I grin to myself. I'm about to show them how a champion celebrates.

Chapter Twelve

BLUE BALLS AND BOMBSHELLS

I HEAD inside the closest building, which happens to be the mess hall. I avoid the main room and follow an empty corridor until we reach a dead end. The doors on each side are all closed which makes me grin, I spin to see them blink in confusion at where we are. I slowly walk towards them letting them look their fill. Drax grins watching me hungrily as Thorn's eyes drop and watch the way my body moves.

When I get close enough, I pounce. Drax catches me as I fling my body at him and I wrap my legs around his waist and my arms around his neck. I slowly lick my lips and his eyes drop to them. His hands drop to my ass and squeeze. I rub myself against him like a cat and he bites his lip. The only noise is our heavy breathing. I wait for his eyes to raise to mine before I smash my lips to his. I show him my need, the extent of the lust coursing through my body. I don't kiss gently, I nip and suck as the kiss turns violent, his lust finally breaking that last shred of control from him. His fingers dig into my ass so hard, it makes me moan against his lips.

A body pushes up behind me and Drax leans me back so Thorn's chest presses against us, holding me up. The angle tilts me so I can run my hands down Drax shoulders to his chest. I pull my lips away and lean my head back as I slowly trace his muscles through his shirt. He watches me with his puffy lips parted, his breathing hard. His eyes are wild and I love every second of it.

Lips meet my neck, distracting me and I arch into it. Drax takes the opportunity and leans forward, licking down the other side of my neck to my pushed out chest. He moves his hands away from my ass, using Thorn to support me. He pushes them under my shirt and slowly traces my skin. I close my eyes as his nimble fingers work closer and closer to my pebbled nipples. Thorn bites my neck, reminding me he's there, it sends a shock right down to my cunt.

Thorn turns my head, stretching my neck as he lowers his lips to mine. He takes his time, gently kissing and licking before sealing our lips together. The kiss is slower and more controlled than Drax's. I get lost in it until a finger lightly grazes my nipple. I gasp into Thorn's mouth and pull back to watch him with hooded eyes. Drax drags his fingertip across one then the other, slowly driving me mad with need.

Leaning closer, I take out some of my frustration by biting Thorn's exposed neck. He pants and stumbles, pushing me closer to Drax. I smirk as I kiss down his neck. Drax thrusts against me as he finally pulls down my bra and twists one of my exposed nipples. The mix of pain and pleasure has my clit throbbing needily. I bring my lips back to Thorn's, our kiss turning explosive as I rub myself against Drax, which rubs my ass back against Thorn. Drax alternates between twisting and flicking both nipples as he kisses down my neck. I almost scream with the need to have his lips wrapped around one. He shoves my top up and the chill hits my exposed breasts, causing them to harden further.

"Fuck, you are so goddamn sexy," Drax's voice is rough and full of desire as his breath hits my left nipple. I take it out on Thorn who starts to move behind me, rubbing, then thrusting slightly. I yank my mouth away to shout at Drax, but he chooses that moment to wrap his lips around my nipple and suck. My eyes nearly roll into the back of my head as I moan. Turning my head back, I watch him through unfocused eyes as he licks and nips at my breast like he did my lips.

Thorn's big hand slides between our bodies and slowly works its way down my front until he reaches my jeans.

"You have to say yes, baby girl." His voice is like velvet.

I almost cry at that, the fact that this big scarred warrior would take the time to make sure this is what I want.

"Yes."

Panting, I look at Drax as he grins around my nipple. With a pop he lets go and moves to the other one, leaving teasing stinging bites in his wake. Thorn flicks open the button and pulls down the zip, the sound loud in the hallway. His hand pushes in and pulls my panties aside. He cups my pussy and applies pressure as I roll my hips against his hand. Drax lets go of my nipple and blows a cold breath on the wet sensitive nub. I moan and grab his head in my hands and pull him towards me. He comes willingly and I push my lips to his.

Thorn pulls his palm away making me whine, his finger tracing lightly down my lips and back up again, spreading my own need around me. One of his fingers dips lightly inside me before pulling out again. Pulling his hand from my pants, he offers his fingers to Drax. I drag my lips away and watch as Drax grins and licks them. Holy sands below.

"Jesus Taz, you taste amazing. I can't wait to have my head between your thighs as I eat you." He grins before diving back to my lips. I can taste myself on him and it only adds to my wetness. Thorn's fingers work their way back between our bodies and into my waiting pussy again.

He circles my clit as it throbs, putting pressure on everywhere but where I need him. I buck, trying to move his finger and he stops. His breath hits my ear making me shiver.

"Be a good girl and you will get what you want," he waits for me to stop moving before starting his maddening circle again.

A throat clearing from somewhere behind us has me blinking the corridor back into view. Drax pulls away enough so I can see Major behind him looking amused. Thorn doesn't stop his circling and I don't pull away.

"What do you need?" My voice is harsh and husky but I don't give a fuck. His eyes don't drop from mine even as his lips stretch into a toothy grin.

"We need to talk."

Really? Right this fucking moment? Thorn presses against my clit, making me buck up into him as I bite my lip to hide a scream.

"Fuck! Right now?" I grunt and drop my head back against Thorn's shoulder. He pulls his finger away and cups my pussy again.

"Yes, I wouldn't interrupt but it's important. I'll wait outside while you get dressed. One minute, Worth, then I'll drag you out myself."

I hear him walk away humming to himself, bloody bastard. I sigh and open my eyes again.

"Play time's over boys," my voice is more even this time. Thorn pulls his hand from my pants and I prop my legs from Drax's waist. I step away so my back is to the wall and grin at their frustrated expressions. I quickly pull up my bra and straighten my top as their hungry eyes track my fingers.

"Aww, it was just getting interesting," Drax pouts at me as I zip and button my jeans. Thorn's face is animalistic and I have to stop myself from jumping them again. I saunter up to them, trying to ignore my needy pussy. I kiss Drax's lips quickly and turn to Thorn. I kiss him and then pull away so my head is between theirs.

"If you're good boys, we can play later." I turn and walk down the hallway and laugh as they both scramble to follow after me.

My head turns back to business at the warning in Major's tone. Something is up and I'm not leaving this time until I have answers.

"You head back to the room, I'll see what Major wants."

"Got it, baby girl. Try not to kill anyone," Thorn smacks my ass as he strides past and I glare at his retreating back, fingering one of my knives, debating throwing it at him in warning. Drax rushes past me, jogging after his friend before turning and walking back towards me, his long legs eating the distance between us. He grabs my waist and spins me around as he kisses both cheeks and then my lips.

"What he said, though if you do, can I watch? It makes me so hard watching you fight." He waggles his eyebrows at me.

"Dirty bastard, I'll think about it."

He winks and drops me gently to the floor before offering me a smirk and chasing after Thorn.

Shit, my pussy throbs again, reminding me why I jumped them in the first place. Can women get blue balls?

"This better be good," I warn Major as I step out of the building. I shield my eyes from the sun and see Thorn and Drax wandering back to the room. My lips twitch at their disgruntled expressions.

"It is, shall we go to my office?" I drag my eyes away from them and meet Major's. I ignore the questions swirling in their depths and nod. With one last look back at the boys as they turn the corner, I follow after Major as he strides away.

MAJOR'S OFFICE is a mix of the old world and the new one. A large clean wooden desk sits in the middle of the room with a comfy looking chair behind it. Paintings cover the deep wood wall and two black leather chairs sit opposite his desk. Weapons ranging from small blades to maces line the wall behind the desk from ceiling to floor. A balcony door is open and the sound of flesh hitting flesh and the crowd filters through with the sunlight.

Major makes his way silently across the carpeted floor to sit behind his desk. He slumps in his seat, rubbing his head, and I notice the bags under his eyes and the stress that lines his face. Whatever has made this usually stoic man lose sleep will not be good.

I plop myself down in one of the comfy leather seats and drop my legs on his desk. He doesn't even comment on my dirty boots touching his clean desk, shit something bad is going on.

I drag my feet off and they fall to the floor with a bang. "What's going on?" I brace myself as he looks up at me.

"I'm sorry kid, I didn't want to tell you. I know you've been sticking your head in the sand ever since you escaped and it worked for you. To tell you the truth, I had hoped you would never come back here," he trails off as he rubs his chin in thought.

"Spit it out, you know I don't do well with half-truths." My fingers bite deep into the arms of the chair as I try and anchor myself. I will myself to stay calm. Major finally looks up at me.

"When I first saw you fight I knew you were a survivor. It was written on your face, the steel and determination to get through whatever you had to," he swallows hard. "You had a hard past kid, I wish I could protect you from this now."

"Major," I growl out the warning.

"He's looking for you."

Those four words stop me like nothing else. Ice runs in my veins as the sound drops away from the room. I drop my unfocused stare to the desk. My saliva tastes like sawdust in my mouth as I swallow repeatedly. Why now? Why after all this time? Haven't I earned my life? Questions and self-pity make me slump in my seat.

The sound comes back into the room with a bang, making my

ears ring. My name being called has me blinking to bring my eyes back into focus.

"Tazanna." My name snaps me out of my funk and with a start, I look at Major. He's crouched in front of me, gripping my clenched hands. His face is pale and full of sympathy.

"Tazanna, did you hear me?" I nod and he drops my hands. I slowly uncurl my fingers from my palms, they leave bloody half crescents where my nails have dug into the sensitive skin. I lick my lips and wipe my hands on my jeans to get rid of the blood, uncaring about the stains.

Major stands with a sigh and makes his way around his desk again. He sits on the edge of his seat and fumbles in his drawer, I just watch him as my world crumbles around me.

He will find me and when he does, the punishment will be unbearable. Living under his thumb again as a slave after being free is something I can't do, I would rather die. I have no doubt that he will find a way to make me his pet again if he gets the chance.

Major offers me an open bottle and I grab it gratefully before taking a huge swallow. When I'm done, I lower the bottle and nod for him to carry on. He leans back and watches me carefully like I'm about to break. It has my hackles rising and I offer him a smile filled with agony.

"I'm fine. How do you know this?" My voice sounds small and so unlike me.

"I don't know how much you paid attention after you left but Ivar has been, well he's been-"

"Spit it out, Major."

"He's unstable."

I laugh bitterly. "He's always been unstable."

Major nods grimly.

"More than normal, kid. They say losing his favourite pet," he winces at the word but I don't flinch, I'm aware of what I used to be. "Well, it drove him crazy. He started punishing his generals, pushing his fighters so hard they died. He turned his sick habits and pleasures on his clan."

Ivar laughs as he slowly twists the pliers in my mouth, pulling the tooth out from its roots. He shows me it clutched between the rusted metal prongs like some sort of prize. The blood fills my mouth and slides down my throat, almost making me choke on it. I refuse to cry or scream; instead, I offer him dead eyes, so lacking in the pain he revels in that he stops laughing and backhands me

I grit my teeth against the memories. I can almost feel the pain and blood, but I manage to push them back.

"I'm aware of his need to watch people suffer. I know how he gets off on other people's pain," I say, Majors eyes flash with misery before they lock down.

"I know, kid. Even his people are questioning his leadership." I blink at that, in a stupor.

"Impossible, they are completely loyal. They never even blinked before." My voice is filled with the shock I feel.

"True, but you push a man far enough, kid, and they will eventually snap. I think he's done that to his people. Half of them are talking revolution with Noah's father at the helm." My heart stops at his name on Majors' tongue and I have to suck in a lungful of air before nodding again. At this point I don't think I can handle any more surprises. He offers me an apologetic wince before carrying on.

"The other half are searching the Wastes and leaving chaos in their wake. Raid after raid, uncaring whose territory they are pissing on." His stare is intense, he's obviously making sure I'm seeing where he's heading. Although I know, I have to be sure.

"They looking for me?" It's his turn to nod.

"Yes. A Reever scav managed to capture one of their men and get him to talk. He owed me a favour so he told me what he could.

This faction of Berserkers thinks finding you and offering you as sacrifice to Ivar The Mad will bring him back."

My eyebrows raise at the name, "Ivar The Mad?"

"That's what they are calling him now, no longer is he Ivar The Destroyer."

Chapter Thirteen

THE HARD TRUTH

"SO, let me get this straight. The Berserkers are split in two, with my ex-boyfriend's dad leading a revolution in their midst and the other half are hunting through the Wasteland, probably causing a war between all the clans, looking for me in hopes that returning me to Ivar will bring their ruthless leader again?"

Major smiles at me. "Pretty much."

It's my turn to rub my eyes.

"Amazing. So that explains all the rumours of raids, but what does this have to do with Dray?" He cocks his eyebrow at me in question and I grin, I did, after all, learn that from him.

"What about him?"

My face freezes. "He said he had a job for me, then sent me a note to meet him here tomorrow." Major pales and jumps up, pacing behind his desk.

"Shit, kid you couldn't just have one mad bastard after you, could you?" My mouth flaps open at hearing him swear.

"It must be my winning personality," I joke dryly. He stops pacing and snorts out a laugh. Slumping back in his chair, he steeples his hands under his chin.

"I haven't heard any rumours, well none out of the usual about him. If he's meeting you here, at least you know he's not going to kill you," he murmurs, almost talking to himself.

My lips twist in a mocking smile. "I don't think he would anyway. He has a strange obsession with me, I think he both hates it and craves it. He offered me safe passage, so I'll meet him and see what the job is." Major nods along.

"I know, he always insisted about being informed about when your fights were."

I blink in shock. "You told him?"

Major leans back and blanked his face, another thing I learned from him.

"Yes, I did. There was no way was I going to deny a pleasant request from the man who killed his own father over leadership. He never caused issues, so I kept on informing him." I look at the desk in thought, my brain has had too much shoved in it recently "I hoped he would save you…" Major's words are quiet and make my jaw clench as a flash of anger heats through me.

"I saved myself. I'm not a princess who needs rescuing, I didn't need a knight in shining armour to ride in on a horse. I can take care of myself." My voice is hard with a threat clearly running through it.

"True, although Dray is more a madman on a motorcycle." He wipes his hand through the air. "So, these men you are with?" He sits back and waits me out.

Stubborn bastard, why do I feel like I'm going to get a sex talk? Sometimes I think he imagines himself as my father, but other times I doubt he even cares enough. I mean how could he when he just walked away when I needed someone? What I told him was true, I can save myself, but as a young girl, Major put stars in my eyes. I yearned for his smiles and our meetings where he would impart fact after fact into my eager head. I thought he cared for me, and when he didn't save me from the fights, it broke something in me, something I'm not sure I can fix. My innocence.

"Are none of your business." I could claim they are a job, although technically true, they have moved far past that now, and no matter how much history and bad blood between me and Major, I still will never lie to him.

"Tazanna," he warns. I sit bolt upright.

"Do not start to lecture me about my life Major, you won't like what happens. You are not my father, you are not my friend, you are a memory from a desperate girl clinging on to any hope in a dark world. One that she built up so tall in her imagination, the real him could never match." I see my words hit home as he flinches like they physically hurt him with their malice.

"I just don't want to see you hurt is all," he sighs and rubs his head as I lock down tight on my memories, unwilling to let them lift their ugly head. "I know what Noah's death did to you, I also saw the way you look at these guys. This thing between you and them is serious, even if you aren't willing to admit it. You lean on them. You never did that with... Anyway, I just don't want to see that again."

His face is open and sincere and it only ignites my anger further. It's the side of him he only ever showed to me, the one we hid behind the walls where he was my mentor and I was a scared little girl. How dare he pretend to care? His words break through the barrier to my past, bringing all the hurt and betrayal back like a freight train. The peace I built between us in the name of work shatters audibly.

"Don't pretend you give a shit about me, Major. I was an investment to you, and a good one at that. Don't let my casual manner fool you, I'm old enough to know now that you could have helped me. You could have saved me. You chose not to. You put your life and business first. I don't blame you for that anymore, you did what everyone does in the Wastes. Put yourself first. But those guys out there? They don't. They have my back and have risked themselves for me. Which is more than I can ever say for you."

He winces at my harsh words as his lips tug down.

"I might not be an amazing person, Tazanna. I might not be

the man you thought I was, but I did try to help you. It might not have been the open rescue like you wanted, but I was always there behind the scenes. Selecting your fighters so I didn't have to see you lose a piece of your soul again as you fought some weak innocent slave. It made your fights harder but I knew you could handle it. Or stopping Ivar from punishing you within my walls; I made that rule to protect you. Or telling the leader of The Berserkers that you needed training, training that only I could offer." His voice is rising with his words. They drag over old wounds, making my heart smash against my chest. "You were the child I lost, Tazanna and it killed me to watch you every day, but I promised myself if you could live through it, then I could watch it. Those meetings where I tried to teach you everything you needed to know to survive this world were the highlights of my day." He stops, his chest rising and falling hard.

"Then why did you lie to me? Why not tell me this?" My eyes want to fill with tears of hopelessness, the ones I never shed when I realized that the man I looked up to wasn't the one I thought he was.

"Because I loved the way you looked at me, so much hope and trust. You hung on my every word, it made the shit I had to do worth it. I'm a selfish bastard kid, I couldn't stand watching that melt away into hatred. But it did anyway. By not telling you I couldn't save you, I watched the last part of you that was still a child wither and die," he slaps his palm against his heart. "That broke my heart Taz. So, you can build me up into the villain in your head, but know this: I am always here, I always had your back, and I always will. I'm not perfect, what person ever is? Isn't it enough I fought that part of me for you? The one which worried about nothing but myself or screamed at me to stop getting involved." His eyes fill as he watches me with hope. The distance between us seems bigger than ever as all our lies, half-truths, and memories drop into it. I wish I could trust him again, that I could fling myself into his arms and cry it all out like I used to. I wish I could find shelter in his arms, but I'm no longer that child. I know being in his arms doesn't mean I'm safe and I know that my tears won't change anything. So I push them down and he watches me do so with a heartbroken expression, the Major he shows to the world cracking to reveal the man underneath.

I know to survive this world he must have done things which changed him. Maybe I would have loved the old Major, or maybe I would have never known him. But we are both not the people we want to be, we are both damaged by the choices we made. I hide it beneath layers and layers of sarcasm and control. Maybe he's right, isn't it enough that he – we - are trying to be more, to be better?

We watch each other for a long time before he breaks the silence.

"I hope one day you will forgive me enough to allow me to earn your trust again. I will never forgive myself, but I want you in my life in whatever way I can have you, and know that I am so proud of you. You are the most resilient, stubborn, caring person I have ever met. We all make mistakes Taz, maybe it's time to start moving on from them." He steels himself, rebuilding himself before my eyes until my mentor disappears and in his place sits Major, leader and executioner of The Ring. I nod and stand to leave, done with this whole day.

"I asked about those men because I do care, and you forget that I witnessed your darkest days. I don't want you going back down that path, it's good to see you smile. Just be careful you don't lean on the wrong people. Ask yourself what do you really know about them?"

I want to scream and shout and defend them, I want to fling his words back in his face. After all, I leaned on him. Instead, I turn calmly to the door, not bothering to reply. I stop when I hold the handle, the metal rough under my hands. I grip it tightly and force the words out. If there is one thing I have learned, it is that you never know when your words to someone might be the last, so they might not be the ones he wants to hear, but they are all I can offer him.

"I don't know if I can ever forgive you, but I want to." I flee before he can reply and I let his words follow me, darkening my steps and making me question the guys. I can see the building in the distance and part of me wants to run into their arms and claim he's wrong. The smarter part of me knows I've been betrayed before.

Is he right? What do I know about them?

I DRAG my feet on the way back to the room. I decide to see what they say when I tell them the news, and if need be, question them later. My insecurities and trust issues make it hard for me to clear my face but I manage it by the time I open the door.

Drax's head drops back on the sofa so it faces me upside down. He grins, making him look strange. Thorn smiles at me from the floor where he is sorting through his bag. Their smiles wash away my doubts, I can still feel them niggling in the back of my head but it's easier to ignore.

"Hey baby cakes," Drax calls happily. I raise my eyebrow at the nickname and wander through the room aimlessly.

"Where's Jax and Maxen?" I end up at the table and frown at the cloth covered lump laying there. I finger the edge as Thorn comes to stand next to me.

"Still with the bikes, apparently one had a problem. That's for you, by the way." He nods at the lump and then darts in and kisses my cheek. With a little grin, he walks off back to his bag. I watch him go, still feeling out of it. Drax meets my gaze and frowns at me.

"Where's my kiss?" he sounds so put out that I laugh. I saunter to him and lean down. Major's words stop me from kissing his lips, but I kiss both cheeks. When I pull away his smile is huge and he watches me tenderly.

"Thanks, baby." He strokes my cheek before I pull away with a deep breath. Heading over to the table, I ignore everything and just concentrate on not blurting out questions at them. I lift the cloth and only get more confused. A denim pair of shorts, a sword very similar to my own but with a skull as the hilt, and a folded letter. I glance at the men but they are talking between themselves, happy enough. I gently touch the skull and run my hand down the blade. It's beautiful. It shines in the light, obviously well looked after. At the bottom of the hilt, there are some bumps and I lean in closer. I squint at the small engravings on the blade.

My destiny

The words are small, but perfectly carved, only adding to the beauty of the blade. Even more curious, I drag my reluctant hand away from the sword and pick up the letter. The writing is neat and the same as the note from the other day.

Thought you might need these – D

Dropping the note, I finger the denim shorts. I'll admit the idea of letting air get to my legs is appealing, I just never wanted to cut my jeans before. Why would he give me these though? And the sword? More questions than answers pile up about Dray.

The door bangs open as Maxen saunters in, Jax on his heels. He flicks me a smile before flopping on the floor near Thorn. Jax nods at his brother before making his way to me. He blinks down at me, his lips curling in a private smile before they look at the sword I'm caressing. The smile grows and he leans in and kisses my head quickly before turning away and yanking his brother's feet off the sofa so he can sit.

Each kiss, each smile, and each little word is pushing them deeper and deeper inside my guard and if Major is right, if they betray me, I don't think there would be anything left of me to fight.

I slump hard into one of the chairs surrounding the table and watch as they laugh and joke between themselves.

My mum once told me that she knew as soon as she saw my dad that he was the one. I never believed in love at first sight. What Noah and I had was a friendship that turned into caring and I was just growing to love him when it all happened, but these four? There's no growing, and time only seems to make it stronger. I was drawn to them that first day I met their eyes and no matter how much I fight against it, they are slowly becoming my reason to smile. The bits and pieces of my broken cold heart are slowly stitching back together again and they are the reason why. So do I trust them or do I let Major's words break this fledgling thing?

Chapter Fourteen

STRIPPED BARE

AFTER I PULL myself out of my funk, I decide we should go for food instead of eating in our room again. They are happy to follow me, so now I find myself surrounded by my men. The mess hall is full, the fighters and masters winding down for the day over a meal and drinks.

At least twenty tables in all shapes and sizes are scattered throughout the utilitarian room. The floor is a mixture of mismatched cracked tile and stone, the walls an unappealing grey. A serving hatch sits at one end of the room, and a table with trays and cutlery next to it. A makeshift bar sits along the back wall, with opened bottles of spirits ready to drink.

I'm waiting for Maxen and Drax to come back with the food when a voice comes from behind me. So far, the others in the room have kept a polite distance. I ignore it, hoping whoever it is will go away. It seems I'm shit out of luck when they round the table to stand in my eye line. My eyebrows rise when I realise it's the slave I saved today. She offers me a shy smile.

"Hi, I just wanted to thank you." She eyes Drax and Thorn appreciatively before sitting down opposite me in the spot between them that Jax had just vacated.

"You're welcome. Was there something else?" She pulls her eyes from Thorn's muscles with effort to focus on me. Jax sits down next to me and pushes some food in front of me. Maxen sits on my other side, eyeing the girl as he adds a drink in front of me. Her eyes rove over them both before stopping on Jax. His face loses all emotion, making me realise he had started to show more around the guys.

"Erm, yeah. I erm-" She looks back at me, "Major told me it's you who I thank for getting me set free, so I guess I owe you a double thanks." I tilt my head in confusion.

"He didn't tell you?"

I shake my head "Oh, well he said he set me free for you and he offered me a job as well. So, I owe you my life. You can't imagine how horrible it was being that pig's slave." I don't correct her, but offer her a nod. She smiles at me before her eyes are drawn back to Jax.

Annoyance flares through me as she eyes him appreciatively. I grit my teeth and down some of the warm beer Maxen brought me. His hand lands on my thigh under the table, making me jump. He grins, which I catch out of the corner of my eye and I roll them.

"Being free does have some perks. You single, honey?"

I almost spit my next mouthful of beer at her. I go to tell her he's mine, but then I think about it. We never spoke about what we are to each other, especially Jax. Yes, we seem to have a connection, but that doesn't mean he won't want to fuck the woman in front of me. She's good looking and obviously wants him. I swallow my protests and wait to see how he reacts. I won't stop him going with her even if it will hurt me. I don't realise I'm rigid until I hear his voice.

"No." His voice is flat and he concentrates on eating, not even giving her the time of day. The fist around my heart unclenches and I draw in a long breath. I put the cup down and pick at my food. She turns to Maxen.

"What about you, cutie?"

Does this bitch ever give up? I eye my fork, debating whether it would be rude to stab it through the eyes she is using to undress him. He starts to rub circles on my thigh. I grind my teeth so hard I can almost hear them crack.

She leans over, flashing her tits at him and smiles seductively. This motherfucker really wants to get stabbed. I'm going to cut off her tits if she keeps flashing them.

"Me and you could have a good time." She lowers her voice, obviously trying to be sexy. To me she sounds like a twat but I could be biased.

"Is that right?" Maxen's voice stops me imagining killing her and instead I turn my fury on him. If this asshole thinks he can flirt with some ho while trying to touch me I'm going to cut off his hand and shove it so far up his-

"Oh yeah, honey." She purrs. He leans back, gripping my thigh to keep me in my seat. Jax's hand drops on my other thigh and I throw a glare at him before turning back to the massive cunt hitting on my men. I don't even debate why I am calling them mine all of a sudden, it just feels right.

"Really? You see, this woman who saved your life today by fighting when you wouldn't, is my current - as you call it - good time. So, not only are you hitting on her man, you are pissing off the only person in here who gives a fuck if you stay alive." The woman pales and turns her eyes on me. No longer sultry, she looks like she's about to piss herself. I bare my teeth at her as Maxen chuckles.

"So what can you really offer me that she can't? She's a strong as fuck fighter which, to be honest, makes me harder than I can ever remember. She's so fucking sexy without trying, and she's the bravest, craziest bitch I have ever met." He eyes her in disdain and it loosens some of my anger.

"You couldn't even free yourself and now you're flinging yourself at any man who will have you. It's sad really, you should take a lesson from Worth here. Get some dignity and learn how to survive in this world, because I have a feeling she won't be saving you anymore."

I have to bite my lip to hold in my smile at the fact he called me Worth, so that no one would know my name. His words wash the anger and my lingering doubts from earlier away. I lean back in my chair and watch her as she cries and tries to stutter out an apology to me.

When I don't say anything, she stumbles up from the table like it's on fire and flees from the room like the hounds of hell are chasing her. My eyes track her out of the door and I debate following her and stabbing her in the stupid tits. Jax grabs my hand away from where I was massaging my knife and squeezes it. Huh, I didn't even know I'd reached for it. Drax and Thorn burst out laughing and congratulate Maxen but my anger is still burning in the background, my demons raising their ugly heads, mingling with Major's words from earlier.

Jax stands from the table and offers me his hand. I blink and look at him carefully. He stands completely still, letting me choose. I look into his eyes for answers but when I don't find any, I gently place my hand in his. He pulls me to my feet and twines his hand with mine.

"We will be back in a minute." He says before pulling me after him.

I follow him silently, he doesn't speak either. He pulls me outside and around until we are around the back of the building and then he lets go of my hand. I miss the warmth immediately but I lean casually against the wall and tilt my head to watch the stars.

"How did you know I needed to get away?" My voice is soft. I am trying really hard but I need to hit something right about now.

"Because it's what I would need." My eyes lower to his, he is standing in front of me with his deep grey eyes searching mine. He steps closer and his eyes dart nervously between mine.

"Why didn't you claim me in front of her?"

I suck in a breath, his words so close to my own line of thinking inside. His eyes dare me to tell him the truth, and I've never been one to back down from a dare.

"I didn't know you were mine."

His arms come up and cage me against the wall so it's just us and the stars above.

"I'm yours. I was yours since you smiled at me, I was yours since you held my brother as he slept. It might be soon, and crazy, but so is this world. When tomorrow is not guaranteed, I refuse to hesitate. So, yes I'm yours, little warrior." His voice is sure and deep and my eyes drop to his lips automatically.

"You haven't made a move like the others," I hear the vulnerability in my voice and want to run away but his arms won't let me. Jax's opinion matters, he understands me even when I don't understand myself. I need to be sure.

"Truth?" He asks hesitantly, shyness overcoming him. Not something I would ever use to describe Jax normally.

"Always, even if I don't want to hear it." He sucks in a breath and watches me intently.

"I don't know how to. I'm not like my brother. Women never really interested me."

"Wait, you prefer men?" I tilt my head in confusion. His cheeks heat and I want to kiss them.

"No. I like women, well one woman. I never bothered before. I couldn't let them close enough to do anything in case they saw my demons and ran. They would. I wouldn't mean to but I would hurt them one day. I can't lose control like that. They were all too weak."

"So, you're a virgin?" Something in me jumps for joy at that. I've never had a virgin. Knowing that he has only been with me? Huge turn on.

"Yes, I'm not ashamed. Fucking some random slut didn't interest me. But I want you Worth, and knowing you're strong enough to handle me?" His eyes catch me in their depths, the fire burning in the grey. My vulnerability and hesitancy disappears. No matter what happens, here at this moment, Jax is mine. This hardened warrior is showing me his demons and asking me to fight them with him. Something inside me snaps and I know my grin is a little evil. All the desire and need from earlier comes rushing back, only heightened by the idea of having Jax at my every whim and control. Having him on his knees, teaching him the pleasure that could be between us. I grab his head and pull it to me slowly. He doesn't resist, allowing me to do what I want. I lick at his lips and nip, not holding back my strength.

I swallow his sharp inhale and cover his lips with mine. Biting and licking, I wait for him to open before teaching him exactly how to kiss me. His lips are unsure and clumsy, but he follows me with pleasure. I pull back to see his unfocused eyes and hear his short sharp breathing.

"Hands on the wall," I demand. He instantly smashes them back on the wall from where they were drifting. I purr and kiss his lips in praise.

"You do exactly what I say or I stop, understood?" I can see the barely controlled power in his eyes and it only makes me wetter. I want to push him, to see him snap and let go of that careful control. I want his darkness. I want his strength and pain and I won't stop until I have it all.

When he doesn't respond, I bite his lip, hard.

"Answer me." He trembles against me but nods. I lower my lips to his again as he chases after me. He quickly learns and has me moaning into his mouth. I pull my lips away and catch my breath. He watches me, his control thinning. Growling, I yank his head back by his hair until his neck is stretched in a long line. He groans and pushes his body closer to mine.

"Stop trying to be in control. I want it all. I want to watch you lose control. You can't break me, Jax, I want you-"

I bite his neck as he moans.

"Rough."

I bite the other side, digging my teeth in deeper. His hips buck against me.

"Hard."

Licking up his neck, I whisper against the wet flesh.

"Wild."

He yanks his head out of my hands, breathing heavily. My eyes lock with his as they flare. His lips twist in a snarl and his control is nowhere to be seen. This is the true Jax, the animal he hides, born from pain and suffering. I can be his control, I know how sometimes you need to let go and trust someone else to catch you. I swear to always be that for him. He drops his lips to mine hard and sucks on my bottom lip. Pulling away slightly, he pulls at it in a stinging bite. My eyes nearly roll back in my head but I know I need to stay in control the first time. After that? I can't wait to see our darknesses meeting. He lets go and I pull my head back.

"Did I tell you to do that?" I keep my voice hard. I grip his jaw in a tight painful grip which has his hips bucking again.

"Undo my jeans." His eager fingers drop to my zip and fumble in their haste. He finally snaps it and pulls on the button until they are undone. I feel him hesitate; it's obvious he wants to touch me, but he puts his hand back on the wall.

"Good boy, touch me." My voice is breathy with the thought of him fucking me, of his fingers buried in me. I won't fuck him this time, not out here where anyone could walk by. No, when that happens, I want him all to myself. But I can show him exactly how much I want him, how much this side of him turns me on.

"Where?" His voice is gravelly as he watches me like a predator, but he's not the only one.

"I want you to play with my nipples. You're going to twist and flick at them both until I'm moaning." He licks his lips as his hands pull away from the wall. He palms my sides and slowly pushes my shirt up, trailing fire in his wake. When he reaches my bra he yanks the cups down and cups my breasts.

He flicks at my erect nipples. I drop my head back to the wall and watch the stark hunger and concentration on his face as he worships my breasts. He twists and flicks as I gyrate my hips, needing more.

"Use your mouth. I want your fingers in me, fucking me."

With a growl, he grabs the sides of my shirt and yanks it over my head. Without hesitating he drops his mouth to my exposed breasts. He locks his mouth on one nipple and sucks. His hand skates down my stomach which clenches in anticipation. He slides his long fingers into my panties. He pulls off my nipple to lave it before switching to the other one.

His fingers slowly inch downwards, caressing me.

"Fuck, you're so wet for me," he murmurs against my nipple.

"Always," I moan as he attacks my nipple, biting hard as he thrusts a finger into me brutally. He pumps another one in, stretching me.

"Yes, fuck yes!"

He leaves stinging bites across my breast as he curls his finger in me before pulling out and pumping in again. His head moves to my other breast as he offers that one the same treatment, leaving red teeth imprints in his wake.

"Rub my clit," I demand. He pulls his fingers out and circles my nub. I almost moan at the empty feeling.

"Keep your fingers in me, use your thumb." I grip onto the back of his head, pulling on his hair in punishment.

His fingers thrust back into me without warning as his thumb circles my nub. I can feel myself clenching around him, so close to coming just from his hands and mouth. I thrash my head from side to side, needing more.

"I want your mouth on me."

He pulls his mouth away from my nipple, his lips swollen and pink. He pants as he carries on fucking me with his fingers.

"Now," I growl. His grin is feral as he slowly pulls his fingers out. Before moving his hand, he lightly slaps at my clit, making me moan again.

"Fuck," I whimper. I watch through dazed eyes as he lifts his wet fingers to his lips and sucks on them. His eyes widen and he groans as if in pain.

"How the fuck can you taste that good?" He grabs my hips and yanks me away from the wall and drops me to the ground before covering me with his weight. I grab his hair again and yank his eyes to mine.

"Fuck me with your mouth and fingers."

He pulls on my jeans until they dangle of one of my ankles and then stares at my half-naked body, the worship clear on his face. Strangely, the thought doesn't scare me.

"You are so fucking beautiful it hurts." He kneels between my parted thighs and rips my panties from my body. I snarl at him as he smirks. He tucks them into his pocket as I watch and then lays down between my thighs. Something about fucking in the dirt makes me wetter, knowing this primal side of him is taking me where anyone can watch.

The cold air hits my pussy, making me shiver before arching when his hot mouth closes over my clit with no warning. Parting my lips, he caresses me as he sucks and licks at me. His fingers thrust back into me, pulling out slowly then pummelling back in. My fingers scramble in the dirt next to us, looking for something, anything, to hold on to.

"Harder," I cry out. He fucks me faster, adding another finger, stretching me in the most delicious way. When he sucks on my clit I come, breaking apart in his arms, my pussy clenching around his fingers, trying to milk him. He moans against my clit and carries on pushing through my tight channel. When I come back down to my body, my pussy tingles from the overload and my sensitive nub cries from the abuse.

"Stop."

He growls before licking my cream, cleaning me with his tongue. I can't do anything but hold on, my fingers gripping his hair. Slowly, he lifts his head, his eyes blazing with his need and his darkness. His chin is wet from me and his lips are even more swollen. His hair sticks up at all angles from my hands and I've never seen anything sexier. I drop my head back to the ground as he crawls up my body. We stare at each other before he gently kisses me, the taste of me on his tongue. I wrap my arms around his neck as his weight pushes me down further into the earth, the feeling comfortable.

He pulls away and watches me. "Mine."

I nod before licking my lips again. He kisses down my jaw to my neck and I turn my face to the trees offering him more access to explore. There, at the tree line, not feet away, is Dray. He watches us, leaning against a tree. His pants are undone and his hand is shoved in them. The sight makes me gasp as Jax bites my sensitive neck, making my toes curl. I watch as Dray slowly pulls out his hand before winking at me and disappearing into the shadows behind him. My heart thunders from the idea of Dray watching us.

Jax lifts his head a small smile on his lips.

"We should get back."

I nod and smile at the peaceful look on his face, his darkness retreating to show me a satisfied version of him. His eyes are warm and loving as he looks at me and his smile is wide and happy. Before I can move, he gently ghosts over my lips again.

"Thank you, my little warrior. I needed that more than you can know." I almost choke. He's thanking me for letting him make me come? I know it's more about letting him lose control, but still.

"Anytime, cutie." His grin grows as he moves back on to his

haunches. His eyes flick over my splayed out body again before standing. He gently pulls my jeans up and I lift my bum to help him. I almost moan at the feel of the rough denim meeting my sensitive pussy. He smirks as if he knows my thoughts and then pulls me to my feet. He rights my bra before gently wiping my back free of dirt.

Turning away, I watch him as he grabs my discarded shirt. Sands below, what an ass. Turning back to me, his lips twitch again obviously seeing where my eyes were. I shrug and pull on the shirt he offers me.

"You keeping my panties?" I tease. He twines his hand with mine as we walk slowly around the building, both of us wanting to prolong this peace before we have to put our shields back up.

"Yes, and so you know, I plan on using them later as I think about you in the shower."

I blink in astonishment. What the hell have I created? A panty stealing monster, obviously.

Chapter Fifteen

Fighting and Forgiveness

BY THE TIME we make it back to the room, I remember I never shared what I learned from Major. There's a lot we need to talk about, so now we are all sitting around the table in our room.

"So, what happened with Major?" Thorn asks as he eyes me and Jax with a knowing smile.

"I want to know what the little she-devil here has done to my brother to make him smile." I laugh at Drax's put out expression.

"I would have thought that was obvious." Maxen winks at me and leans his arm over the back of my chair. Jax sits with a smirk on his face, not the least bit bothered.

"You're just jealous. And I don't even know where to start with Major," I rub my head as the mood plummets and everyone turns serious.

"That bad?" Drax's smile has disappeared and he's watching me with concern. I swallow hard. There is a decision I need to make. Do I trust them or not? I look around, meeting their waiting eyes. Each one causes happiness to bloom in my once dead chest. Thorn with his steadfast strength and smile, Maxen the warrior, Drax the charmer and Jax the one whose demons match my own.

"It's not a pretty story and things are about to get a whole lot harder."

Drax leans back in his chair with a smile. "Ain't ever been

easy, babe. Anything that is worth having isn't." Thorn nods and Jax squeezes my hand. I turn to Maxen.

"I told you, we have your back." He squeezes my shoulder, and I take strength from it. Steeling myself, the words spill out.

"I was a slave for Ivar, he's the leader of The Berserkers. I was his little pet...when I won my freedom, he hated it, but he had to honour The Ring's rules. I managed to slip out before he could corner me and I haven't seen him since." Every one of their faces darkens with each word, but I don't hide. If they show pity, I need to see it.

"Apparently losing me has driven him mad. He's an evil man - that I didn't lie about. He takes great pleasure in torturing people. He used to reserve that for me and his slaves. I was the only one who didn't break, that only seemed to spur him on. I was his favourite, he got rid of all the other slaves until only I remained. It meant I had his sole focus and tender care. Major told me that the clan has split into two factions. One who thinks bringing me back to Ivar will let him regain control of his anger and bring him back to sanity - well as much as he ever was. They are raiding everywhere in the Wastes, causing wars and crossing territories looking for me."

"And the other faction?" Thorn's jaw clenches like he has to spit the words out.

"They want to overthrow Ivar. I know the man who is leading it, he's a good man. Lost, but good."

"Is this what Dray wanted?" Maxen rumbles next to me.

"I honestly don't know, it must be. I'm the only member of The Berserkers to ever walk away, so it makes sense that if they are breaking territory rules, he would come to me."

"Can we trust him?" Drax looks around "If you meet him, is he planning on giving you to the faction searching for you to make them stop?"

So, he finally gets where my thoughts have spun to. I trace

the wood on the table and don't meet their eyes. I take time to sort through my feelings, and what I know of Dray before I answer.

"I don't know. My instincts scream that I can trust him, but I've been wrong before." My words end on a choke and I push away from the table to pace.

"So what do we do?" Jax asks, breaking into my thoughts. I turn to the table and grip the back of the chair. I can almost feel the awaiting storm; one growing closer, ready to leave devastation in its wake. One that my words will start, but even sensing that, they are still on the tip of my tongue, raised by my insecurities and the need to not trust anyone.

"I meet him, I see what he wants. If he betrays me, I kill him." The words are like acid on my tongue. The idea of being able to kill him is nearly impossible but it's my heart that rebels against it. The crazy bastard is a weakness for me, I just hope he doesn't know it. Major's other words come to me as I meet their eyes, needing to see the answers written there.

"Can I trust you? Why are you here? What are you looking for?" The world stutters as my accusations hit them like blows. Jax turns rigid and Drax looks crestfallen. Thorn's lips tug down and I daren't look at Maxen.

"Where is this coming from?" Thorn asks, his fists clenching on the table.

"It's strange timing that you turn up as the raids start. How do I know you don't work for Ivar? That you won't betray me?" My last words are quiet but it's like a bomb goes off. Maxen pushes away from the table and turns to me, furious. Drax looks at me like I've kicked him and Thorn watches me in anger.

"You never asked why we were here. You really think we would work for slavers?" Maxen spits out the word and glares at me, his nostrils flaring and his chest heaves. Despite the anger, and the fight we are in, I can't help but notice how sexy he is when he's angry. All alpha male and hard, his body a weapon and his tongue sharp like barbs.

"I don't know. I hope not, but I have to know."

Jax slides his chair back, breaking mine and Maxen's stare off. I look into his eyes to see they have frosted again, my sweet Jax disappearing.

"Then how could you touch us, thinking we are evil? What does that say about you?" Before he turns, I see the heartbreak in his eyes and mine shatters in my chest as he walks out the door and shuts it gently behind him. Drax stands, and without looking at me, follows his brother, leaving me with Thorn and Maxen. I look between them and Thorn stands with a sad shake of his head. Walking past me, he stops.

"So you know, we aren't looking for you. If you had asked, we would have told you why we are here." With that, he stalks after the others, leaving Maxen and I alone with his anger.

"Maxen, I-" He holds his hand up and glares at me.

"He's right." He stomps towards me and stops with just a breath between us. The need to reach out to him is strong, but I'm scared he would step away. Regret is bitter on my tongue and my heart lays in tatters once again. Major did not break this, I did. I took the only happiness I know and twisted it.

"You're scared of how you feel about us, so you are using this as an excuse so that you can go back to hiding, living your miserable life. You need to learn to trust, Worth, before you push everyone away," he turns and walks away from me and into the bathroom, slamming the door behind him.

My chest turns tight as I try to suck in air. My eyes fill with tears I won't allow to fall. Is he right? Did I push them away because I'm scared? But, most importantly, is it too late? Have I broken this thing between us?

UNWILLING TO STAY in the room, I leave and hide away in the training grounds. I don't know how long I've been punching and kicking the dummy when I hear a noise over the top of my racing heart and exhausted breathing. Spinning, I watch as Dray pushes off the wall and strolls towards me. Shit, how long has he been there? Stupid, shit, he could have been anyone. He could have gotten the drop on me and I wouldn't have even noticed, too worried about my stupid hurting heart. This is why it is better to feel nothing.

The memory of him watching me and Jax flashes in my mind, making my nipples harden. Bloody hussies. It seems they do that if one of the men even bothers to look in my direction recently.

"You ready to tell me what the hell that note was about?" I scowl, covering my desire. He stops in front of me, his lithe body relaxed. His eyes drink me in before meeting mine.

"You're welcome for the sword," he grins and buries his hands in his jean pockets, drawing my gaze to his thick thighs. I snap my eyes back up, but he smirks at catching me looking.

"I didn't say thank you." Exhaustion has me rubbing my head. It's been a hell of a couple of days. My anger and guilt are still hovering over me like clouds, making me unable to think properly. "I don't want to play games right now Dray, just tell me what you want."

His face changes and he steps forward until our bodies are almost touching. He cups my cheeks and raises my head. I know I should pull away, but honestly, I could use all the comfort he's offering right now.

"Never any games between us. I'm not a soft man and you're not a soft woman. This world ripped all kindness and caring out of me when I was a child. I can't be what you need right now. I see it in your eyes: the need to be reassured, but I refuse to lie to you or pretend I know how to do that. I am a warrior, so I might not be able to hold you and offer you pretty words, but I can offer you the things I do well." Opposite to his harsh words, his fingers gently stroke my cheek, sending a shiver through my body. How can it react to him so strongly, like he is the spark that starts the fire in my body?

"What's that?" I find myself asking. His eyes don't warm, but at this moment, I am exactly where I want to be.

"Strength. You always have my strength."

My tongue darts out to moisten my bottom lip and he follows it with his thumb, making me swallow hard. He's right, he never lies to me. I might not know the man standing in front of me very well, but at this moment, he's allowing me to ask. I might not like the answers, but he would never hold anything back.

"I don't need pretty words. All I ever want is the truth. I don't need your comfort, I need to get rid of this energy in me."

His grin is a little evil but has my panties dampening.

"Fighting or fucking. It's your choice." His voice is as cold as his eyes.

I watch him, knowing I could have him right now. I can see and feel his need. It would be harsh and brutal like the man himself, but if I cross that line with him, there's no going back.

"I don't want to fuck. I want to fight." He nods, the need still in his eyes.

"Both are pretty much the same to me." He's right, the lust quickly turns to bloodlust in his eyes. The image of me and him beating the shit out of each other, of not having to hold back, of just being the monster they created, has me snarling with the same need he feels. His grin turns feral. I know he can take it and return it and that makes me hotter than hell. I never need to hide the darkest parts of me with him. He sees them, and revels in them, twisting them with his own. So no, he will never be the man who holds me and tells me everything will be okay. But I don't need that, I never have. I know the evil that waits around each corner, the darkest parts of a person's soul. No pretty half-truths will make me feel better, but taking it all out on him might.

"I've been wanting to do this since I saw you spill that Seeker's guts in your first fight. I've never seen anything as beautiful as you rising from the sand, covered in your enemy's blood, a stolen blade clutched in your hand. You looked like a fucking queen, the way you tilted your head in defiance."

The memory of that fights rises. I remember my eyes meeting his in the crowd and what felt like an electric bolt hitting me.

"Enough talking." Stepping back, I let his hands drop. He rips his shirt over his head and tosses it away. His eight pack is revealed, all solid mass with clear sharp lines. A delicious V leads down to his low riding jeans as does his happy trail. Scars, burns and bruises mar his chest, showing me how much of a warrior he is. He is like the wildness in this world, the death and destruction around him, suiting him, accepting him. Looking into his eyes, it's easy to see why so many fear him and whisper about him in reverence, but it only serves to amp up my desire. My anger wraps around it, twisting me inside until I don't know whether to jump him or attack him.

He waits, letting me look my fill. He doesn't pose or show off, just stands loose and waits for whatever I throw at him. That thought breaks the last shred of my control and with a speed I didn't even know I had, I run at him, my previous exhaustion melting away to brutal unrelenting anger.

I slide at the last minute and jump to my feet behind him. I jab his sides before dancing away. He spins, already striking, faster than I thought possible. His fist catches my exposed face, the force snapping it sideways. A grin to match his graces my lips at the fact he didn't pull the punch, it allows the chains holding back my demons to snap. I whirl at him, brutally hammering with punches and kicks. He blocks and returns as we dance across the training grounds. I start to flag after about ten minutes and I can tell he still has more stamina. He manages to put me to the ground, standing over me with his eyes alight.

Time to show him why I'm the champion. Grabbing a fist full of sand, I fling it into his eyes and push up, jumping. Wrapping my legs around his neck, I twist in a dirty move, rolling him under me so my thighs bracket his face. Without missing a beat, his legs wrap around my throat and yank me down. Applying more pressure, I grit my teeth against the burning in my throat. Rolling us to the side, I manage to shimmy out of the hold while releasing my legs. Not giving him a second to act, I grab his arms and throw his body so he lays on his front, his arm at an angle behind him.

From this, I can control his movement. He pulls, yanking his arm. I have a split second to decide whether to let him go or dislocate his arm. I let go and he dislodges me before pinning me to the floor.

We stare at each other, our chests heaving, the adrenaline running through our sweaty bodies. The rest of the world drops away, leaving just me and Dray.

"Give up?" He grins as he talks, the sweat trickling down his face and dripping onto my chest. With a smirk, I roll us and lean over his hips. His hard length hits my core, making me wiggle.

"Never."

His grin is full of amusement and his cold eyes blaze.

"Good. Draw?" He asks. I'm betting he has never had to draw in his life, although neither have I. I know he's talking about more than the fight, if I agree, I'm meeting him halfway. I'm reaching out to him. I nod and roll off to lay next to him in the dirt. We both stare at the sky for a while before his voice breaks the quiet of the night.

"I need your help."

My head snaps to the side to see him looking at me intensely.

"With what?" I ask shocked.

"I'm calling a Summit. It's the only way to deal with the

Berserker threat. They are getting stupid, and with no proper leader, it could spill over all the borders, creating a war none of us can win. Not with our infighting anyway."

"What does that have to do with me?"

"They trust you. Everyone knows your rep and plenty of men out here owe you their lives or loyalty because of what you did in The Ring. Us leaders don't trust one another, but having the Berserker champion come to them? That just might work."

"That's crazy," I protest, sputtering at the idea.

"Maybe, maybe not. If anything, they will be curious and want to lord their power over you so they will come."

"So, what, you want me to round up the most feared men in the Wastes?"

"Not exactly. I got Reeves to agree to attend the summit here, only the Worshippers haven't answered my call," he sounds angry. I'm betting he's never heard no before.

"So you plan on saving the Wastes?"

"Don't give me more credit than I deserve. I don't give a fuck whether the Berserkers wipe them out, but if they do, they reach more land and people. That will upset the balance and leave me at a disadvantage. War will devastate all the clans. Ivar needs to be dealt with. I'm not asking for miracles, if I call a summit, I can see where the others stand while seeming like a good ally."

I go quiet for a while, thinking through his logic. "I will die before I go back to him, you know that right?" I stare at him, letting him see the truth in my words.

"I know. If it comes to that; if I - you- we - can't stop him, I'll kill you myself before he gets his hands on you." Some of the fear dissipates in me at that, I know he will keep his word. My chest loosens and I let go of the worries I've held since I heard they were looking for me.

"So you want me to go The Worshippers?" I try changing the subject, done with thinking about the past.

"Extend the invitation. I know you have ex-fighting friends there. Use your connections and then be back for the Summit." He makes it sound easy.

"What why? Why do I need to be here for the Summit?"

"Beside the fact you know more about The Berserkers than anyone else in the Wastes? You're smart, and if we are to win this, we will need your survival instincts. Besides, having you there might calm the clans and stop us from tearing each other apart before Ivar can."

"When's the summit?" I groan, he couldn't have asked for something easy could he?

"Twelve days." He smiles as my eyes narrow at the late warning.

"Who else will be there?"

"Major, Reeves, you, me, and a representative from The Rim." He turns on his side to face me, propping his head on his arm. He looks younger right now, without all the weight and expectation of leading on his shoulders.

"Why do you think I'll do this?"

"I could feed you lies about how you want to save people which, although true, isn't the main reason. Revenge. Your time to make him pay for everything and if you save innocent lives along the way, that's a bonus for you. You're the only one who can do this. You're smart, resourceful and even the leaders have a grudging respect for you. We need you. I need you."

"Fuck."

He laughs, throwing his head back before looking at me. My pulse races at how close we have gotten and I grudgingly bring my mind back to business.

"Fine, I'll leave tomorrow morning." I flop back on the sand, his stare still burning into me. Wait! "You presumptive bastard! Is that why you sent me the sword?"

"Yes, do you know whose it was?"

"No," I answer honestly, the curiosity getting the better of me.

"Ivar's. I stole it from him and it's been in my clan ever since. It's said to be the sword that saved the Wastes from invaders before the clans were split."

Sands below, the idea of touching a sword Ivar used makes me feel sick. "I don't want that thing."

"Ivar wasn't always evil. He's a man changed by the Wastes like we all are. Plus, the sword has more history than that. It is rumoured to be King Killer."

"From the siege which won his castle?" I try to recall the history one of the warriors told me when I was a child about the castle he called home, pre-waste.

"Exactly. It's fitting really." He lays back down next to me, closer than before, the stars shining down on us. It's beautiful, but I know somewhere under the same sky is Ivar. That takes some of the beauty away.

"Why?"

"Because if we succeed and kill Ivar, and have no doubt that we will have to, they will need a new leader. I can't think of anyone better to hold it."

I can't think of anything like that. I struggle to even manage myself, never mind a whole clan. I'm quiet for a while. I know I should get up and leave but my own questions keep me here. If I go to The Worshippers, there's no guarantee I'll come back. It bolsters my courage and I find myself asking something I've wanted to know for years.

"Why didn't you come back?" I resolutely look at the sky, the only way I can get through this conversation.

"I planned on it. Apparently being imprisoned puts a hindrance on plans, I'm not saying I would've ridden in like your knight in shining armour, but I would have found you a place in my clan; bought you from Ivar if I had to. I would have done whatever it took to get you." I nod, and my word vomit continues.

"Did you really kill your father?"

"Yes." The word is a growl and I turn to him in shock, although I don't know what I expected.

"Why?" I ask, more curious than anything. He looks at me, his eyes alight with hate.

"Because he was a monster. He was a bad father and a worse leader."

"And that earned him his death?" I'm not judging, just trying to work out what he means.

"Yes. If he had stayed in power, our people would have died. The only way to stop his reign of terror was to kill him, something I happily accepted. In fact, I relished it, watching the dawning fear in his eyes as I gutted him." Watching his face change as he speaks about his people, I realize something about this crazy man. He cares for them.

"Okay." I turn back to the stars.

"What? No protests and cries of disgust?" He sneers, but underneath, I sense his hesitation. Did he fear my reaction? The man who kills and rips people apart with his bare hands?

"No. If you say you had to do it, I believe you. If I had the chance, I would kill Ivar without hesitation." When he doesn't speak, I look at him "I know who and what you are, Dray. No hidden feelings blind me to the animal you are. In all honesty, it's refreshing. I wish I could accept myself like you do..." I trail off as a brilliant smile, devoid of his usual mask breaks free.

"You do not see yourself clearly. You still worry what people will think of you. You have survived that which would break others. Maybe it's time you embrace the side of you that kept you alive. I'm betting it would be magnificent."

My heart warms at his words, the truth hitting me like a ton of bricks. Nodding, I push myself to stand. Needing to walk away before I give in to the sexual tension between us, I stop at his next words.

"Nothing will stop me this time, or for the rest of my life. I will always come for you." He declares it like a promise. Turning, I march up to him and hover above him.

"Why? I don't get why? You barely know me."

"Time doesn't matter to me. I've been tortured for an hour before and it felt like months and I've watched you for years and that feels like minutes. I know you. I know what even you hide from yourself. You are my soulmate." He shrugs like it's obvious.

"You believe in soul mates?" I sputter.

"Yes. I might not know how to love, but I know when my soul is pulling me back to you every time, no matter what."

"Have you ever thought I don't want to be your soulmate?" I choke on the word.

"It's not a choice, you can fight it all you want." He smiles at me.

"And you don't want to?" I ask incredulously.

He snarls and jumps up, his feral grin back.

"I did. For the first few years after I met you, I watched as my soul withered with every punch, whip and broken bone you endured. I offered you a chance, it was going to be a place in my clan. In hopes it would stop whatever this pull is. When I finally came round to the fact that something in me will always want you, I stopped fighting but then it was too late. I was imprisoned by my father, and when I got free, you were gone. I don't plan on making that same mistake again. I will take you in whatever way I can. And right now, I want you beside me as we fight."

"Not behind you?" I snark.

"Never. You are a warrior, a Berserker Queen. I would be proud to stand by your side, not the other way around. Now you must get some sleep. It will be a hard couple of days. Unless you want to fuck?" He grins before blending back into the shadows like they welcome him with open arms.

Soulmates. I balk. Sands below, he's crazier than I thought.

Motherfucking soulmates! I snarl and stomp away, but deep inside preening at the words and my stomach is filled with warmth. I must be as crazy as he is, and where does this leave me and the four other guys I'm drawn to?

I spend the walk back planning the next couple of days. I wonder if they will come with me? I have faced down insurmountable odds in The Ring. I have been tortured, abused, betrayed and almost killed more times than I can count. But the idea of facing them again sends more fear into me than facing down any fighter.

What if they turn away from me? What if they don't want me anymore? What if I hurt them too much? In trying to protect my own heart, I tore theirs out and stomped on it. My Jax, who trusted me to watch his brother and to see his demons. Drax, who fell apart in my arms as his nightmares haunted him. Thorn, who no matter what, I know would always have my back and nothing I did could ever disgust him. And Maxen. The man who taught me to care again, to open my heart. To finally lean on someone and find out what a family means. I face the door, my heart beating double time, my palms sweating, and my chest tight.

I can't lose them. I don't know what's going to happen in the future. I don't know if Ivar will find me or if the other clans will kill me on sight. Hell, I could die in my sleep at the hands of an assassin. But I can't live another minute without telling them how I feel, no matter if they don't forgive me. Steeling my nerve, I open the door to face my future, whether that will be by their side or knowing I could have been. I'm done hiding.

Chapter Sixteen

Honesty Train

THE DOOR SLAMS shut behind me, announcing my arrival. They all ignore me as they dig into the food on the table. Gritting my teeth, I walk over to where they all can see me and clear my throat. Maxen lifts his head, his expression cold.

"I'm sorry," I have to push the words out, but once they are said a weight lifts off my chest, "I have trust issues." I cross my arms defensively and wait. Maxen sighs and offers me a sad smile, his face softening.

"I'm sorry too, Mi Alma, I shouldn't have snapped like that."

The relief is staggering, but I look at the others. Drax smiles cheekily at me but sadness still lingers in his green depths.

"I can think of ways you can make it up to me."

Rolling my eyes, I face his brother. Jax sighs and my heart clenches. I look for any sign of the man I know he hides but it's like he's completely locked away from me.

"I can understand where you were coming from, but it hurt." Swallowing, I nod. "But I forgive you. We are all going to make mistakes, but let's promise to be truthful with each other from now on."

Nodding vigorously, I smile at him and he returns it. It brightens his whole face, sending my heart into overdrive. Okay, one more to go. Thorn doesn't lift his head from where he's staring intently at the table. His shoulders are tight with tension and he actually flinches as I step closer.

"Thorn?" When he doesn't reply, I find myself in front of his chair. With my usual confidence returned, I plop myself in his lap, making his head snap up, his eyes locking with mine in shock. Cupping his cheek, I lean my forehead against his.

"I'm sorry, big guy." His eyes close in bliss and he eventually sighs and wraps his arms around me. In his arms, all the tension and worry fades away, leaving a warmth that spreads through my whole body. How could I ever think I didn't know them when my body reacts like this to them? He doesn't speak but the tightness around his eyes speaks volumes.

Looking into his eyes, I know if I hurt him again this deeply, it will be the end. Here and now in his arms, I vow to trust him, even if I don't like the outcome. Breaking our silent conversation, he sighs out his next words.

"I guess I forgive you then."

I dart in and kiss him before wiggling to face the others. I don't bother moving off his lap; I think I might need the comfort of his arms before the end of this conversation. A part of me rejoices as they tighten and when he nuzzles into my hair, I almost squeal. I haven't lost them. Remembering my vow to be honest, I nibble my lip before ploughing right in.

"Okay, while we are on the honesty train, I met with Dray," Jax's eyes narrow but the rest just wait for me to carry on, "He told me what he wants from me and I agreed to the job. Know that before I tell you, you don't have to go with me."

"As if, sweet cheeks," Drax snorts. Maxen's lips twitch and he rubs his thumb across the plump bottom one, making my eyes follow. Clearing my throat, I bring my train of thought back to the conversation.

"Right. Okay. Well, there's been a summit called. He needs me to go to the Worshippers and extend the invitation to their leader."

The words are going down like a lead balloon. Their muttering blends into each other.

"Well, shit," Drax smiles grimly at me.

"Pretty much. Reeves has already agreed to come. Dray's thinking is I might be able to use my connections to get us in to see the Worshippers safely." I wiggle on Thorn's lap, causing him to grip my hips tightly and bite my earlobe. My pussy clenches in response, making me bite my bottom lip against the groan that wants to escape. I raise my eyes and they lock on Drax's heated ones. Thorn nips my flesh again, harder this time. My eyes stay locked with Drax's as he watches me rub myself on Thorn.

"And can you?" Maxen asks, oblivious to the sexual tension. Reluctantly, I pull my eyes to him.

"Honestly, I don't know. I've let people live in the ring, I've shown mercy and made friends, but that doesn't mean they will betray their clan for me. The Worshippers aren't known for being social." My voice is rough with my desire, almost velvety.

"We are coming with you," Jax's voice rings out, firm and resolute.

The last shred of doubt falls away. I was worried about going alone. It gets tiring watching your own back, and after being spoilt with them for the last couple of days, I don't want to go back to being alone. The realisation strikes me like a lightning bolt, freezing me in my spot.

I don't want to be alone anymore, maybe I never did. My inner wall is nowhere to be found, destroyed by these men. This is the turning point. I could push them away again and they would walk away. Everything in me screams at that idea. Or I could bring them with me. They might not like what they find, but it's a risk I'm going to have to take. Decision made, I lean back against Thorn.

"Then we leave after breakfast in the morning. It's at least a three-day ride if we are going flat out. With the raids, I'm not planning many stops, so pack enough and be ready for a hard ride." I twine my fingers with Thorn and he squeezes reassuringly. My conversation with Major resurfaces and so does my curiosity.

"So, what are you doing here?" I hold my hand up to forestall the argument "I'm not accusing you of anything. You said I should have asked, so I am."

They look between themselves before Maxen clears his throat, "Officially, we were hired by the cities' government to come to the North and scratch out an agreement with the leaders."

"And unofficially?"

"They want us to spy on the clan leaders. Also, there are rumours of a place buried in the Wastes unaffected by the world around it. A paradise. The cities are dying. What they don't want anyone to know is they don't have enough power or food to hold them for much longer," Maxen's voice is hard and laced with anger. Shit, I didn't realise it was that bad down there.

"They want you to find this place?" I raise my eyebrow in question.

"Yes, they want us to scout it, then report the location back." Leaning back, he watches me carefully.

"That place doesn't exist. Don't get me wrong, I've heard the rumours, but that's all they are: rumours. All that's left out here is death and destruction, and if you're lucky you find a slice of happiness."

"Maybe, maybe not. It doesn't matter anyway," Drax points out happily.

"Why not?" I tilt my head to the side to watch him, but it's Maxen who answers again.

"We never planned on going back. If this place existed, we planned to seek sanctuary."

"And if it didn't?" The questions swirl in my brain to fast to keep up.

"We would stay in the North. Better we die because of our

mistakes out here than at the hands of the government who are culling the poor to stay on top," Jax almost spits the words out, the venom clear to hear. He clenches his hands into fists on the table, his skin mottling with the force.

"They wouldn't-" gasping at my imagination throwing image after image at me.

"-they are. Only a small amount for now, but enough for us poor bastards to know. The rich will live while we die like rats on their streets, protecting their walls, collecting their food," Thorn grumbles behind me.

"So why did they trust you with this?"

"Thorn was born up here. We may have overstretched his knowledge and connections to make sure they sent us. Plus, they've used us for missions before. We are their elite fighters. We fight and hunt like Northerners. It makes us lethal, they like that." Maxen smile is devious, shooting a bolt of desire straight to my pussy. The image of hundreds of people being killed soon dampens it. There's just one more thing I need to know...

"So you don't plan on going back?"

He smiles at me as if he knows where I'm going with this. As sick as I feel at the mass murder happening down South, I know I have to concentrate on one problem at a time. It's not like I can ride in there and save everyone, even if I want to.

"No." They all answer unanimously, their voices blending together like a chorus of my favourite song.

"So what will you do?"

Thorn chuckles into my hair and kisses my neck. My heart throbs at the unexpected gentleness.

"We were hoping you would keep us," his breath hits my sensitive neck as he speaks, causing me to shiver.

"Either that or we stalk you across the Wastes. Your choice really," Drax winks, but I have a feeling he's serious.

"Fuck, you're all mad," I groan, but inside I'm happy dancing at the thought of spending the rest of my days, however many that may be, with these warriors.

"You love it," Drax declares happily.

Damn right I do. Having not one, but four, maybe five, men that can keep up with me? Who needs paradise?

STARING OUT AT THE WASTELAND, the night's breeze brushes against me. The guys went to bed a while ago. I told them I would be in after packing up. But really, I needed some space, just to try and think of a plan that won't get us all killed.

"Can't sleep?"

Jumping, I turn around to see Maxen leaning against the door frame. I didn't even hear him come out, my thoughts too distracted by what is to come.

"No, I keep thinking of different ways we can get into The Worshippers compound. Paths to follow, our options if captured..." I trail off, rubbing my head.

"You are going to give yourself a headache at this rate."

I nod and lean back against the stone barrier of the balcony.

"Tell me something about you," I beg, needing something to distract me. He reclines against the wall of the building, the moonlight lighting his perfection. I let my eyes run down him before meeting his.

"What do you want to know?"

"Anything," I say softly, my mind turning to the gutter at his half-naked form.

"Drax told you how we all met, but he never told you why. My mum was a whore, I never even knew who my dad was. She wasn't a bad person, just distant. It was hard for her to raise a baby while still trying to work. I used to have to lay in bed at night as her clients came by. One night, I was only nine, one of them got rough.

I ran in and used the bat she kept for safety. Between us, we ran him off..."

"What happened?" I ask, his face is distant as if reliving it even now.

"He came back. I was asleep. He brought his friends. They beat her and dragged me out of my bed. The bastard made me watch as he hurt her. She was barely conscious but she told me to run. She used the last of her strength to attack him. It offered me a distraction. I slipped out of his friend's hands and under the table. I ran to the door, but I couldn't leave her. I looked back, but there was so much blood and the men were coming towards me." He breathes in, his eyes locking on mine, filled with ghosts. "I left her there, I ran away and left her to die. By the time I got the local wardens to come, it was too late."

"Maxen-"

"I lived on the streets after that, and that's when I met them." He jerks his head inside, and I can see the love he has for his brothers.

"You love them."

He nods, before slipping out of his relaxed position. I watch him hungrily, his story not dampening my need for him. One which he only fuelled the other day.

"I would die for them, they are my family."

He stops in front of me, cupping my face.

"I can't stop thinking. I'm worried I'm going to get you all killed. This mission is crazy and none of your business." I don't let myself look away. I let my weakness come to the front. "But I want you with me."

"We are coming with you, like it or not. You can't get rid of us."

How do I make him understand all the worries and thoughts rattling around? Unable to let them go, my control too tight?

"I can't stop. My mind won't switch off."

"Then let me help you."

"How?" I ask, looking into his eyes like he is my saviour.

"I'll get you out of your head for a while."

His lips descend to mine, and he kisses me softly. I steady myself on his shoulders as I kiss him back. He sucks on my bottom lip, making my nails dig into his shoulder. All the tension, teasing, and need have me groaning into his mouth. I won't hold back this time. I made that choice tonight.

Still kissing me, he picks me up and puts me on the stone railing, his hands running up from my parted thighs to the sides of my breasts. He moves between my legs, as his hands reach my face.

He cups it softly as his kiss turns brutal, making me ache with need as he devours my mouth.

I break away panting, as he continues to kiss down my face to my throat. I arch it to the side for him. He pulls away, and his hands move to my jeans, flicking open the button. Making sure to watch me, he slowly pulls down the zipper. Bracing on my hands, I let him pull them off along with my panties. He moves back between my legs, his rough trousers grinding into my pussy as he smashes his lips to mine.

His hands make short work of my top, and soon I am naked before him. He pulls away again and steps back, drinking in my body. It makes sense I would have Maxen first. My rock, the man who pushes me. I know he will catch me when I fall, and right now all I want is to lose myself in him.

"Take your pants off," I order. He grins, but slowly unbuttons them. They fall to the floor, showing me bare skin. He's naked under them, his long thick length standing proudly between his legs.

He moves fast, slamming his lips to mine as he parts my legs further. His hands seem to be all over, one flicking and playing with my nipple until I am moaning and arching into his touch, needing more. The other drawing circles on my inner thigh, so close to where I need him.

His lips leave mine, and my head drops back, my eyes on the stars above us as his lips wrap around my nipple. He sucks until I am gripping his hair harshly.

"Maxen, fuck," I moan.

His fingers finally move where I need them. He lightly runs them over my pussy, making it clench in anticipation. He smiles against my breast as he circles my clit with that same maddening control.

"If you don't fucking-"

I cry out as he flicks my clit. He rubs it in circles as I move against his hand. Before I can swear at him again, he slips a finger in me, stretching me before another joins in. He doesn't give me time to get used to them before he is fucking me shallowly.

Even though I am here in the moment, my control still stays with me. His mouth leaves my breast, as he finger fucks me.

"Let go," he growls.

"I don't know how," I plead as I arch up into his hands. He brutally bites my neck, making my pussy clench around his fingers.

"You will. I want all of you. I want that careful control gone until you're wild for me. Until you're riding my cock, your cries filling the air as you come."

His dirty words have me moaning. I start riding his fingers as they turn harder and faster. But still I need more, I need him.

"I need you in me," I say breathlessly. He continues to fuck me with his fingers and I grab his hair. Pulling his head up, I dart forward and bite his neck like he did to me.

"In me, now," I order.

Something in him snaps, and as I pull away, panting, his eyes turn deadly. I drop my head back as his fingers pull out of me, leaving me empty. I feel him line his cock up at my entrance, as my pussy begs for him.

He grabs my throat, the pressure bordering on pain, but it's enough for me to shed that last bit of control. To leave him fully in charge. Using his handle on me, he pulls my head back up to look at him. As our eyes connect, he thrusts into me punishingly, squeezing my throat at the same time. I couldn't cry out even if I wanted to, and knowing the others are in the other room only adds to the thrill. All I can do is sit and take it as our eyes stay locked and he fucks me, rough and hard like the man himself, his eyes smouldering as they watch me. I arch into him, increasing the pressure and he groans before pulling out. Snapping my head up I move quickly, jumping down from the railing and jumping him, pinning him to the cold stone floor. Leaving him at my mercy.

I grin down at him, my dark side coming out to play. I don't worry about hurting him, or him being scared. In fact, his eyes are telling me to give him everything. I plan to do exactly that.

I grab his cock with one hand, as I line him up. I keep my eyes on him as I slowly slide him in. When he bottoms out I moan, my head falling back to appreciate the full feeling.

His hands grab my hips, bruising in their grip. It has me tightening around him and he groans before moving me. I start to help him, riding him hard and fast, chasing my orgasm. He helps me, but lets me do what I want to him.

I can feel it building, winding me tighter and tighter and when he flicks my clit, I come with a moan. He thrusts into me through my orgasm and while I am riding the high, he flips us.

Blinking to bring myself back to earth, I lay my head back on the stone.

"My turn, Mi Alma."

He fucks me hard and fast, his hips slamming into mine as he holds me. I'm soon winding back up again, my pussy milking him as he brands me. My nails scratch down his back, trying to pull him as close as possible to me. Grabbing my face, he clenches my jaw, making my eyes open to meet his.

"Look at me as you come, Mi Alma. Watch me as I make you mine."

I cry out as I come again. He watches me the whole time before his thrusts turn harsher. He comes with a roar, me watching him like he did me.

We lay panting underneath the stars, our eyes locked together.

Clapping has me looking over his shoulder to see Drax at the doorway.

"Well, that was quite the show. Shall I show you how much better I am now?"

I groan and lay my head back, my body shaking with the aftershocks.

Eventually, I leave the boys to it and slip away to clean up. The truth is I need a minute away from Maxen's intensity and Drax's laid-back attitude. I'm not running, not this time. Just a breather. I flick on the bathroom light and have a quick wash in the sink. My skin is glistening with sweat as I smile at myself in the mirror. Maxen was right though, he did get me out of my head for a while.

I'm just drying off when the door opens. Drax slips in and leans against it, his cocky smile in place.

"I'm hurt darling, I thought I would be your first," he pouts at me before his eyes drop to my body. He slowly checks me out, and when his eyes reach mine they are alight with lust. My pussy pulses, and I nearly groan.

"Maybe you're just not as hot as you think you are," I say, slowly drying off, letting him watch as I run the towel over my skin. His eyes follow it greedily.

"Keep telling yourself that babe, now at least kiss me goodnight."

Dropping the towel, I saunter towards him, I use his chest to balance before bringing his head down to mine.

"All you had to do was ask," I murmur against his lips. I lick along the seam and he moans. Grinning, I nibble on his plump lower lip.

"Wouldn't you prefer a different kind of kiss goodnight?" I ask softly against his lips.

Pulling back, I meet his unfocused eyes.

"Wha-What did you have in mind?" he asks, his voice rough and needy.

I drop to my knees in front of him, and his eyes widen. I have to swallow a little of my pride, but I trust Drax and if his breathing is anything to go by, this should be fun. I don't ever really do this, it leaves you too vulnerable, too little control. But since I am throwing everything else out the window, why not this too?

I flick open his pants and grab his hardened length. He is thinner than Maxen but no less impressive. Letting him watch, I lick around the tip, almost groaning at his taste.

"Go ahead babe, let me see what you are made of."

Smiling, I stretch my mouth around his length as I slowly suck him down. Hollowing my cheeks, I let him bump the back of my throat.

I keep my eyes rolled up to his as I suck him as far down as I can. Pulling back up again, I scrape my teeth along his length. He groans, his hands in my hair tightening as he thrusts helplessly into my mouth. He pants above me, his eyes begging. I was so wrong. If anything, I have more control. Watching this man writhe above me is a power in itself.

"Fuck, please baby."

I pop him out of my mouth and as he goes to protest again, I swallow him back down. Further than before, until I see his eyes roll back into his head. He cries out, his thrusts turning wild as he picks up speed. I stop playing with him and let him fuck my mouth. Watching him has me squirming against the tiles, the cool feels amazing against my overheated flesh. Knowing right now, he would do anything, be anything for me, makes me want to pull him down here with me. But I hold back, wanting to watch him come, wanting that power over him as he is helpless to me.

"Taz, I'm going-," he tries to groan out, but I take that moment to pull back and suck on the tip.

He comes with a yell, his come spurting down my throat as I swallow it all back. When he's spent, I pull away from him and lean back on my haunches.

He leans against the wall, looking like he is about to fall over as I casually get to my feet and wipe the corner of my mouth. I wink at him before turning and wrapping the towel around me. I slip past him, the door half open.

"Goodnight," I whisper before slipping out into the darkened room, an evil grin on my face.

"Jesus Christ, I think I've met my match," I hear him groan out, making me laugh lightly.

THE NEXT MORNING arrives too soon, and I groan as I get up. My body is sore in the best way. No one said anything, but they all must have heard what I did last night. Yet they act the same. We have a quick breakfast, the conversation light and normal, relaxing some of my fears.

After breakfast, we pack up quickly, smiling at each other, all of us ignoring the looming shadow that our mission causes. It's going to be easy right? All we need to do is get across the Wastelands, avoiding Berserkers, ferals and cannibals, before arriving at the settlement of a known cult. Somehow get inside without getting killed and convince them to attend the summit. Oh, and then get back across the Wasteland and plead my case to get all the leaders of the northern clans to kill a mad berserker king. And I thought winning my freedom was hard.

The early morning sun outside chases the shadows of The

Ring away, leaving an almost heavenly glow about. Major and Dray are whispering as they head towards us, obviously on their way to our rooms. I lean against the building and wait. It doesn't take them long to notice me, their conversation stopping as they approach. Major gives me an unreadable look, but Dray gives me his usual savage smirk.

"You ready to leave?" Dray hops up on the stone wall next to the stairs to the building and lounges there, watching me. A ray of sun shines down on him, highlighting his toned half naked body. His eight pack glistens, making my mouth water, his fingers trail lightly over them, teasing me. I narrow my eyes at him and turn back to Major who's watching it all play out.

"You really okay doing this, kid?" The worry in his voice softens my anger towards him. We might not have everything sorted but who knows what will happen at The Worshipper's? I don't want our last words to be in anger.

"Someone has to," smiling, I push off the wall as I speak. "Besides, it gets me out of your hair, old man."

He smiles grimly at me. We both know the odds of me making it back. Sighing, I walk towards him. Wariness enters his expression, saddening me. I stop in front of him and tilt my head back to meet his eyes.

"If anyone can do this, it's me."

"I know-" sighing, he rubs his eyes which I notice have massive black bags under. His worry is palpable. "Is there anything you need me to do?"

"Help Dray set up the summit, spread some rumours that I've gone towards his territory," His eyebrow raises at that and I grin. "His men are good enough to take on Berserkers and it might buy me some time to get through the Wastes without being attacked."

He throws his head back as laughter tumbles out. When he looks at me again, his eyes are bright with happiness and pride.

"When did you get so smart?" Leaning in, I kiss him on the cheek.

"I learnt it from the best. Help me this time Major, and I might just forgive you," I mean it as a joke, but his face steels with determination.

"Anything for you kid." Grabbing the back of my head, he kisses my forehead. "Please come back to me," he whispers before turning on his heel and marching away. Not before I see the glistening in his eyes though.

Swallowing past the lump in my throat, I turn back to see my guys watching me, their support obvious. I wink at them before strolling to Dray.

"I'll be back in ten days with your answer, and if I'm not, then you have it either way." Hopping down, he leans against the wall facing me.

"If you aren't back in ten days, I'll burn this whole fucking Wasteland down looking for you." We smile at each other, the fact that he's being serious only making me happier.

"I'll get everything ready here, give them hell." He swoops in before I can move and kisses me hard. Blinking in shock, I watch as he swaggers away whistling to himself. A throat clears behind me and I wince. Shit, what will they think? Turning, I notice Drax's sly grin and Thorn's red cheeks. They start to file past me, Drax chuckling as he goes. Jax is last and he stops in front of me.

I twist my hands nervously and then still them when I notice. Meeting his eyes, I search for how he feels about Dray kissing me. This thing between us is so new and fragile.

"While you were screaming around my tongue last night, I saw him watching us -" Holy sands below, I open my mouth to explain, when he carries on "- I don't mind, I see the way he looks at you and the way you look at him."

"What way is that?"

"You need him, the way you need us. We each offer you something different. I offer you the feeling of being in control and the fact I will never leave you or judge you. Dray shows you how to embrace your anger and be the warrior you are without being ashamed."

"The others?" I ask curiously, unsure what to say.

"Maxen shows you it's okay to lean on someone; he's your rock. Thorn is your softness, the stuff you hide away. He brings it out in you and shows you it's okay to feel. Drax teases you, pushes you, and makes you play for what I'm guessing is the first time in your life."

"You might not understand why you're drawn to all of us, but you need us as much as we need you. Don't question it, just go with it." With that bombshell, he walks away, leaving me flustered.

Chapter Seventeen

Close Call

THE FIRST COUPLE of hours are uneventful. We are on a stretch of road that used to be a motorway, with cars, buses, and trucks abandoned everywhere. Their insides burnt out or covered in spray paint. Dust covered land stretches as far as the eye can see on each side, and the only noise is the sound of our bikes. We pass a shell of a fuel station, among other destroyed buildings. The whole drive I see my men looking at me every now and again, only for them to smile when I notice. I'm debating stopping for a break, as we have to slow down to manoeuvre between the cars when I spot something on the road ahead of us.

A bridge over the old road, with a darkened pass underneath. The barriers that used to be on either side of the bridge are crumbling with the stone falling to the road below. One side of the bride is collapsed, with it laying on the road in rubble. The sun doesn't penetrate its shadowed interior and my gut clenches.

Slowing down, I squint into the awaiting darkness. Pulling behind an old sports car, I wait for the others while not taking my eyes off it. My instincts are screaming at me, and they are never wrong. We could go around but it would take us an extra day, an extra day of us being hunted by Berserkers in the Wastes. Plus, if I'm late back, I have no doubt that Dray will storm to The Worshippers and slaughter them all to find me.

"What's up, babe?" Drax asks as he pulls next to me. He has a crossbow strapped to his leg and crisscrossing blades on his chest. His green eyes peer at me with caring as he waits patiently. I can feel the others behind me, waiting for my lead.

"There's something or someone in there," I say, looking back to the pass.

Drax blinks at me then looks to the darkened stretch of road.

"How do you know?" Maxen calls at a low volume.

"I just do." Stroking my blade attached to my left leg, I debate our options.

"So, what are we doing?" Drax asks again, his eyes still peering into the darkness. Even now, my heart clenches at their trust. I shake away the warm feeling and gesture at his crossbow.

"I know you hit that guy the other day, but are you any good with that?"

He grins at me blindingly.

"Babe, I'm good with my hands, don't worry."

I snort and turn back to the road. Straightening my back, I grab one of the swords crossing my back. It just so happens to be the one Dray gave me.

"Get ready to fight. If it's feral dogs, we are better trying to outride them but keep them off you if you can. Their bites carry infection. If it's cannibals, don't get surrounded, they work together to bring a person down and they will eat you then and there. Cover each other's back and let's get this shit done. You ready?"

Drax nods while the others mutter agreements. No one questions me going first and the warm feeling starts again. Fucking feelings. It was so much easier when I pushed all that behind the wall. Cracking my neck, I hold my sword in one hand with it resting loosely on the handle, while my other grips tightly to the gas.

"Shout if you get overwhelmed."

"Wait, what if it's Berserkers?" Thorn asks softly.

"Then you fight like the devil it's self is trying to get you and pray it's enough." I don't think about what will happen if we lose, I can't or I'll be tempted to turn them around. Not for me. I can handle what they throw at me, but I couldn't stand them hurting my men. Somewhere over the last twenty-four hours, my priorities have shifted from staying alive to keeping the parts of my scattered heart around me alive. Let's hope they are as good of fighters as I think.

Revving the bike, I slowly crawl towards the pass. Just when I think I might have been wrong, an arrow whizzes through the air, grazing my cheek. Pain explodes in my face but I use to it sharpen my senses. Ignoring the blood trickling, I shout to Drax.

"On the bridge above, two men!" I don't wait for him to answer. I kick off my bike and draw my other sword. Crouching, I wait for the shadows moving in the pass.

I hear a shout and then a cry of pain before a man tumbles down from the bridge and splatters before me on the asphalt, a bolt through his left eye. Another scream soon echoes. It's silent for a moment before a war cry sounds and men charge from the darkness, their weapons gleaming in the light. Their mouths open with their battle cry and death gleaming in their eyes. Their dirty odour hits me as my focus narrows on the approaching gang. At least fifteen men, all armed, all clearly know how to use their weapons. Gripping both swords tightly, I swing them in an arc. Grinning as I wait.

My sword clashes with the first man, blocking the mace being swung towards my head. I grin from where our faces are inches apart and head-butt him. He stumbles back with a cry, and I don't waste any time slitting his throat, twirling with the movement to meet the swing of another man. On and on, I swing and parry as we dance back and forth, the sounds of dying men and pain our music. This man is more cautious than the first and clearly knows how to use his weapon.

Eventually, he falters and I move behind him and cut the tendons behind both knees. He falls to the floor and I sheath one sword before pulling his neck back and slicing.

"Taz, behind you!" Drax screams from where he is fighting back to back with his brother. I duck, narrowly avoiding a knife which clatters to the floor. Spinning low, I roll until I'm at the man's feet. He fumbles for his sword at his waist, but he's too slow and I gut him before he can raise it.

Pain explodes in my shoulder, forcing a grunt from me as I tumble forward. Catching myself on the floor, I roll to avoid the blade arcing down where I just was. Ignoring the burning in my shoulder, I snap my sword up to meet his. My attacker snarls down at me, his face wild and covered in sweat. I kick out, forcing him back and flip to my feet. I raise my sword, ready to jump at him when he screams and twists around, showing me the bolt in his back. Silently thanking Drax, I use his distraction to hack at his neck. Blood sprays as he falls to his knees, more blood bubbling at his mouth. The poor bastard is still alive. I keep hacking, ignoring the screams and squelching, my whole world narrowing to killing him. Blood splatters on me from my desperate swings, his head almost removed from his neck. His axe lays on the ground next to him.

Stopping, my chest heaving from my short sharp breaths, my cheek stinging and my shoulder burning, I turn with wide eyes to check everyone else. I can't see Drax and Jax, but Thorn is holding his own against two big men. His face is fierce and darkened by anger, his moves precise with his long sword. He spins, parries and cuts, his feet fast for such a big man. I tighten my hold on my sword to help, not that he needs it, when a noise drags my gaze to the open area near the bikes. Something large hits my back, causing me to fall to my knees and then tumble onto my side. Pain races through me from hitting my injured shoulder.

A man stumbles towards me, roaring as he does. My eyes spot

Maxen over his shoulder. He comes striding through the fray like the devil, blood and bodies painting the ground in his wake. I watch from the ground as he hacks at a man's neck who stumbles into his path. With a roar, he rips the man's head off. A grin splits my face as it flies through the air and into the man above me. Using the momentary distraction, I heave myself up, spinning and impaling him on my blade as I go. Blood gurgles from his lips as I slide my blade out. I turn my back on him as he falls to the floor, dead. I make my way through the fray to Maxen, striking anything that gets in my path. Without words, we turn back to back. Only four men remain that I can see. Two charge at us as Maxen takes one and I face the other. I block his swing and then stumble, my wounds weakening me as my shoulder screams.

Maxen blocks my weak side and with a shout, kicks out with all his might, sending the man attacking me tumbling into Thorn's waiting sword. Thorn offers me a smile before moving to my other side. The three of us slowly push back, our attention on striking and covering each other until we stand in a circle of bodies. My chest heaves and my arm drops limply with exhaustion. My eyes search for more targets but I spot the twins first.

Drax and Jax stride towards us, blood and dirt covering their faces, their eyes alight with the thrill and adrenaline of their kills. Side by side the sight floors me, my warriors walk towards me, their eyes meeting mine with our shared fear, triumphant and caring.

"Well, that was fun," I say humourlessly. We all laugh before looking around at the carnage.

"Check for anything useful and see if any are alive, they were too organised to be a random attack." They all nod and we separate in our search, me favouring my bad arm.

A weedy scream sounds from behind the car Maxen is approaching and a body flies at him. He slides, avoiding it, and spins. Maxen leans back, his back leg bent and his front out straight so he is almost touching the floor. He twirls his sword with a feral grin, his bare chest gleaming with his sweat. He gestures for the guy to come to him. I grip my sword, ready to help if need be. The man hesitates before rushing in.

Maxen twirls and dances around the man, his blade flashing in the light, an extension of his arm. His movements are fluid and brutal as he plays with his kill. Maxen opens small cuts on the man as he goes until the man eventually drops to the floor, either from pain or blood loss. The man's fingers grasp at the gravel and sand as he tries to drag his body away. Maxen watches me as he skewers the man trying to crawl away, his eyes locked on mine as he twists his sword into the flesh beneath him. The man's death cries fill the air as does the scent of piss and shit. Maxen's hair streams past him and in this moment, I lose myself to the warrior that is Maxen.

When I offer no judgement or protest, just simple acceptance, his stance loosens and he prowls towards me. Blood smatters one cheek and a cut weeps on his pec. His hair curls around his shoulders, darkened with his sweat from battle. His obsidian eyes darken with need as I stay rooted to the spot. I've never seen anything so glorious, so formidable and he's all mine.

When he reaches me, he grabs my waist, and uncaring about the blood, smashes his lips to mine ferociously. I wrap my legs around his waist and grab his hair, pushing my fingers through the long locks as I give as good as I get. My cheek huts as our faces hit together, the pain and pleasure mixing together as he grips my ass and massages. His shoves his tongue in my mouth as we duel for control. Pulling back, he nips at my lip and lowers his head to mine, leaving our swollen lips inches apart. His wild eyes watching me.

"Fuck, if I had less control I would throw you to the ground and fuck you right now."

My pussy clenches and I'm tempted to dare him to do it but Thorn's yell interrupts. I sigh and unwrap my legs. He lets go, letting me slide down his body to the floor, his hard, slick muscles sliding seductively against me.

"Later," I promise.

"Later."

We both turn to the others to see Thorn yank the arm of a boy no older than eighteen from inside the darkened pass. He throws him on the ground in disgust in front of me.

"The rest are dead, I found this one hiding like a coward in the tunnel."

The boy cries, snot and tears mixing on his pale face. Ruby red hair sticks up in a small mohawk and he has both eyebrows pierced. His green eyes meet mine in desperation as his bottom lip trembles. Sighing, I crouch in front of him. He flinches back, watching me like an executioner.

"Why did you attack us?" I ask gently. Killing men who attack me is one thing, but I can't kill a scared boy just because he was part of it. Especially when he is offering me no violence.

"S-sor-ry." He cries before scrubbing at his red puffy eyes. He's shirtless and I can see the 'R' carved above his heart. Fucking Reeves.

"Why are the Reeves after me?" I add a threat to my voice, hoping I don't have to carry through.

"Tt-hey aren't."

Getting annoyed, I snarl. He jumps back and lets out a cry.

"Fuck kid, I'm not going to hurt you okay? I just need to know why you attacked us." I scrub my head before sitting down, crossed legged in front of him.

"You-u won't h-hurt me?" He asks.

"No."

"Why?" I sigh. Why indeed.

"Because you're a kid. Because I'm betting this wasn't your idea. Because you could have tried to kill my man there but you didn't."

"There's a bounty on your head." His words rush out and then he waits like a slave waits for the whip to crack.

"Shit. The Reeves took the bounty?"

He shakes his head and watches me, calming slightly when I don't move.

"No. T-Man said Reeves wouldn't find out about it. We were warned not to fuck with you or with Berserkers, but Reeves is on his way to The Ring and T-Man wanted to make some money." I'm guessing T-Man was the leader of this little group.

"So Reeves has nothing to do with this?" he nods as I gesture round at the bodies. "And these are the only ones who took the bounty?" he nods again.

"The rest are loyal to Reeves or you. T-Man always wanted more yanoe." He rubs his fingers together, not bothering to finish his sentence.

"Okay kid, anything else?" He thinks about it, his eyes clouding in concentration before shaking his head.

"Okay, head to the Ring and tell Reeves what happened. Tell him to clean his clan up before I get back or I will." He jumps up, nodding as he goes, his lanky body swaying.

"No problem." He scuttles away before stopping. "Oh, erm I wasn't supposed to hear but the Berserkers are heading to Seekers territory looking for you, so you should be okay this way." I smile at him before he sprints to the closest bike and speeds away.

"Well, at least one thing is going our way." I heave myself up and turn to my men. "We grab anything we can use and keep going. We aren't stopping until the sun sets." Drax groans, but winks at me. Jax walks towards me as the others pack up some food and weapons and load our bikes. He slides his finger along the cut on my cheek gently.

"Too close, way too close, little warrior," he says softly.

I place my hand over his, making him hold my face. I nod,

shaken now that the adrenaline has left my body. He's right, it was too close and this was supposed to be the easy bit of the mission.

WE'RE all wound tight the rest of the journey, the landscape changing as we ride cautiously. The kid might have lied to us or maybe he was telling the truth, either way, I'm not taking the chance. We ride past buildings, destroyed bridges, even what once was a loch. Exhaustion courses through my body, but I push on until the sun dies and the moon and stars shine. The temperature cools enough to be comfortable and with a grumble, I pull up next to a broken building. From what I can see, the roof is completely gone and one of the outer walls has a huge hole in it, but it's better than sleeping outside. We park our bikes out back and silently unload, all of us lost in our thoughts. I slide inside, the moon allowing me to see. Rubble and debris fill the floor apart from one sheltered corner. I drop my bags there and lean against the wall.

"Okay, I want two on watch at all times. One at the hole, one at the door. We can have a quick meal. No fire to cook anything, as we don't want to draw attention, then we bed down, switching every three. Get as much sleep as you can. We leave at first sun's rays." With that, I drop to my ass and pull the food from my bag. We sit in a circle and share it between us, the glances heating and the touches prolonged until my body screams at me to rest. Thorn must sense it as he smiles gently at me.

"Maxen and me will take first, then switch out with the twins."

I go to protest when he covers my mouth with his hand.

"You're injured, let us do this one thing for you." Stopping myself from licking his palm, I nod and he smiles brightly at me. "Get some sleep, sweetheart." He kisses me gently before heaving himself up and disappearing to the front door. Maxen stands and stretches, my eyes automatically checking him out. He winks before leaning in and kissing my head.

"Be good, Mi Alma." Then he disappears as well. I roll my eyes and pull my jacket from my bag and use it as a pillow. Jax and Drax move about, getting ready as I curl on my side facing the opening and close my eyes. A body slips behind me and one in front. An arm from behind slips under my neck and one around my waist pulling me close. A hard warm body meets my back. I squint my eyes and look into Drax's. He winks before turning over, giving me his back. He wiggles closer and sighs when I bury my face in it. Draping my arm around his waist, I hug him to me.

"Good night, little warrior," Jax whispers into my hair. I fall asleep smiling.

I'm so tired that I don't even wake fully when they change over, only enough to roll off Jax's arm and onto Maxen's waiting chest. Thorn leans on my back, his head heavy in a good way as I sprawl on Maxen.

"Go back to sleep, Mi Alma."

"What does that mean?" I ask groggily. He kisses my head and hums.

"It means 'my heart'." A goofy grin breaks out and I bury my face in his wide chest to hide it. He laughs and Thorn groans before smacking my ass.

"Sleep."

And I do.

Sun shines into my eyes stirring, me from a nightmare-less sleep. I blink as Thorn's snoring face comes into focus in front of me, his skin shimmering in the beam of sunlight making its way through the hole. My head is cushioned on Maxen's arm where he's wrapped around me. Thorn's legs are trapping mine and our hands are entwined over my heart. I know I should move, we need to leave after all, but I find myself watching him, until he swallows and his eyes crack open, I know I should be embarrassed watching him like a creeper but maybe Dray's ways are rubbing off on me.

He smiles sleepily at me, his eyes almost closed and my breath catches. He's beautiful, not something I would call a man but it suits him. Even the scar in his eyebrow doesn't detract from that, only making me more attracted to him.

"Mornin' baby girl." His voice is rough from sleep.

"Morning," I whisper.

He drags me out of Maxen's arms who moans and rolls over, giving his back to us. Our faces are inches away as we look at each other, smiling.

"I'd be happy waking up every day to your beautiful face. You're in here," he thumps his chest and then holds my hand over his heart "deep, Tazanna Worth." The openness on his face almost undoes me and I remember Jax's words. He said Thorn was my softness. Maybe he's right because suddenly words spill out of my mouth.

"You found the heart I didn't even know I had anymore. I have rough edges, big guy. I'm angry, sarcastic, and always see the worst in people. How can I be good enough for you four, for each of you?" My insecurities raise their ugly head but I know I need his answer.

"You might be all of those things but you're also kind, caring, and you try to save everyone, even when you know you shouldn't. You let us in despite everything you've been through and fought through nightmares so bad most would die or give up. You're so strong and so brave. It's us who aren't good enough for you, but we will never give you up. Your ours baby. We never want anyone to hide behind us. Seeing you there next to us, riding into battle with you leading us. Your dad was wrong. You're not a princess, you're a fucking queen. Your darkness is how you survived and you don't see yourself clearly at all. I'd happily die for you Taz, but more importantly, I'd live for you."

Noah's sorrow and death come to my mind, how angry I was that he didn't fight anymore. That he could leave me so easily. Looking into Thorn's eyes, I know he's right. He would die protecting me, but he would always fight with everything in him to get to my side again. Something Noah would never do.

"You're just now letting yourself feel, to find out who you really are after you've been hiding it all your life. I can't wait for that day where you embrace every part of you, darkness and all. You'd be unstoppable, a woman who knows when to give mercy, but also when to take it. One willing to fight, or to die for her friends and people. Feeling fear or happiness doesn't make you weak, they make you stronger than ever."

Leaning forward, I brush my lips over him. We keep the kiss soft and light. I pull back and look into his shining eyes.

"Thank you, for staying with me."

He kisses my forehead, each cheek and my lips softly.

"Always, baby girl."

After mine and Thorn's heart to heart, I wake Maxen and we all have a quick breakfast. I can see the lack of sleep weighing on the guys, but they are in surprisingly good moods and so am I. We laugh and joke through breakfast and even as we pack up. When I sit astride my bike, they all drop quick kisses on my lips before mounting theirs. With a smile, we set off for day two.

Chapter Eighteen

Heartache and Mistakes

DAY two of our journey is uneventful; we ride hard, not even stopping to eat or rest. We ride through a ghost town, the buildings still standing but empty. The glass on the shop windows broken, with their goods laying scattered on the floor. A child's bike lays in the middle of the road, and further down a stuffed teddy.

On the way out, four bodies hang along a pole as a reminder of the world we are in. Clearly a family, caught by some rogue scav. A small boy who can't be any older than ten hangs at the end. I don't know why, but I can't seem to look away from him. His striped t-shirt has a rip and holes in it, showing his malnourished chest. His little legs are encased in dirty tattered black shorts. One foot has on a trainer while the other is bare, the trainer lost to the street below. His baby blue eyes are open and staring lifelessly at me, his terror and pain seemingly etched forever in their depths.

Next to him hangs a young girl. Her dress is ripped down the middle, showing the whole world her not fully developed breasts. The animals even took her knickers. Logically, I know she is dead, but it makes me feel sick knowing that she has been left like this. Her mother is in almost the same state next to her, only she has clearly been tortured. Where one of her nipples used to be, only blood and a hole remain with a clear teeth imprint. Blood covers all of her rounded stomach and her bare feet show some of her toes missing.

The father is naked, his balls and cock obviously cut off. His chest is a mess of cuts and stab marks and his face is drenched in blood.

I pull my bike to the side, away from where I had stopped just before them. I can't leave them like this. I jump from my bike, and without saying anything, look around for a way to get them down, my mind screaming the entire time.

"Baby girl?" Thorn asks. I move away when he tries to touch me, and I see his face fall. His hurt spears through me, and I quickly grab his hand and hold it to my cheek. Letting his warmth comfort me, I close my eyes.

"I can't leave them like this. They deserve to be able to rest in dignity."

"Okay," he says, he kisses me softly and keeps a hold of my hand.

"Let's get them down," he orders. The others nod grimly, and I watch from the safety next to Thorn as Drax climbs the pole and carefully cuts down one after the other. Each time a body falls to the floor, it feels like a knife twisting in my gut.

When the dad's body lands on the floor with a squelch, the skin over his head flaps open. They tried to skin him! Anger runs through me. Unable to stand here, I move over to the girl. I try not to look into her eyes as I cover her up. I do the same to the mom and turn back to my guys.

"We can dig a grave around the back of that shop. Let's give them some peace."

They nod and follow me, each one of their faces filled with the anger and sadness I feel at this senseless torture and murder.

WE ALL HELP TO dig the graves and bury them. When the last bit of soil covers the bodies, something in me loosens. Thorn fashions a cross for each out of some wood and I kiss his cheek in thanks. We stand at the edge of their graves, our heads bowed. Each sending our own words with the bodies.

With one last look at the dirt, we turn back to our bikes, walking in silence. We mount our bikes and set off again, this time more subdued, the reminder working to keep us on our toes. By the time the sun sets, I calculate we should arrive at The Worshippers settlement by tomorrow afternoon. We camp out under an old bridge and build a fire to cook some meat we brought with us, courtesy of Major.

"So, what's the plan for when we get there?" Drax asks around a mouthful. Leaning back on my arms, I stretch my legs out, the muscles aching from riding all day.

"Honestly, I don't know. I'm going to wing it." He chokes on his next mouthful and Jax thumps his back grimly.

"Wing it?" Drax chokes out before grabbing his water and downing it. I nod, amused.

"Yup, I'm going to approach the gate and hope they don't kill me on sight. They shouldn't; I'm a woman and they often collect them for their leader to serve as his concubines."

"That's the plan?" Thorn asks incredulously.

"I know—" I scrub my head. "If I had more time I would have sent word to some men I trust within his cult, but I didn't."

"Hey—" Maxen scoops my legs up and massages the tired muscles. "We follow you, we get through this together and then head back." Nodding, I lean my head back against Thorn's shoulder next to me.

"I think you should wait somewhere they won't see you until I secure our passage," I say around a blissful moan at Maxen's talented fingers. I'm almost too engrossed to notice the look they share over my head.

"Sure thing, babe," Drax winks and carries on eating.

When we finish, we put out the fire and station two people on watch again. I volunteer first, noticing the tiredness in their eyes, plus I've never been around people for this long before. It's tiring, and I could do with some space to sort through my chaotic thoughts. Maxen takes one end of the bridge and I take the other as the twins and Thorn sleep.

Looking out into the darkness, I think back on the past week. I've changed so much, I can feel it already. I'm not as harsh, and my emotions pulse once again in my body. I have something to fight for again and not even the darkness and horror of my memories can take that away.

Major was right. I had been burying my head in the sand hoping it would all go away. These men changed that. They brought the colour back into my world and yanked me out, kicking and screaming. They don't pretend everything is good, but they stand beside me when it gets bad.

Analysing my feelings, I think I might love them a bit. It's new and tentative but it's already so much stronger than with Noah. What we had was desperate, seeking something to hold onto to keep us afloat in a world of pain and torture. The thing between me and the guys now, no matter how strange, pulses with happiness and a partnership. Footsteps behind me have me whirling with my blade drawn. Drax holds his hands up in mock surrender before plopping down next to me. Shaking my head, I sheathe my blade and look back out into the Waste.

"I need to tell you something, in case anything goes wrong tomorrow. I need you to know." Turning with a blink, I look into his serious face. His eyes are full of nerves and something else.

"Know what?" Tilting my head to the side, I eye my usually playful twin. He swallows before licking his lips.

"I love you," he stares shyly at me, the words floating in the air between us. My chest warms and happiness bursts to life in me, my chest warms as I feel the broken pieces of my heart sealing together as my eyes fill with tears. But panic immediately follows the happiness making my heart beat double time.

"Wh-" I choke out but a howl has me jumping into a crouch with my blade in my hand once again.

"Taz-"

I hold my hand up and close my eyes, listening hard.

"Sweet cheeks, please say something." Opening my eyes, I look at him, his face looks stricken. I don't want to say it back, not until I'm sure, but I need to give him something. I open my mouth when a twig breaks close by.

"There's something out there." His face falls and closes down but he nods. He crouches next to me, but he feels a million miles away. Shit, I need to fix this but I need to protect us first. I can accept his distance, but I can't accept him dying because I was busy pouring my feelings out.

A howl sounds off in the distance again, making me clutch my knife tighter.

"Stay behind me," I warn before sneaking around the chunk of stone I was sitting on. There. Moving in the shadows are at least three ferals. Drax must see them too because he swears and I hear him draw a knife.

"What do we do?"

Grinding my teeth, I wait to see if they move closer.

"Wait. I don't want to kill them if we don't have to."

"Why?" He whisper-shouts.

"Because it will draw a pack and then we are fucked." He swears again and I have to agree. We stay crouched there as they sniff about before yipping at each other and taking off in the other direction. I barely breathe until I can't hear them anymore and then I still wait. A good twenty minutes later, I relax my position and turn to Drax.

He glances at me, then sheathes his knife. He looks at the

ground, his face hard. Fuck, I hate sharing feelings, but if it will bring back my Drax, I'll suck it up.

"I've been in love before." His head snaps up as he watches me warily. "I know I mentioned it to you."

He nods. "What happened to him?"

Noah's dead body flashes in my mind, making me fall back on my ass. "He died."

He sucks in a breath and sits cross-legged in front of me. "What happened?" He grabs my hand and squeezes, offering me comfort. I sigh and look into his eyes.

"He was one of Ivar's general's son's. We were friends at first, both of us being around the same age. We had to hide it, me being a slave and all. We grew up, growing closer as we did. But he was training to be a warrior and I was Ivar's pet. He used to come to my room every night and treat my wounds from the day, and every time I could see his heartbreak. He was soft, too soft for this world. His dad thought it could be trained out of him, but I knew better." Looking down, I play with Drax's fingers.

"We fell in love. It wasn't sudden and all-consuming, but slow and warm. I needed someone, anyone, and he felt the same way. Once Ivar caught us kissing, he punished me." I release my death grip on his fingers and he lifts my chin up with his other hand.

"How?" he asks softly. I refuse to look away, to be embarrassed about what I endured.

"He tied me to the post on the steps of his castle and whipped my bare back. When he was done, I was half dead. He left me there overnight. I remember the crows circling me as I watched the night turn to day. Ivar released me the next evening. Noah came and looked after me that night. I could feel his helplessness and anger. I just never expected him to do anything about it. The fool attacked Ivar." Licking my lips, I carry on.

"Ivar was going to kill him as Noah's dad stood by and watched, because if he pleaded for his son's life, it would be seen as a weakness. Ivar found an even better way to punish him. He threw me in The Ring. Noah knew if I lost I would be raped and killed in front of everyone. But I won, so Ivar kept putting me back in."

"What happened to Noah?"

"He couldn't stand by and watch me fight, but I had changed by then, the blood and pain consuming me, my only thoughts on survival. He wanted to run away, I knew it wouldn't work. Ivar would find us, hell we wouldn't even get out of the territory." Stopping, I suck in a breath as the memories cloud my vision.

"I remember I had just won my fifth match. I was so fucking proud of myself, high on the adrenaline and blood. Ivar was happy, too happy. He told me to rest that night which was unusual. Even if I won, Ivar found an excuse to try and punish me. When I got to my room, I found Noah hanging from my ceiling." My heart breaks all over again, my cries loud in my own ears.

"Oh, babe..." I look at Drax, the pain fresh in my eyes as the tears I didn't cry then fall now.

"He couldn't fight, he wouldn't live for me. Instead, he let his hate and anger consume him and left me all alone."

"Baby, that's not—"

"I know. I do. I was so angry at first, so fucking angry at him. I used it in my fights but eventually, I realized how lost he must have felt to do that." Shaking my head, I grab his hand again.

"I get why he did it Drax, but I can't forgive him. I needed him and he left me. Ivar used it to hurt me, he laughed and wouldn't remove his body until we left back for Berserker land. I had to sit in that room for days, watching the only person I care about fade away. Major refused to let me stay in that room after that." Drax's arms wrap around me as I cry silently into his shoulder.

"Fuck, I had a point, I did." Pulling myself away I face him. "What I'm trying to say is, I hardened my heart, what was left of it. Now I don't know anything else, but you four have wormed your way in there. I care for you Drax, I do. I can't say the l-word again, not yet. But whatever is left of that broken thing in my chest is yours."

His smile is brilliant, and like the sun rising, it banishes the dark from the land. He cups my cheek gently and kisses me with such tenderness I have to fight off more tears.

"I can live with that until you're ready."

We spend the rest of watch wrapped around each other, laughing and joking, telling each other secrets no one else knows. If someone had told me before that this is where I would be now, I would have laughed. I would have hated myself for showing any weakness, but these men taught me that I don't always need to be strong and that letting myself feel doesn't make me less capable.

THE ENTRANCE to the small town is blocked by numerous old, abandoned vehicles, including a school bus, a truck, and a lorry. Houses surround the other two sides, with no passage in between them. The third and final side is the church. One road in, one road out. Everything leads back to the church. Fucking Worshippers. Last night went quickly, and we packed up this morning, each touch longer than the last. Before I mounted up, I kissed them all, something that now felt like goodbye as we now face the cult's settlement.

With a sigh, I turn to look at my men once more before stepping out from behind the trees with my arms up in surrender. My instincts are screaming at me to fight, but for once I don't let them rule me. I hear the guys swear behind me but I concentrate on the guards who are now rushing around and shouting at me. Slowly, I walk until I'm feet away from the entrance to the settlement. Stopping, I wait, sweat pouring down my spine as I fight to stay still. To not reach for my weapons. To not protect myself.

The bus blocking the way partially moves, allowing four men to slip out. The red patch stitched on the sleeves of their jackets marks them as Worshippers. They quickly surround me.

"Name?" One demands, his gun pointed at me. So, this is where they all disappeared to.

"Worth." They visibly inhale before squaring back up to me, their weapons closer.

"Why are you here? We could kill you." Another one warns.

"I know. I have a message for Priest." They shuffle nervously and I smirk, the stories by Worshipper fighters are coming in handy. I just hope I can spot someone I know, and soon.

"What message?"

"It's for Priest, and I don't see him anywhere."

"You think we would let a Berserker cunt in to see our leader?" he laughs.

"You worried that you can't handle one little girl?" I say sweetly. A gun gets shoved into my back, making me grunt.

"Oh, so the four men we just caught in the woods aren't yours?" One of the men asks.

Fucking son of a -

"They are, but I figured you wouldn't shoot if I came first."

"Five of you, that's all?" The first one asks.

"That's all," I say honestly.

A familiar guard steps through the gate and rushes to my side, his smile genuine. The massive scar across his neck is healed from the last time I saw him. His head is still shaved, and he's still a big bastard. Probably just a little smaller than Thorn. I met Cal my second year at The Ring when we got paired in a gladiator tandem style fight.

"Worth, you crazy bitch." He slaps my back in greeting before pulling away and glaring at the guards.

"Let her in," he orders.

"Sir?" One of them asks, his weapon dipping in hesitation. I really have to control myself so I don't grab it.

"That's an order, grunt," he snarls at them, his face reminding me of why he survived so long in the fights before Priest decided to pull him out.

"Yes, sir."

Cal turns back to me with a smile. "Come on, what are you doing here? Finally ready to accept my marriage offer?" I laugh as I follow behind him. Turning, I see Maxen and the guys following, looking sheepish.

"I need to see Priest."

"Worth, I don't even think—"

"I wouldn't ask if it wasn't important. You know that," I interrupt, my voice hard.

He sighs before looking us all over.

"Fuck, only because I owe you my life. I'll see what I can do. Until then, you can wait at my house." I nod my thanks and follow him through the streets.

Well looked after houses line the road to the church. Men carrying various weapons walk freely, their heads up as they glare at us. Women rush by in red robes, their hoods up. Something is niggling at me looking around and I can't figure out what. I keep walking, my eyes taking everything in.

"There are no kids," I say eventually around a frown. All these women and not one child? Cal looks back at me and then around as some guards come closer. I nod my understanding and follow quietly behind him.

He reaches a house which looks the exact same as the others and ushers us in. Standing in the living room, I cringe at the colourless furniture. Everything is in shades of grey, even the walls. Cal looks out the window and then back at us.

"Stay here while I go see what I can do about that meeting."

Nodding, I grab his arm on the way by.

"Thank you, Cal."

"It's the least I can do, and hey maybe you'll agree to be my wife after, eh?" Laughing, I let him leave and turn back to my men with my hands on my hips.

"What happened to staying hidden?" I fume. Maxen drops to the sofa and watches me with his head tilted back.

"No offence, Mi Alma, but did you really think we would let you waltz into a known cult village alone?" Crossing my arms, I glare at him. Thorn smiles and shuffles to me before pulling me into a hug that drags my feet off the floor.

"Fine," I groan, unable to stay mad at them, as I uncross my arms and wrap them around his neck. He turns with me still in his arms and dumps me in Maxen's lap. Maxen's arms instantly wind around me as Drax and Jax lean against the wall, watching us.

"So, I guess we wait?" Jax asks as he looks around the room. Nodding again, I lean back against Maxen's chest. I just open my mouth when the front door explodes open and men in hoods come pouring in.

Jumping up, I draw my sword, as does Maxen. With a roar, we attack but there's too many of them. I drop at least three but more swarm in. I watch in horror as Thorn goes down with four on top of him, fighting like a beast.

Drax falls with a cry and Jax jumps in front of him. Ducking, I avoid the man trying to knock my head off. Maxen shouts as he tries to cut a path to me from where we are separated by bodies. I keep fighting even as Maxen disappears from sight.

"Stop, or we kill him," a voice shouts. Breathing hard, I look around wildly until I see a hooded man with a knife to Jax's throat. He's fighting, trying to get free, but stops when the knife nicks his throat.

"Drop your sword," the man warns. Grinding my teeth, I lock my eyes with Jax. He shakes his head, but I let my sword drop from my hand. Curling my now empty hands into fists, I face the man.

"Let him go," I warn. He laughs and nods at a man next to me. The last thing I see is Jax growl as something slams into the back of my head with a sickening crunch.

Chapter Nineteen

Priest

WITH A GROAN, I come to. I wince when the light hits my sensitive eyes and I narrow them quickly, looking around. My men are spread out in front of me in a row, all chained to the floor. Their iron shackles surrounding both wrists, connected to a chain bolted to a ring in the floor. They watch me warily and then their eyes flick behind me. Nodding to show I understand, I slowly push up. Chains rattle, drawing my gaze down to my own bound hands. I growl and yank on them uselessly. Panic wells as old memories slam into me.

"Mi Alma."

His voice brings me back as I look to Maxen, my rock. He stares at me, offering comfort in the only way he can. Calming, I stop tugging on the chains and concentrate on breathing. My head is pounding and my mouth feels like cardboard. I slowly look over my men to make sure they aren't hurt. Jax has a trickle of blood at his neck, Maxen has a black eye and Thorn's hairline is cut. Drax has a cut cheek. So altogether not bad. I push myself into a standing position and turn as much as the chains will allow me to.

There, watching everything, is a man with the hood of his cloak pulled up. I'd guess he is the man from before.

"So, you're the one they are looking for?"

Yep, the one from before. His voice grates on my sensitive

nerves and sends pain shooting through my head. With a flourish, he pulls the hood down, revealing an average looking man with salt and pepper hair. I don't bother talking but my eyes run over the room, trying to find a way out. Two more men stand at the only door in and out of what I'm guessing is a basement. The stairs leading up look old and decayed and the smell of damp and musty air has me nearly sneezing. A small window is letting in the light in the corner, so we can't have been out that long unless it's been twenty-four hours.

"You will answer me when I speak or there will be consequences." His voice is full of unwavering condescension, like he expects me to cower and beg. I straighten my spine and meet his gaze boldly before smiling slowly. He snarls before his face wipes clean.

"As you wish." He steps towards me, watching for any sign that I will give in. I keep that same sarcastic smile in place and brace myself for the pain I know is coming. I'm betting this guy isn't nearly as good at torture as Ivar.

Stopping before me, he grabs my cheek in a rough grip before his hand runs to the back of my head and presses in the wound his men made. Searing agony races through me. I hear my men shouting and growling, but I tune them out. I bite my tongue to stop my cry from coming out as pain spikes through my head again when his thick fingers press harder. Dots dance in front of my gaze, but I lock my feet in place. When I don't make a noise, he looks at me in confusion. Stupid fuck, if he only knew that I perfected the art of staying silent. After all, any little noise would only spur Ivar on. He loved to hear me scream and cry, it was his own version of ecstasy.

Anger darkens his face as he cocks back his fist and punches my stomach. The air is knocked out of me and I bend over, catching my breath. When I can breathe normally, I ignore the pain and straighten once again with that same sarcastic smile on my face. How boring and predictable. I mean really, could he not get creative with his techniques? Using his fists, how primitive.

"I'm going to skin you alive you son of a bitch!" Drax shouts from behind me, the hate clear in his desperate voice. My men carry on shouting threats but I focus on the man in front of me. If I offer them reassurance it would be a lie, I know I can survive this I just wish they didn't have to watch.

"Are you the one The Berserkers seek?" he shouts, spittle flying from his mouth and hitting my cheek. When I don't answer, he pummels into my stomach with both fists in quick succession. Sucking in air, I gasp as I bend over to protect it. He grasps my hair and yanks my head back until I'm looking at him. In his hand, he has one of my blades, the knife shining in the light. Oh, this is going to hurt.

"Answer me," he warns in a deadly voice. My smile is slow and pained but it does the job. With a snarl, he slams the knife into my already pained shoulder. I swallow back the scream, biting my tongue in my efforts. Swallowing rapidly I suck down the blood and bile. *Motherfucking twatbag, wanker, dog fucker-*

"Are you Ivar's pet?" His voice cuts off my internal creative insult stream.

"I'm going to kill you," I warn. He flinches as he watches me, probably seeing his death written in my eyes.

Blood dribbles down my lip and on to my chin and I spit it at him. Laughing crazily, I watch as he recoils and wipes his face on his cloak.

"Fucking crazy bitch. Fucking animal!" He screeches as he rubs his face desperately.

"You missed a spot," I gasp out between painful laughs. He backhands me, my face snapping to the side before I turn to face him only to watch as he rushes up the stairs, still scrubbing his cheek. For a torturer, he sure doesn't seem to like blood, I muse.

"Follow me and lock the door behind you!" He screams at the

guards at the door. They rush out after him as I hear the tumbler on the door drop into place. Spitting the rest of the blood on the floor at my feet, I grimace at the pain radiating throughout my whole body. I feel like I went ten rounds in The Ring.

Sands below, I forgot how much I hate torture.

"Baby, answer me please!"

"Tazanna, answer me this second!"

The voices blend together, their anger and worry hurting my sore head.

"Fuck, I'm fine. Chill." It goes quiet and I manage to turn slowly in my chains, being careful not to move too fast in case I pass out or throw up. I'm going to rip that motherfuckers cock off when I get my hands on him, then I'm going to feed it to him and sew his mouth shut. The thought helps lessen my anger, not by much, but enough to think clearly.

I face the guys and offer them what I hope is a happy smile. It must fall flat because Drax looks close to tears, Jax looks murderous. My sweet Thorn is cold and Maxen? Sands below, I would not want to be on his bad side at this moment.

"Are you okay?" He enunciates every word slowly like he's trying to control his anger. Looking into his eyes, I see death. His chest seems double its normal size and his arms are bulging against the chains on his wrists. His nostrils are flaring.

"Yeah, I've had worse. He hits like a pussy," I laugh, but they all stare at me. Then turning to each other only Maxen's eyes stay on me like if he looks away he might explode. I hear them start to discuss a plan, but I tune them out, making one of my own. Fuck! My head hurts. It feels like that time I went on a four-day binge. Damn, that was a good week. After I get out of this, I am grabbing a bottle, or two, or whiskey, and locking us all in a room.

Ignoring them, I reach up and finger the blade the man left in my shoulder. What an idiot. I knew if I got him mad enough he would forget it was there. Gritting my teeth, I grip the handle firmly. My eyes lock on Maxen's as I pull it from my shoulder.

"TAZ!"

"FUCK."

The agony rocks me as the knife rips through muscle and skin. When it slides free, I drop my head and breathe deeply to stop from passing out. My ears are ringing and my eyes are unfocused. That can't be good.

"Baby, what the hell—" My ears pop and I can hear them again.

"I'm fine." Lifting my head, I see them all trying to get out of their chains to reach me, their worry palpable. The smell of my blood seeps into the room as it runs freely from my wound. At least it doesn't smell old down here anymore. I look at my shoulder with a frown. Damn, another scar. Well, not like it will make much of a difference, but soon I will be all scar tissue. I finger the edge of my ripped top around the wound. The end of the world sure is hard on a girl's wardrobe.

"You ready to blow this joint?" I ask as casually as I can with the pain still riding me. I drop my hand from my shoulder and face them again. Jax snorts out a desperate sounding laugh as the rest blink at me incredulously.

"Alright, boys. Watch and learn, and keep the volume down will you? I don't want them hearing and coming to check things out while I'm mid-escape." They all nod and I wink. Relief hits their faces. Shit, I guess I look worse than I feel.

Cracking my neck from side to side to try and relieve the pressure, I grip the blade in my mouth and concentrate on the chains. I felt the pull in the cuffs earlier and know I can break free. I guess Ivar did teach me some things.

Shimmying my hands into my jeans pocket, I grab the tiny piece of a soda can that I keep in there, just in case I was ever caught again. Pulling it out I slide it into the teeth of the cuff and push it down over the serrated edges until it meets the middle. Pressing the cuff into my leg it locks in tighter squeezing painfully before it catches. Then I easily slide the cuff off. Repeating the same on the other hand, I drop the cuffs to the floor and grab the knife from my mouth. Looking up, I see they are all blinking at me until Maxen laughs humourlessly. I throw him a wink and look around.

"Ok, next part. I'm going to pretend to be passed out where they cuffed me. You are going to scream and shout until they come down. You tell them you think I'm bleeding out. When they check, I'll take them both out and get you free okay?"

"Just get us out now!" Drax whines.

"No, if they come down and see you free they will run back up and warn them before we can stop them. We can't get out of the door with it locked. We need to do this one at a time okay? Plus, yours are shackles. Mine were only cuffs, that trick won't work."

I wait for them to nod before slipping into a ball on the floor over my cuffs. Looking up once more, I eye them.

"That motherfucker who stabbed me is mine, the rest upstairs are yours."

They all grin this time, every single one filled with longing for blood. Laying my head down, I cover the knife and wait. They start screaming, the words blending into one another. I listen and smile when I hear the door unlocking. They stop screaming and wait as the booted feet descend the stairs.

"What the fuck is going on?" A man snarls behind me. I didn't hear the door lock again so the plan is good.

"She's bleeding out. I think he hit an artery!" Drax cries dramatically. I stick my tongue out at him and close my eyes.

"God damn it," the man curses before his boots sound on the cement floor as he walks around me. The air changes in front of me and I can see him through my slitted eyes as he crouches down. Fuck, where is the other guard? With no time to waste, I pop up and slice his throat. Covering his mouth, I watch as the blood spurts from the wide neck wound. When his eyes dim, I slowly lower him to the floor.

"One down, one to go." Hearing movement upstairs, I search the man and come across the keys. Throwing them to Maxen, I slide towards the stairs and peek around. The guard's silhouette is clear as he stands with his back to the open door. What an idiot. Throwing my guys one last smile, I tiptoe silently up the stairs. At least the pain in my head is receding a bit, leaving me less sluggish.

"Taz, wait," Thorn hisses. I ignore him and keep going until I'm nothing but a silent shadow behind the man. Not wasting any time, I cover his mouth with one hand and stab him in the back with the other. Twisting the blade, I feel him slump against me. Sliding him through the door, so he is hidden in the darkness of the basement, I let him slip down the wall until he lays in a heap. I press my fingers to his neck to feel his pulse weakening.

Searching through his pockets, I find another knife. Why couldn't he have a sword? I can hear Maxen swearing as he fumbles with the keys. I slide around the door and eye the hallway. One end leads to what I'm guessing is the front door. Cocking my head, I listen to at least three men talking in a room at the other end. Using the shadows, I slide across the floorboards silently. When I reach the door frame, I peek around before pulling my head back. Okay, four men. I jump when a hand rests on my shoulder. Drax looks grim next to me.

"Maxen and Thorn are going upstairs to check. Jax will take the front door." His whisper is almost silent and I nod my understanding.

"Four men," I whisper back.

"Two each." He grins at me and darts in for a quick kiss before rushing across the open doorway next to me to stand on the other side of the frame. He drops his fingers from three, to two, and then one. We both burst into the room at the same time, my knife already in motion through the air. It hits a man through his shoulder and he falls with a cry. Running, I use the table as a leapfrog and land on him, pulling the blade out as he falls to the floor. Rolling away, I fling myself to my feet and hold both blades out, waiting. Another man charges at me and I spin to avoid the punch and cut his back as I go. He cries out, but swings around like a bull, managing to catch my injured shoulder.

I snap, and fling myself at him, hacking as I go. Until he's nothing but a bloody carcass on the floor. Rolling to my feet, I throw my knife at the man trying to sneak up on Drax. With a grin, I grab my sword from the table. I blame the head wound for me not noticing it sooner, and then I gut the man whose shoulder I injured.

"My sword, asshole." Turning to Drax, I see him nod as the last man falls to the floor. He tosses me my knife which I jimmy into the waistband of my jeans. A banging sounds on the stairs and I watch in amusement as Maxen drags in the crying torturer. His nose is burst like a grapefruit, his blood mixing with his tears. Maxen throws him on the floor before walking over to me. He gives me a once over before swooping in for a quick hot kiss.

"He's all yours, Mi Alma." I grin as he steps back.

"On the chair please, Drax," I instruct as I wipe my sword on the dead man at my feet. Thorn saunters in with my other sword in his grasp and I smile gratefully at him. I would have hated to have to burn this place down looking for them. Nobody touches my fucking weapons.

Drax drags the man into a kitchen chair and pushes him down none too gently. Using the table to steady myself, since the adrenaline is retreating and the pain returning, I lean back in front of him.

"Are you working with the Berserkers?" I ask kindly as he watches me in fear. He swallows hard but doesn't answer. I was really hoping he wouldn't. Straightening, I wait.

"I warned you what I would do..." I whisper before driving my fist into his stomach. Gasping, he bends over. I grab his hair like he did to me and yank his head back.

"Are you working for the Berserkers?"

"Y-yes," he wheezes. Letting go of his head, it drops down before he lifts it up with a glare.

"Is your leader?" I ask.

He licks his lips and I grin. Using the same knife he stabbed me with, I slowly push it into his shoulder. He screams raggedly as it cuts into his flesh.

"Please, please stop. I'll tell you!" I stop but don't remove the knife. "No, only some of us," he cries. He shivers in pain and then cries when it jolts the knife.

"Does Ivar know I'm here? And don't lie to me," I warn, my mouth on his ear with the blade still in his shoulder. He whimpers but doesn't answer. Smiling ferally, I twist the knife and pull my head back. I slowly slide the blade out, widening the wound as I go. He screams wordlessly and the smell of piss hits the air.

"I'm only just getting started. You do know that I learnt from him right? That I know all his little tricks? The best ways to keep your subject alive as you play with them. The places that cause the most pain..." I lick my lips, tasting my own blood and he whimpers again.

"No, he doesn't know. I needed to be sure it was you- please, please just let me go."

"Let you go?" I ask.

He nods, "I told you everything," he cries.

"Oh, darling I'm not letting you go. I'm going to have some fun until your leader arrives. I'm betting they heard the screams by now and then I will give you to him." His eyes widen further. "Oh yes, I've heard all about the ways he treats traitors."

He throws his head from side to side as his words blur together pleadingly. Jax comes into the room. "Your friend and some men are heading this way." I sigh sadly.

"Guess our time's up, buddy. Don't worry, I'm sure you'll get what you deserve." Stepping back, I swing myself up on the table and wait.

Not one minute later, Cal marches through the door, his footsteps loud as he hurries to where we wait. He stops, looking at me and then the man in the chair.

"You look like shit." He steps further into the room, letting the men in behind him. I tense but don't move.

"Thanks, I guess they decided I needed a facelift." He snorts and then looks in disgust at the blubbering man in the chair. "You okay?"

I nod and wince as my shoulder pulls.

"Yeah, did you sort out that meeting with Priest? It seems we have a lot to talk about." The man in the chair screams at his leader's name and throws himself on the floor trying to crawl through the men's legs.

Cal sighs and rubs his face wearily. "Yes. Come on, I'll take you there, he'll want to know what went down here." Turning to the other men, he points at the bag of shit on the floor. "Bring him with us."

Sliding off the table, I go to Maxen, and ignoring everyone else, I twine my good hand with his, seeking comfort. Smiling down at me, the love is clear in his eyes. My body tires now, the adrenaline is running out and I use him to help support myself.

"Come on, Mi Alma. Let's go extend your invitation."

WE ARE MARCHED across the town and into the church. Guards stop and stare and whisper between themselves. Ignoring them, I keep my hand in Maxen's, uncaring if it looks weak.

The church rises before us like some avenging god, flags with suns on them proudly displayed. Grey bricks make up the church, with a towering bell tower in the middle. Two open brown wooden doors are framed by carvings and gargoyles.

Cal ignores everything and quickly marches us through the open doors and down the centre walkway. The red faded carpet is branched off into the wooden pews, light flowing into the area from big arched windows on each aisle.

A lone man waits at the end of the altar. Holy shit, he's actually dressed in priest robes. I guess the name makes sense now. I stop before him, my men spread out behind me protectively. I frown at the skeletal figure in robes he is bowing to, the statue looking like the personification of death.

Priest's hair is cut short, black and wavy, styled to perfection. His face is clean shaven and looks friendly but his eyes say differently. He's small, smaller than I expected. He's about my height, and skinnier than nearly every man in here. He doesn't even feel powerful, he feels like a regular man. Not even one I would fear. Yet, there must be something about him. He couldn't lead a cult or be so feared if not.

"This is Worth, my lord." Cal bows and steps back into the rest of the guards. Priest eyes me, his gaze cold and calculating. Intelligence shines in his eyes, so different from the craziness I expected of a cult leader.

"I hear you were attacked." His voice is smooth and cultured like we are discussing meal choices.

A strained laugh busts out of me, making him arch his eyebrow at me. "You could say that. It seems you have some traitors in your midst," I offer. His face loses all emotion, it's like looking at a statue. One that can kill you without even lifting his arm. He looks at the guards, and without speaking, they drag my kidnapper forward.

"This man?" Priest asks as he slowly walks down the steps towards him.

"Yes. He admitted he is working for the Berserkers and so are some in your-" I cut off at the word cult and cough out the next part "church." He smiles knowingly before it wipes clear and he looks to the man at his feet.

"Oh, Gabriel. You know what the price for this betrayal is? I can't have one of my flock betraying our faith." Gabriel struggles and screams raggedly through the gag someone must have put on him. Priest gestures idly.

"Take him to Jophiel. Get me the truth and the names of the other men working with him." The guard nods and drags him away. Poor bastard.

"Now that nasty business is out of the way, would you like a drink?" Priest offers, watching me idly.

"No thanks. I'm here to extend you an invitation and you can understand when I say I would like to be in and out of here as soon as possible."

Tsking, he stops in front of me. "Fine, champion, my man tells me you are trustworthy. He is loyal so I shall believe him, but only so far."

I nod in understanding, the blood is still dripping from my wound, soaking into my shirt and I'm starting to feel weak from it.

"I would be inclined to trust you more if you pass a test," he offers. Cal makes a noise but falls to his knees as Priest looks at him.

"What test would that be?" I ask, willing to do anything to hurry this up. There is something wrong about this place.

"Sacrifice, you must lose that which is precious, to show your devotion." Inside I panic, what the hell does he mean sacrifice?

"How?" I ask slowly. I can almost sense my men shifting with unease.

"Sacrifice what is yours. Give freely to our God for judgement."

Fuck, does this guy always speak in riddles? My head is hurting from earlier, and trying to think through this is causing pain to batter against my nerves. His eyes drop to my blood for a split second, but it's enough for me to know what he means. Gritting my teeth, I pull out a blade and hold it against my wounded shoulder. Careful of the blood glistening on the end, I hand it across to Priest. He smiles at me before turning to the altar.

He kneels before it, the knife balanced on his hands in an offering. I don't even try to figure out his mumbling before he uses his fingers to spread my blood on the face of the skeleton.

He speaks again before nodding and standing. Turning to face me, he offers my blade back. I hesitantly take it and slide it away.

"You are to be trusted. You are strong, with a great destiny about you. You will lead us from the darkness."

Ookkaay. Time to get off this crazy train.

"Now, for the reason why you are here," he says conversationally, my blood still coating his fingers. While I watch, he raises them to his lips and sucks them clean. Nope, not today crazy. I can't wait to get out of here.

"There has been a Summit called," I rush out. His eyes widen and then close down.

"What for?"

"The Berserkers. As you can see, they are getting bolder. They are attacking clan lines and soon there will be war. The Seekers and Reeves both wait in a parlay at The Ring. They ask you to join them in four days."

"Interesting. Alas, I fear you are right. My flock have been attacked at our borders. They even tried to take one of my wives." He shivers, his eyes shining with sadness. His emotion is clear but there's something off about it like he's unsure if it's right and is faking it.

"Do you accept the invitation?" I ask tiredly, my pain making me bold or stupid.

"Can I ask you one thing, champion?" He says, stepping closer.

I nod, gritting my teeth.

"Will you fight with us? If that is what it comes to? Will you fight the Berserkers or will you run away again?" He sneers the last part, ignoring the anger on my face. My voice is clear as day as it rings out around the church like a declaration.

"I run from no one. I will fight again. I will kill Ivar The Destroyer and I will stop this war. On your God and mine, I swear it." Dramatic, but it seems to do the trick. His smile is shark-like as it stretches across his lips.

"You may tell them I shall be there. I make no promises of treaties, but I shall attend the summit after I clean my flock of these pesky traitors." With that, he whirls and walks back to his altar, clearly dismissing us. Fine by me. I stumble against Maxen and he wraps his arm around my waist. Cal eyes the guards before stopping in front of me.

"Looks like The Champion is back." He leans in to whisper the next. "Be careful on the road back and I shall see you at the Summit." Nodding. I turn, and without waiting for the others and using Maxen as a crutch, I walk out of the church.

Chapter Twenty

Bittersweet

WE HURRY FROM THE SETTLEMENT, women and men stopping to watch us as we wait impatiently for the bus to move from the gate. Maxen binds my shoulder, staunching the bleeding, but I still feel weak. Even walking to the bikes seems to tire me. I keep pushing myself step after step, only concentrating on the road in front of me.

I can't quite manage to ride so I sit in front of Drax on my bike. He leaves his bike at The Worshippers. I have to fight my eyes closing. I'm that bone tired, my whole body seems to shut down. At least we survived the cult though, even if it wasn't exactly smooth. Now to get back to The Ring and The Summit before Dray goes all medieval and starts burning down The Wastes looking for me.

I need to try and clean my wounds at some point as well, an infection can set in too easy out here and that would mean my death. I don't bother telling the guys that my body is burning up and that I can already feel an infection setting in from my wounds yesterday. I just pray we get back to The Ring in time to get it under control. All I can seem to care about at the moment though is Drax's arms holding me to him. Offering me his strength.

"Just hold on babe, only two days ride if we don't stop."

I nod and lean my weight back against him. I must doze off because the next thing I know, Drax is crying out behind me as the bike swerves and flips.

I fly from it, the sound of metal grinding on the concrete as the road rushes up towards me. I land with a sickening crunch. My body is numb and I can't seem to kick my brain into action, instead, darkness is closing in and my eyes are blurring. I fight it with everything in me but I am dragged into unconsciousness, kicking and screaming.

Groaning, I flick my eyes open. My head is banging and all I can see is the grains of dust on the road in front of me, stained red from my blood. I must lose a couple of seconds again because when I come to again, I see Drax a couple of feet away, his eyes closed and an arrow sticking from his back. Gasping, I push myself to my feet, my body protesting but all I can focus on is Drax. I stumble to my feet and over to him, my body swaying and blood pumping from my wounds.

"Taz!" Thorn yells. I must miss a few seconds again, which can't be good, but when I come back to, I see the others fighting Berserkers just down the road from us. I have no time to be scared or let the anger at them take hold. Shakily, I pull my sword and hesitate. I can't leave Drax alone but I can't let my guys fight this battle, no matter how good they are - Berserkers are better. I hesitate for too long and Thorn goes down, his body slumping against the ground, where it lays unmoving as a Berserker stands over him letting out a war cry. His blonde braids flying as he bangs his chest, his symbolic shield strapped at his side. Crying out, I stumble across the ground, intent on getting to Thorn to protect him, only to stop when I hear running feet from behind me.

Whirling, I see another Berserker warrior with his eyes locked on Drax. I fling myself across the distance and cover Drax's body as the man's axe is about to drop. Closing my eyes, I wait for the death blow. When it doesn't fall, I lift my head. A knife sticks from the man's chest as he tumbles to the ground, his shield falling to his side. Not wasting any time, I turn, worriedly feeling for Drax's pulse. It's weak, but still there. Sands below, there is no way for us to win this. Not with Thorn and Drax down and me half dead. Maybe, just maybe, if I hand myself over they will leave my guys alone? But I know better than that, so it looks like I have a choice. Try to run and save myself, or die fighting with them.

Pushing myself to my feet, I stand in front of Drax, both of my swords held before me. They die, I die. I won't die on my knees either, but fighting with everything in me. I just pray we meet again, in another life where we have a chance to be together. Breathing deeply, I let everything else go. I become the monster, The Champion. I will die the way I lived, fighting to the last breath.

The next couple of minutes are a blur as I fight and slash like a demon. I ignore the pain and weakness and keep urging myself to go faster. I don't know where the others are but I can't afford to worry. My whole world becomes protecting the man I love. I don't hold myself back, no worries about my life anymore. I will take as many of these bastards with me as I can.

Chest heaving, I misstep and a punch hits the side of my head. Another rains down as I fall to the ground. The Berserker above me rains down hell, kicking every part of me he can. I crawl to Drax and cover his body as the man carries on with his attack.

I try to fight away the encroaching darkness but my body is shutting down. Maybe I'm dying, I think casually. It's sad that it is now, just as I started living. I wish I could see them one more time, tell Drax that I love him too. Tell all of them how lucky I was to know them. Have them hold me, just once more. But that's not the way the world works. Death isn't pretty and people don't always get to say goodbye, that's why living every day, every second like it's your last is so important. I regret now that I didn't. I let fear and shame cloud everything until I was nothing more than a body, an empty shell, going through the motions.

I hear something in my body crack as the man carries on his assault. Leaning forward, ignoring the agony in me, I kiss Drax's lips one last time, smearing my blood on him.

"I love you too," I whisper, my voice cutting off as I cough up blood.

The last thing I see as I cover Drax's unconscious body is Jax fighting like a demon to get to us. His horror-stricken eyes meeting mine as he calls out to me, heartbroken, the knowledge in his eyes that he will be too late. I try to let him know it's okay, and that I'm sorry I got them into this. I spot Maxen behind him, standing over Thorn, roaring like a beast. A white, blinding light cuts through everything before everything goes dark. My last thoughts are for the men who hold my heart and a prayer that we will meet again.

WHAT THE EVER-LOVING-FUCK? If this is death, does it have to be so bright?

I slam my eyes shut and wait before slowly opening them again, allowing them to adjust to the bright sunlight streaming in. With a gasp, I snap upright, remembering what happened. My stomach rebels and pain shoots through me but I push it away. Drax! Shit, where are they? I need to get to them, I need to know they are okay. In my panic, I slide off the bed I was laying on and try to stand, only to fall to the floor with a grunt. Looking down, I see I'm only in my bra and panties and a huge bandage is wrapped around me from ribs to the bottom of my stomach. Road rash from hitting the ground, after falling of the bike, covers my left thigh and bruises cover most of my body. I hate to think about what my face looks like. That's when the pain hits again and I nearly writhe on the floor with the force of it. It's like my whole body is an open wound, the agony races through my veins as I bite my tongue to stop from screaming. I have a feeling that if I start, I won't stop.

Breathing through it, I let my body adjust. When it's at a more manageable level, I sit up slowly and grasp the edge of the bed to pull myself up to sit on it. Frowning, I poke at my ribs and stomach. Shit, shit, shit. Bad idea. Closing my watering eyes, I wait until the pain retreats again. Breathing deeply, I open my eyes again and finally take in the room I'm in.

Glass windows run from ceiling to floor, the source of the sunlight. My eyes linger on them, but I force myself to look around. The room is white and looks like hospital rooms from when I was little. I'm sitting on a single bed with a metal railing, which is one of the only two pieces of furniture in the room. The other, a chair, sits in the corner of the room with a red bit of material draped over it. Swinging my eyes around, I try to remember what happened. The last thing I saw was bright lights. So it has to have something to do with that. A red blinking light in the corner of the room catches my attention and makes me scowl. A camera is perched way up out of reach, fucking perverts. I look around for my weapons and only get even more pissed when I don't find them. Standing shakily on my feet, I make my way to the chair, wondering if they are hidden there. It takes a while since I'm unsteady on my feet, but eventually, I reach it.

Fingering the silky material draped across the chair, I lift it. I cringe when I realise it's a dress. Fucking brilliant. How the hell am I supposed to fight in this thing? The back is cut low, almost too where my bum would be and then falls in a waterfall. The train is so long I'll probably slip on it, the front is higher neck. Unwilling to wear the impractical material, I look around for anything I can use as a weapon. I really don't want to be caught half naked, but it's better than not being able to move and fight.

Making my way to the bed, I slump back down, seeing nothing

of use. Frowning at my feet that are leaving dirty footprints on the pristine checkered floor, I try to get my muddled brain to figure out a plan. My usual calm and collected self is nowhere to be seen, instead, I'm terrified about what has happened to my men. Ugh.

I slam my fists on the bed in frustration and the pillow moves with the force, showing something shiny underneath it. Looking around again, I put my back to the camera and pull the blade out from its hiding space. Despite the circumstances, I find myself smiling. Only four men know I sleep with a blade under my pillow. It means at least one of them must be alive. But how?

A buzz from behind me has me spinning, keeping the blade hidden behind my thigh. The door that I didn't notice before, slides open and a man steps through with a hesitant smile on his face.

He's older than the last time I saw him, wrinkles line his eyes and his cheeks are red from the sun. But that smile I would remember anywhere, the corners stretch so far I always imagined it would one day stretch over his whole face. He even still has the little white scar under his lip, from when I accidentally head-butted him.

"Daddy?" My voice is rough, but shock courses through me, making me forget the thirst that is settling in. How is this possible? What the hell is going on? His smile widens and he steps further into the room. I warily eye the man who raised me. He's wearing a clean white dress shirt open to show the tank underneath, his black pants are tucked into brown boots. He's bigger than I remember, more muscle. He has salt and pepper hair now, but still, those bright blue eyes. Eyes that I used to see every night in my dreams, eyes I begged for in my darkest, weakest moments. Now here they are, watching me. Looking exactly as I remember. How is he alive? Why now? Why him? Questions run rampant in my battered and abused brain, as my heart clenches from the pain of seeing the only remaining member of my family, one I thought long dead. He watches me cautiously, but his face is reflecting pure happiness.

"Hi, Princess, welcome home."

ABOUT THE AUTHOR

K.A Knight is an indie author trying to get all of the stories and characters out of her head. She loves reading and devours every book she can get her hands on, she also has a worrying caffeine addiction.

She leads her double life in a sleepy English town, where she spends her days at the evil day job and comes home to her fur babies.

Read more at K.A Knight's website.

https://www.katieknightauthor.com/about

ALSO BY K.A. KNIGHT

Books By Katie:

Keep your eye out for Katie's other works.

Their Champion Book Two

Coming later this year

Circus Save Me

October 2018

Auroras Coven

Coming later this year

Voyage To Ayama

Pre-Order coming soon, turn the page for a sneak peek!

FOLLOW ME ON SOCIAL MEDIA

If you want to stay up to date on everything K.A Knight, join my Facebook group and follow me on Instagram

Facebook
https://www.facebook.com/groups/1981652728766816/

Instagram
https://www.instagram.com/katieknightauthor/

SNEAK PEEK: VOYAGE TO AYAMA

Dawnbreaker Book One

TRANSMISSION LOG 00015
DATE: 2032
MISSION: 43, COLONY
SHIP: DAWNBREAKER
DESTINATION: AYAMA

>…………….. Accepted
> Any news from Ayama? Rumours have gotten around, there must be a break in the chain of command. A rebellion naming themselves The Saviours has started, they claim to know. Advise on how to proceed?

CHAPTER ONE

A YEAR AGO

OUR HOUSING UNIT is still a mess from my birthday two days ago. I plop my bag down on the table and clear the remaining cake and presents away, I've just spread my books out on the metal table when the bing sounds from the comms unit. I groan, what now? My mother's voice breaks through my thoughts.

"Indy, you there?" Her velvety voice comes over the speakers, as if she is in the room.

With a sigh, I trudge to the comms unit in the kitchen, pressing the talk back button. "Yeah, everything okay?"

"Yes love, how was school?"

I'm betting she's knee deep in some secret experiment right now, she has been for weeks. I barely see her or dad with the exception being my birthday, and school, really? More like college.

"Fine, I should be able to graduate soon," I say smugly, thinking of the disbelief on my tutor's face when he read my results.

"That's nice darling," her voice is distracted and I can hear her tinkering with things in the background.

"I'm also thinking of piercing my nipple, maybe both, and then chaining them together."

"Hmm, whatever you think." Her voice is far away and it's obvious she's not even paying attention. My lips twist, she doesn't mean to be ignorant, but when she's working, she's miles away.

"What's up?" I ask in a defeated tone.

"Hmm, oh! Me and your father will be working late tonight."

I snort, when don't they? I don't mean to be pissy. I know they have important jobs and I'm busy too; trying to beat Effie to see who can graduate first.

"Ok," my chipper reply is forced. It's strange for the first year on board I was so angry with them for pulling me away from my friends and boyfriend and well -- Earth. Now that I've grown up a bit, I can understand why, I just miss spending time with them.

"Could you bring us some cake? Your dad is moaning for some," I can hear the smile in her voice and my dad shouting a reply in the background. I smile, despite the loneliness in me.

"Sure, be right there." At least I will get to see them today, maybe I can get them to pay attention for long enough to tell them about my application approval to join flight training once I graduate. Grinning, I imagine their reaction. They will be so proud; my dad's chest will puff up and he will say something stupid like, "I never doubted you." My mum will hug me and tell me how proud of me she is. The youngest pilot ever recorded, that's my aim at least.

"Thanks, honey," her voice is distracted again. I cut off the comms and grab some cake, putting it on a plate with a lid over it. I don't bother grabbing my jacket, the ship has been warmer than normal lately, so my basic white t-shirt and functional pants - the cool ones with all the pockets - will be fine. I place my hand on the release scanner at the door to our private housing area and make my way to the labs.

When they first told me I would be coming to space, I imagined the ship to be tiny and cramped. It's the complete opposite. The hallways are well lit and massive, bigger than my old school. The ship has its own swimming pool, theatre, dining areas, the labs and then housing. It's split up into sections: upper, middle and lower. Original, I know. Upper is for crew only, the middle is where I am, it's for the scientists and high up civvies. Lower is for the rest. Under the lower is the storage areas and I'm not sure what else. I suppose it has to be big, we are a colony mission after all; on our way to a new frontier -- Ayama.

The colony has already been started there and we are the third trip. Only the best of the best get to go; a fresh start they said. I should have expected my mum and dad to get picked, but it was still a shock when they sat down and told me. And the tests? Ugh. Every medical, psychological, and physical test you can imagine. Plus they tested my skills, intelligence, and what I wanted to do.

The journey is supposed to take five years, plenty of time for me to graduate and earn my pilots license. Then, at least when we get to Ayama I won't be stuck on the ground doing some menial job, not that there's nothing wrong with that. But I crave excitement, always have. My mother says I'm an adrenaline junkie, my dad says I take after him. He's a mechanic's son, he studied engineering at university where my mother was studying. They met in first year and fell in love. The rest is history, as they say. My mother worked her way up, as did my father.

I smile and nod at people as I pass, they nod back with friendly smiles. Everyone around here knows me. My mother runs the labs and my father is one of the head engineers for the ship. My eye is caught by a flash of black. I notice a few guards stand around talking. I make eye contact with one; he's tall. He's probably a couple of years older than me and just filling out from his growth spurt. His eyes are what stop me though, grey. Unusual. His skin is a dark tan, not from sunlight, not up here, so it must be his natural skin tone. His hair is short and black and almost blends into the usual guard's uniform. He turns away from me as someone nudges him.

Carrying on, I look in the labs as I pass. It's one thing I enjoy about space, people from all over the world got picked to go. The opportunity to learn new languages and meet new cultures was the only thing I looked forward to.

My mum's lab is at the very end. It's basically a giant square and runs the whole length of the end of the ship. I can see the airlock door up ahead, apparently for the lab's safety in case any part of the hallway is compromised. I stop when an alarm I've never heard before blares to life. The ship rocks, throwing me into the wall; that's not supposed to happen. I run my eyes around, the guards are running down the corridor towards me.

Explosion in the main lab.

The speaker blares to life, the automation voice loud to be heard over the siren. Wait, main lab? No!

I whirl to my mum's lab and run, the guards behind me. A panic like I've never known hits me. I sprint faster, pumping my arms the last few feet, my eyes honing in on the door. I'm driven totally by instinct.

I skid to a stop outside the door and try the scanner. It blinks red. I slam my hand down, again and again, trying to see through the glass.

"Come on!" I shout desperately. If I can just get the door open, I can get them out.

A bang on the glass has me freezing, my hand still on the cushioned scanner. My mum's face appears. I'm the spitting image of her, apart from my eyes which I get from my father. Her long brown hair is tied on top of her head. Heart shaped face, with brown eyes staring back at me. Tears are rolling down her face and I start to panic even more. My mother doesn't cry. She's the strongest person I know. The day I came home with a broken arm from Tommy pushing me off the slide, she sat me down and talked me through the pain in a logical way. She told me to never let anyone see that they get to me. My first heartbreak, my grandad dying, our blowout when I refused to come to space. Nothing, she keeps her emotions in check and thinks logically, unlike me.

I watch as the tears drip down her face, each one a blow to my racing heart. The guards are shouting behind me. I ignore everything as I look into my mother's hopeless eyes. A bang sounds from somewhere in the room making her flinch, but she doesn't turn around. Looking behind her, I scream when I spot my father's crumpled form on the floor. She steps in my way, blocking my view of him and puts her hand on the glass, a sad smile on her beautiful face.

"I'm sorry, baby," her voice is muffled by the layers of steel and glass between us.

No, no, no. Shaking my head, I smash my palm again and again on the scanner only for it to blink red each time. Frustration burns through me, fighting with the panic clawing at my throat.

"Indy."

I ignore her and the guards, as I try and get through the door. I could circumvent the scanner, but that would take time I don't have. I could kill the circuit board with a-

"Indy, look at me." The voice is stern, the one she uses when I'm in trouble. I freeze and do as I'm told for once in my life, my eyes reluctantly dragging back to hers, as if not looking will make it okay.

"I love you, baby. Be brave and always look for the truth. I'm so proud of you." I put my palm over the glass mirroring hers, each word hammering home my heartbreak. My chest tightens as my heart struggles to beat, the pain indescribable.

No, she can't be saying goodbye. The tears finally burst from my overfilling eyes like a waterfall as a strained sob emerges.

Someone grabs me and drags me away from the door. I fight them kicking and screaming, trying to get back to her.

She stays there watching me, the tears dripping steadily down her face. That horrible smile twisting her lips as she faces death. Something explodes behind her making her cringe, but even then, she doesn't look away. Her eyes tighten, and her lips start to turn blue, her shallow breaths puffing against the glass. I keep fighting, needing to be there, needing to save her.

She starts gasping for breath and I fight harder. I hear a grunt behind me and the arms holding me loosen. I jump forward, running back to her. I'm tackled again and lifted in the air. I kick and fight as I watch her suffocate, her eyes dim, and she slumps against the door as I scream.

The noise of the guards, the siren, and everyone else start to blur together. I'm turned into a chest, a broad one. I notice the name Barrott stitched onto the guard uniform before my head is gently pressed to it.

"Don't look," the deep voice warns from above me.

I try and fight, bashing my fists against his chest. He lets me as sobs rack my body. He doesn't speak or fight back, just lets me pummel his chest until I'm out of energy. I slip to the floor, him following, still cushioning me. Looking into his face through tear-filled eyes, I realise it's the guard from earlier.

"No," I whisper as his face fills with sorrow.

"I'm so sorry."

"No!" I shout it and turn to the door, he allows me this time. The guards are surrounding it, all with grim expressions. One is shouting into the control panel.

"Tell me how this happened!"

"I don't care, keep the door sealed."

I ignore them all, instead, I look at my mother's body against the glass. I know she's dead, so is my dad. It's now just me. I'm alone in space.

"Not alone." The chest vibrates against me as he speaks.

I don't remember saying it out loud, but I must have because Barrott answers. I ignore him and everyone around me, staring at my mother's open dull eyes.

Eventually, I'm taken away. Barrott lifts me in his arms and strides down the ship. I don't care. I don't care where we are going or who he is. My mind is numb, and I can't feel my body. I know this is shock and I should be bothered, but I let the numbness fill me up.

I'm taken to the medical wing where they check me over. The doctor tries to talk to me, but I ignore him, so he turns to Barrott instead. My eyes lock on the floor replaying my mums last moments again and again.

Barrott crouches by my side where I sit on a cot. I pay no attention to him, I can see his mouth moving out of the corner of my eye, but it seems like a lot of effort to focus on the words. *I wonder what happened to the cake I was carrying,* I think idly.

Eventually, Effie comes in and throws herself around me sobbing. I don't even try to return the embrace, my arms like lead at my side. She cries into my shoulder, her words floating over my head. Her father, Howard, stands in the curtain door hesitating, heartbreak on his face. He's just lost his best friend. I know the feeling.

The next couple of days are a blur. I don't sleep much, Effie takes me to their housing unit and stays by my side the whole time, assuring me she's there for me. Howard tells me not to worry about anything, that they will look after me. They tell me how sorry they are all the time, I hate the sympathy and pity in their voices.

It's the day of the funeral -- if that's what you want to call it. I stand in front of the wooden boxes containing my mother and father. My emotions are fighting the numbness, but I need it now more than ever. The whole ship is here; the first two deaths ever recorded in space. Some are being nosey, some are crying, and some just want to see the orphan girl break down.

I won't. I won't show them that. I catch Barrott's eyes where he stands to the side watching me, but I ignore him too. I won't let anyone know how much I'm suffering. How could they possibly understand? I won't let them think I'm the broken girl, when in reality my heart is with the two wooden boxes being pushed into the airlock.

They can't keep the bodies on board, one of the doctors told me, so they will be purged into space. There was a ceremony where my mum and dad's colleagues spoke. I didn't listen to a word. None of it matters.

The buzz of the airlock closing sends a stab through my heart, but I block it out. I watch as the outer door opens, and they fly out into the abyss of space. A lone tear rolls down my cheek and I swipe it away before it can fall. I push back the tears by gouging my nails into my thigh, they will be the last ones to fall in front of anyone. I stand there until the crowd breaks, going back to their own lives, and their own families.

I stand there alone on that platform until a throat is cleared behind me. I turn slowly. Barrott is watching me, concern and something else in his eyes. Still not bothering to speak, I watch him, and eventually he sighs.

"Come on, I'll take you to the Jenkins' quarters. That's where you are living now right?" He winces at his words. I step towards him, and I can see Effie and Howard hesitating at the door, waiting for me. I won't be going with them. I need to be alone with my grief. I need to be somewhere I can break down, somewhere filled with my family.

I shake my head.

"No. I'm staying in my family's unit," I ignore his protests and walk through the whispering people who stayed behind to watch. I hold my head high and walk through, ignoring their stares and remarks. I meet the eyes of a bald man standing next to a woman with jet black hair. They nod at me. Striding through I count the steps back to my unit. Back to my empty house and life. Only then will I break down and let myself feel. I will be like my mother, I will not show them anything. They will never have it to use against me.

Printed in Great Britain
by Amazon